DECK THE HALLS
WITH FATAL FOLLY

SUPPER WITH MISS SHIVERS
by Peter Lovesey
The Ghost of Christmas Past sends a young
woman a curious invitation that may hold the
answer to a thirty-year-old death.

THE SANTA CLAUS CLUB
by Julian Symons
Formal dinners can be murder . . . but how was
the tycoon done in between the entree and
dessert? And was the killer still in the room?

SANTA'S WAY
by James Powell
'Twas the night before Christmas and Santa
was—dead. 'Tis the season for murder,
mayhem, and 18.5 percent interest in this
hilariously grim crime-fantasy about Christmas
gone commercial.

*And twelve other tales of holiday mystery
that guarantee you'll have yourself
a scary little Christmas.*

D0720469

MYSTERY PARLOR

☐ **THE DEAD PULL HITTER by Alison Gordon.** Katherine Henry is a sportswriter—until murder pitches a curve. Now death is lurking in her ballpark, and she's looking for a killer on the dark side of glory days and shattered dreams. (402405—$3.99)

☐ **HALF A MIND by Wendy Hornsby.** Homicide detective Roger Tejeda had an instinctive sense for catching criminals. But now he's working with a handicap: his last case left him with a skull fracture, black-outs and memory lapses—which make it that much harder to figure out who sent him a gift box holding a severed head. . . . (402456—$3.99)

☐ **THE CHARTREUSE CLUE by William F. Love.** Although a priest with a murdered girlfriend wasn't exactly an original sin, the irascible, wheelchair-bound Bishop would have to use leads that included a key, a letter, and a chartreuse clue to unravel the deadly affair. (402731—$5.50)

☐ **MRS. MALORY INVESTIGATES by Hazel Holt.** "Delightful . . . a British whodunit that works a traditional mode to good effect." —*Cleveland Plain Dealer* (402693—$3.99)

MURDER UNDER THE MISTLETOE

And other stories
from *Ellery Queen's
Mystery Magazine*
and *Alfred Hitchcock's
Mystery Magazine*

Edited by Cynthia Manson

A SIGNET BOOK

SIGNET
Published by the Penguin Group
Penguin Books USA Inc., 375 Hudson Street,
New York, New York 10014, U.S.A.
Penguin Books Ltd, 27 Wrights Lane,
London W8 5TZ, England
Penguin Books Australia Ltd, Ringwood,
Victoria, Australia
Penguin Books Canada Ltd, 10 Alcorn Avenue,
Toronto, Ontario, Canada M4V 3B2
Penguin Books (N.Z.) Ltd, 182-190 Wairau Road,
Auckland 10, New Zealand

Penguin Books Ltd, Registered Offices:
Harmondsworth, Middlesex, England

First published by Signet, an imprint of New American Library,
a division of Penguin Books USA Inc.

First Printing, November, 1992
10 9 8 7 6 5 4 3 2 1

CONTENTS

INTRODUCTION

Murder Under the Mistletoe is the third in a popular series of books presenting tales of crime and detection in which Christmas settings play a significant role. The stories were selected from the archives of the world's leading mystery magazines, *Ellery Queen's Mystery Magazine* and *Alfred Hitchcock's Mystery Magazine*.

This book's two predecessors are *Mystery for Christmas* and *Murder at Christmas*, but one need not have read either of the earlier books to enjoy this latest anthology.

In this collection we have a splendid lineup of authors and their well-known series detectives, including favorites like Mortimer's Rumpole of the Bailey, Joyce Porter's Hon. Constance Morrison-Burke, and Margery Allingham's Albert Campion. For lovers of the classics, there is also a Christmas offering from Sir Arthur Conan Doyle, featuring the incomparable Sherlock Holmes.

Special attention is due, we think, to three stories that capture the spirit of Christmas with great poignancy and intertwine it expertly with mystery and intrigue: "The Carol Singers" by Josephine Bell, "Supper With Miss Shivers" by Peter Lovesey, and "Noel, Noel" by Barry Perowne. We love all the stories that follow, but these three have a special place in our hearts—we hope they find one in yours as well.

—*Cynthia Manson*

MURDER
UNDER THE
MISTLETOE

THE SANTA CLAUS CLUB

by Julian Symons

It is not often, in real life, that letters are written recording implacable hatred nursed over the years, or that private detectives are invited by peers to select dining clubs, or that murders occur at such dining clubs, or that they are solved on the spot by logical deduction.

The case of the Santa Claus Club provided an example of all these rarities.

The case began one day a week before Christmas, when Francis Quarles went to see Lord Acrise. He was a rich man, Lord Acrise, and an important one—the chairman of this big building concern and the director of that big insurance company and the consultant to the Government on many matters.

He had been a harsh, intolerant man in his prime, and was still hard enough in his early seventies, Quarles guessed, as he looked at the beaky nose, jutting chin, and stony blue eyes under thick brows. They sat in the study of Acrise's house just off the Brompton Road.

"Just tell me what you think of these."

These were three letters, badly typed on a machine with a worn ribbon. They were all signed with the name James Gliddon. The first two contained vague references to some wrong done to Gliddon by Acrise in the past. They were written in language that was wild, but unmistakably threatening.

"You have been a whited sepulchre for too long, but now your time has come . . . You don't know what I'm going to do, now I've come back, but you won't be able to help wondering and worrying . . . The mills of God grind slowly, but they're going to grind you into little bits for what you've done to me.''

The third letter was more specific. ''So the thief is going to play Santa Claus. That will be your last evening alive. *I shall be there,* Joe Acrise, and I shall watch with pleasure as you squirm in agony.''

Quarles looked at the envelopes. They were plain and cheap. The address was typed, and the word *Personal* was on top of the envelope. ''Who is James Gliddon?''

The stony eyes glared at him. ''I'm told you're to be trusted. Gliddon was a school friend of mine. We grew up together in the slums of Nottingham. We started a building company together. It did well for a time, then went bust. There was a lot of money missing. Gliddon kept the books. He got five years for fraud.''

''Have you heard from him since then? I see all these letters are recent.''

''He's written half a dozen letters, I suppose, over the years. The last one came—oh, seven years ago, I should think. From the Argentine.'' Acrise stopped, then said abruptly, ''Snowin tried to find him for me, but he'd disappeared.''

''Snowin?''

''My secretary. Been with me twelve years.''

He pressed a bell. An obsequious, fattish man, whose appearance somehow put Quarles in mind of an enormous mouse, scurried in.

''Snowin? Did we keep any of those old letters from Gliddon?''

''No, sir. You told me to destroy them.''

''The last one came from the Argentine, right?''

''From Buenos Aires to be exact, sir.''

Acrise nodded, and Snowin scurried out. Quarles said, ''Who else knows this story about Gliddon?''

"Just my wife." Acrise bared yellow teeth in a grin. "Unless somebody's been digging into my past."

"And what does this mean, about you playing Santa Claus?"

"I'm this year's chairman of The Santa Claus Club. We hold our raffle and dinner next Monday."

Then Quarles remembered. The Santa Claus Club had been formed by ten rich men. Each year they met, every one of them dressed up as Santa Claus, and held a raffle. The members took turns to provide the prize that was raffled—it might be a case of Napoleon brandy, a modest cottage with some exclusive salmon fishing rights attached to it, a Constable painting.

Each Santa Claus bought one ticket for the raffle, at a cost of 1000 guineas. The total of 10,000 guineas was given to a Christmas charity. After the raffle the assembled Santa Clauses, each accompanied by one guest, ate a traditional Christmas dinner.

The whole thing was a combination of various English characteristics: enjoyment of dressing up, a wish to help charities, and the desire also that the help given should not go unrecorded. The dinners of The Santa Claus Club got a good deal of publicity, and there were those who said that it would have been perfectly easy for the members to give their money to charities in a less conspicuous manner.

"I want you to find Gliddon," Lord Acrise said. "Don't mistake me, Mr. Quarles. I don't want to take action against him, I want to help him. I wasn't to blame—don't think I admit that—but it was hard that Jimmy Gliddon should go to jail. I'm a hard man, have been all my life, but I don't think my worst enemies would call me mean. Those who've helped me know that when I die they'll find they're not forgotten. Jimmy Gliddon must be an old man now. I'd like to set him up for the rest of his life."

"To find him by next Monday is a tall order," Quarles said. "But I'll try."

He was at the door when Acrise said casually, "By the way, I'd like you to be my guest at The Santa Claus Club dinner on Monday night."

Did that mean, Quarles wondered, that he was to act as official poison taster if he did not find James Gliddon?

There were two ways of trying to find Gliddon—by investigation of his career after leaving prison, and through the typewritten letters. Quarles took the job of tracing the past, leaving the letters to his secretary, Molly Player.

From Scotland Yard, Quarles found out that Gliddon had spent nearly four years in prison, from 1913 to late 1916. He had joined a Nottinghamshire Regiment when he came out, and the records of this Regiment showed that he had been demobilized in August 1919, with the rank of Sergeant. In 1923 he had been given a sentence of three years for an attempt to smuggle diamonds. Thereafter, all trace of him in Britain vanished.

Quarles made some expensive telephone calls to Buenos Aires, where a letter had come from seven years earlier. He learned that Gliddon had lived in the city from a time just after the war until 1955. He ran an import-export business, and was thought to have been living in other South American Republics during the war. His business was said to have been a cloak for smuggling, both of drugs and of suspected Nazis, whom he got out of Europe into the Argentine.

In 1955 a newspaper had accused Gliddon of arranging the entry into the Argentine of a Nazi war criminal named Hermann Breit. Gliddon threatened to sue the paper, and then disappeared. A couple of weeks later a battered body was washed up just outside the city.

"It was identified as Gliddon," the liquid voice said over the telephone. "But you know, Señor Quarles, in such matters the police are sometimes happy to close their files.''

''There was still some doubt?''

''Yes. Not very much, perhaps, but in these cases there is often a doubt.''

Molly Player found out nothing useful about the paper and envelopes. They were of the sort that could be bought in a thousand stores and shops in London and elsewhere. She had more luck with the typewriter. Its key characteristics identified the machine as a Malward portable of a model which the company had ceased producing ten years ago. The type face had proved unsatisfactory, and only some 300 machines of this sort had been made.

The Malward Company was able to provide her with a list of the purchasers of these machines, and Molly started to check and trace them, but had to give it up as a bad job.

''If we had three weeks I might get somewhere. In three days it's impossible,'' she said to Quarles.

Lord Acrise made no comment on Quarles's recital of failure. ''See you on Monday evening, seven thirty, black tie,'' he said, and barked with laughter. ''Your host will be Santa Claus.''

''I'd like to be there earlier.''

''Good idea. Any time you like. You know where it is—Robert the Devil Restaurant.''

The Robert the Devil Restaurant is situated inconspicuously in Mayfair. It is not a restaurant in the ordinary sense of the word, for there is no public dining room, but simply several private rooms, which can accommodate any number of guests from two to thirty. Perhaps the food is not quite the best in London, but it is certainly the most expensive.

It was here that Quarles arrived at half-past six, a big suave man, rather too conspicuously elegant perhaps in a midnight-blue dinner jacket. He talked to Albert, the *maître d'hôtel,* whom he had known for some years, took unobtrusive looks at the waiters, went into and admired the kitchens. Albert observed his activities with tolerant amusement. "You are here on some sort of business, Mr. Quarles?"

"I am a guest, Albert. I am also a kind of bodyguard. Tell me, how many of your waiters have joined you in the past twelve months?"

"Perhaps half a dozen. They come, they go."

"Is there anybody at all on your staff—waiters, kitchen staff, anybody—who has joined you this year and is over sixty years old?"

Albert thought, then shook his head decisively. "No. There is no such one."

The first of the guests came just after seven. He was the brain surgeon, Sir James Erdington, with a guest whom Quarles recognized as the Arctic explorer Norman Endell.

After that they came at intervals of a minute or two—a minister in the Government, one of the three most important men in the motor industry, a General promoted to the peerage to celebrate his retirement, a theatrical producer named Roddy Davis who had successfully combined commerce and culture. As they arrived, the hosts went into a special dressing room to put on their Santa Claus clothes, while the guests drank sherry.

At 7:25 Snowin scurried in, gasped, "Excuse me, place names, got to put them out," and went into the dining room. Through the open door Quarles glimpsed a large oval table, gleaming with silver and bright with roses.

After Snowin came Lord Acrise, jutting-nosed and fearsome-eyed. "Sorry to have kept you waiting," he barked, and asked conspiratorially, "Well?"

"No sign."

"False alarm. Lot of nonsense. Got to dress up now."

He went into the dressing room with his box—each of the hosts had a similar box, labeled *Santa Claus*—and came out again bewigged, bearded, and robed. "Better get the business over, and then we can enjoy ourselves. You can tell 'em to come in," he said to Albert.

This referred to the photographers who had been clustering outside and who now came into the room specially provided for holding the raffle. In the center of the room was a table and on this table stood this year's prize—two exquisite T'ang horses. On the other side of the table were ten chairs arranged in a semicircle, and on these sat the Santa Clauses. The guests stood inconspicuously at the side.

The raffle was conducted with the utmost seriousness. Each Santa Claus had a numbered slip. These slips were dropped into a bowl, mixed up, and then Acrise put in his hand and drew out one of them. Flash bulbs exploded.

"The number drawn is eight," Acrise announced, and Roddy Davis waved the counterfoil in his hand. "Isn't that *wonderful?* It's my ticket." He went over to the horses and picked up one. More flashes. "I'm bound to say that they couldn't have gone to *anybody* who'd have appreciated them more."

Quarles, standing near the General, whose face was as red as his robe, heard him mutter something uncomplimentary. Charity, he reflected, was not universal, even in a gathering of Santas. More flashes, the photographers disappeared, and Quarles's views about the nature of charity were reinforced when, as they were about to go into the dining room, Erdington said, "Forgotten something, haven't you, Acrise?"

With what seemed dangerous quietness Acrise answered, "Have I? I don't think so."

"It's customary for the Club and guests to sing *Noel* before we go in to dinner."

"You didn't come to last year's dinner. It was agreed then that we should give it up. Carols after dinner, much better."

"I must say I thought that was *just* for last year, because we were late," Roddy Davis fluted. "I'm sure that's what was agreed. I think myself it's rather pleasant to sing *Noel* before we go in and start eating too much."

"Suggest we put it to the vote," Erdington said sharply.

Half a dozen of the Santas now stood looking at each other with subdued hostility. It was a situation that would have been totally ludicrous, if it had not been also embarrassing for the guests.

Then suddenly the Arctic explorer, Endell, began to sing *Noel, Noel* in a rich bass. There was the faintest flicker of hesitation, and then guests and Santas joined in. The situation was saved.

At dinner Quarles found himself with Acrise on one side of him and Roddy Davis on the other. Endell sat at Acrise's other side, and beyond him was Erdington.

Turtle soup was followed by grilled sole, and then three great turkeys were brought in. The helpings of turkey were enormous. With the soup they drank a light, dry sherry, with the sole Chassagne Montrachet, with the turkey an Alexe Corton, heavy and powerful.

"And who are *you?*" Roddy Davis peered at Quarles's card and said, with what seemed manifest untruth, "Of course I know your name."

"I am a criminologist." This sounded better, he thought, than private detective.

"I remember your monograph on criminal calligraphy. Quite fascinating."

So Davis did know who he was—it would be easy, Quarles thought, to underrate the intelligence of the round-faced man who beamed so innocently to him.

"These beards really do get in the way rather," Davis

said. "But there, one must suffer for tradition. Have you known Acrise long?"

"Not very. I'm greatly privileged to be here." Quarles had been watching, as closely as he could, the pouring of the wine and the serving of the food. He had seen nothing suspicious. Now, to get away from Davis's questions, he turned to his host.

"Damned awkward business before dinner," Acrise said. "Might have been, at least. Can't let well alone, Erdington." He picked up his turkey leg, attacked it with Elizabethan gusto, then wiped his mouth and fingers with a napkin. "Like this wine?"

"It's excellent."

"Chose it myself. They've got some good Burgundies here." Acrise's speech was slightly slurred, and it seemed to Quarles that he was rapidly getting drunk.

"Do you have any speeches?"

"What's that?"

"Are any speeches made after dinner?"

"No speeches. Just sing carols. But I've got a little surprise for 'em."

"What sort of surprise?"

"Very much in the spirit of Christmas, and a good joke too. But if I told you it wouldn't be a surprise now, would it?"

Acrise had almost said "shurprise." Quarles looked at him and then returned to the turkey.

There was a general cry of pleasure as Albert himself brought in the great plum pudding, topped with holly and blazing with brandy.

"That's the most wonderful pudding I've ever seen in my life," Endell said. "Are we really going to eat it?"

"Of course we're going to eat it," Acrise said irritably. He stood up, swaying a little, and picked up the knife beside the pudding.

"I don't like to be critical, but our Chairman is really

not cutting the pudding very well,'' Roddy Davis whispered to Quarles.

And indeed, it was more of a stab than a cut that Acrise made at the pudding. Albert took over, and cut it quickly and efficiently. Bowls of brandy butter were circulated.

Quarles leaned toward Acrise. "Are you all right?"

"Of course I'm all right." The slurring was very noticeable now. Acrise ate no pudding, but he drank some more wine, and dabbed at his lips. When the pudding was finished he got slowly to his feet again, and toasted the Queen.

Cigars were lighted. Acrise was not smoking. He whispered something to the waiter, who nodded and left the room. Acrise got up again, leaning heavily on the table.

"A little surprise," he said. "In the spirit of Christmas."

Quarles had thought that he was beyond being surprised by the activities of The Santa Claus Club, but still he was astonished by the sight of the three figures who entered the room. They were led by Snowin, somehow more mouselike than ever, wearing a long white smock and a red nightcap with a tassel.

He was followed by an older man dressed in a kind of gray sackcloth, with a face so white that it might have been covered in plaster of Paris. This man carried chains which he shook.

At the rear came a middle-aged lady, who sparkled so brightly that she seemed to be completely hung with tinsel.

"I am Scrooge," said Snowin.

"I am Marley," wailed the gray sackcloth, clanking his chains.

"And I," said the middle-aged lady with abominable sprightliness, "am the ghost of Christmas past."

There was a murmur round the table, and slowly the murmur grew to a ripple of laughter.

"We have come," said Snowin in a thin mouse voice, "to perform for you our own interpretation of *A Christmas Carol*—oh, sir, what's the matter?"

Lord Acrise stood up in his robes, tore off his wig, pulled at his beard, tried to say something. Then he clutched at the side of his chair and fell sideways, so that he leaned heavily against Endell and slipped slowly to the floor.

There ensued a minute of confused activity. Endell made some sort of exclamation and rose from his chair, slightly obstructing Quarles. Erdington was first beside the body, holding the wrist in his hand, listening for the heart. Then they were all crowding round, the red-robed Santas, the guests, the actors in their ludicrous clothes. Snowin, at Quarles's left shoulder, was babbling something, and at his right were Roddy Davis and Endell.

"Stand back," Erdington snapped. He stayed on his knees for another few moments, looking curiously at Acrise's puffed, distorted face, blueish around the mouth. Then he stood up. "He's dead."

There was a murmur of surprise and horror, and now they all drew back, as men do instinctively from the presence of death.

"Heart attack?" somebody said. Erdington made a noncommittal noise. Quarles moved to his side.

"I'm a private detective, Sir James. Lord Acrise feared an attempt on his life and asked me to come along here."

"You seem to have done well so far," Erdington said dryly.

"May I look at the body?"

"If you wish."

As soon as Quarles bent down he caught the smell of

bitter almonds. When he straightened up Erdington raised
his eyebrows.

"He's been poisoned. There's a smell like prussic
acid, but the way he died precludes cyanide I think. He
seemed to become very drunk during dinner, and his
speech was blurred. Does that suggest anything to
you?"

"I'm a brain surgeon, not a physician." Erdington
stared at the floor, then said, "Nitrobenzene?"

"That's what I thought. We shall have to notify the
police." Quarles went to the door and spoke to a disturbed Albert. Then he returned to the room and clapped
his hands.

"Gentlemen. My name is Francis Quarles, and I am a
private detective. Lord Acrise asked me to come here
tonight because he had received a threat that this would
be his last evening alive. The threat said: 'I shall be there,
and I shall watch with pleasure as you squirm in agony.'
Lord Acrise has been poisoned. It seems certain that the
man who made the threat is in this room."

"Gliddon," a voice said. Snowin had divested himself
of the white smock and red nightcap, and now appeared
as his customary respectable self.

"Yes. This letter, and others he had received, were
signed with the name of James Gliddon, a man who
bore a grudge against Lord Acrise which went back
nearly half a century. Gliddon became a professional
smuggler and crook. He would now be in his late sixties."

"But dammit man, this Gliddon's not here." That was
the General, who took off his wig and beard. "Lot of
tomfoolery."

In a shamefaced way the other members of The Santa
Claus Club removed their facial trappings. Marley took
off his chains and the middle-aged lady discarded her
cloak of tinsel.

"Isn't he here? But Lord Acrise is dead."

Snowin coughed. "Excuse me, sir, but would it be possible for my colleagues from our local dramatic society to retire? Of course, I can stay myself if you wish. It was Lord Acrise's idea that we should perform our skit on *A Christmas Carol* as a seasonable novelty, but—"

"Everybody must stay in this room until the police arrive. The problem, as you will all realize, is how the poison was administered. All of us ate the same food and drank the same wine. I sat next to Lord Acrise, and I watched as closely as possible to make sure of this. I watched the wine being poured, the turkey being carved and brought to the table, the pudding being cut and passed round. After dinner some of you smoked cigars or cigarettes, but not Acrise."

"Just a moment." It was Roddy Davis who spoke. "This sounds fantastic, but wasn't it Sherlock Holmes who said that when you'd eliminated all other possibilities, even a fantastic one must be right? Supposing that some poison in powder form had been put on Acrise's food—through the saltcellars, say—"

Erdington was shaking his head, but Quarles unscrewed both the salt and pepper shakers and tasted their contents. "Salt and pepper. And in any case other people used these. Hello, what's this?"

Acrise's napkin lay crumpled on his chair, and Quarles had picked it up and was staring at it.

"It's Acrise's napkin," Endell said. "What's remarkable about that?"

"It's a napkin, but not the one Acrise used. He wiped his mouth half a dozen times on his napkin, and wiped his greasy fingers on it too, when he'd gnawed a turkey bone. He must certainly have left grease marks on it. But look at this napkin."

He held it up, and they saw that it was spotless. Quarles said softly, "The murderer's mistake."

"I'm quite baffled," Roddy Davis said. "What does it mean?"

Quarles turned to Erdington. "Sir James and I agreed that the poison used was probably nitrobenzene. This is deadly as a liquid, but it is also poisonous as a vapor, isn't that so?"

Erdington nodded. "You'll remember the case of the unfortunate young man who used shoe polish containing nitrobenzene on damp shoes, put them on and wore them, and was killed by the fumes."

"Yes. Somebody made sure that Lord Acrise had a napkin that had been soaked in nitrobenzene but was dry enough to use. The same person substituted the proper napkin, the one belonging to the restaurant, after Acrise was dead."

"Nobody's left the room," said Roddy Davis.

"No."

"That means the murder napkin must still be here."

"It does."

"Then what are we waiting for? I vote that we submit to a search."

There was a small hubbub of protest and approval. "That won't be necessary," Quarles said. "Only one person here fulfills all the qualifications of the murderer."

"James Gliddon?"

"No. Gliddon is almost certainly dead. But the murderer is somebody who knew about Acrise's relationship with Gliddon, and tried to be clever by writing the letters to lead us along a wrong track. Then the murderer is somebody who had the opportunity of coming in here before dinner and who knew exactly where Acrise would be sitting. There is only one person who fulfills all of these qualifications.

"He removed any possible suspicion from himself, as he thought, by being absent from the dinner table, but he arranged to come in afterwards to exchange the napkins. He probably put the poisoned napkin into the clothes he discarded. As for motive, long-standing hatred might be enough, but he is also somebody who knew that he would benefit handsomely when Acrise died—stop him, will you.''

But the General, with a tackle reminiscent of the days when he had been the best wing three-quarter in the country, had already brought to the floor Lord Acrise's mouselike secretary, Snowin.

RUMPOLE AND THE SPIRIT OF CHRISTMAS

by John Mortimer

I realized that Christmas was upon us when I saw a sprig of holly over the list of prisoners hung on the wall of the cells under the Old Bailey.

I pulled out a new box of small cigars and found its opening obstructed by a tinseled band on which a scarlet-faced Santa was seen hurrying a sleigh full of carcinoma-packed goodies to the Rejoicing World. I lit one as the lethargic screw, with a complexion the color of faded Bronco, regretfully left his doorstep sandwich and mug of sweet tea to unlock the gate.

"Good morning, Mr. Rumpole. Come to visit a customer?"

"Happy Christmas, officer," I said as cheerfully as possible. "Is Mr. Timson at home?"

"Well, I don't believe he's slipped down to his little place in the country."

Such were the pleasantries that were exchanged between us legal hacks and discontented screws; jokes that no doubt have changed little since the turnkeys unlocked the door at Newgate to let in a pessimistic advocate, or the cells under the Coliseum were opened to admit the unwelcome news of the Imperial thumbs-down.

"My mum wants me home for Christmas."

Which Christmas? It would have been an unreasonable

remark and I refrained from it. Instead, I said, "All things are possible."

As I sat in the interviewing room, an Old Bailey hack of some considerable experience, looking through my brief and inadvertently using my waistcoat as an ashtray, I hoped I wasn't on another loser. I had had a run of bad luck during that autumn season, and young Edward Timson was part of that huge south London family whose criminal activities provided such welcome grist to the Rumpole mill. The charge in the seventeen-year-old Eddie's case was nothing less than wilful murder.

"We're in with a chance, though, Mr. Rumpole, ain't we?"

Like all his family, young Timson was a confirmed optimist. And yet, of course, the merest outsider in the Grand National, the hundred-to-one shot, is in with a chance, and nothing is more like going round the course at Aintree than living through a murder trial. In this particular case, a fanatical prosecutor named Wrigglesworth, known to me as the Mad Monk, as to represent Beechers, and Mr. Justice Vosper, a bright but wintry-hearted judge who always felt it his duty to lead for the prosecution, was to play the part of a particularly menacing fence at the Canal Turn.

"A chance. Well, yes, of course you've got a chance, if they can't establish common purpose, and no one knows which of you bright lads had the weapon."

No doubt the time had come for a brief glance at the prosecution case, not an entirely cheering prospect. Eddie, also known as "Turpin" Timson, lived in a kind of decaying barracks, a sort of highrise Lubianka, known as Keir Hardie Court, somewhere in south London, together with his parents, his various brothers, and his thirteen-year-old sister, Noreen. This particular branch of the Timson family lived on the thirteenth floor. Below them, on the twelfth, lived the large clan of the O'Dowds. The war between the Timsons and the O'Dowds began, it seems, with the casting of the Nativity play at the local comprehensive school.

Christmas comes earlier each year and the school show was planned about September. When Bridget O'Dowd was chosen to play the lead in the face of strong competition from Noreen Timson, an incident occurred comparable in historical importance to the assassination of an obscure Austrian archduke at Sarejevo. Noreen Timson announced in the playground that Bridget O'Dowd was a spotty little tart unsuited to play any role of which the most notable characteristic was virginity.

Hearing this, Bridget O'Dowd kicked Noreen Timson behind the anthracite bunkers. Within a few days, war was declared between the Timson and O'Dowd children, and a present of lit fireworks was posted through the O'Dowd front door. On what is known as the "night in question," reinforcements of O'Dowds and Timsons arrived in old bangers from a number of south London addresses and battle was joined on the stone staircase, a bleak terrain of peeling walls scrawled with graffiti, blowing empty Coca-cola tins and torn newspapers. The weapons seemed to have been articles in general domestic use, such as bread knives, carving knives, broom handles, and a heavy screwdriver. At the end of the day it appeared that the upstairs flat had repelled the invaders, and Kevin O'Dowd lay on the stairs. Having been stabbed with a slender and pointed blade, he was in a condition to become known as "the deceased" in the case of the Queen against Edward Timson. I made an application for bail for my client which was refused, but a speedy trial was ordered.

So even as Bridget O'Dowd was giving her Virgin Mary at the comprehensive, the rest of the family was waiting to give evidence against Eddie Timson in that home of British drama, Number One Court at the Old Bailey.

"I never had no cutter, Mr. Rumpole. Straight up, I

never had one," the defendant told me in the cells. He was an appealing-looking lad with soft brown eyes, who had already won the heart of the highly susceptible lady who wrote his social inquiry report. ("Although the charge is a serious one, this is a young man who might respond well to a period of probation." I could imagine the steely contempt in Mr. Justice Vosper's eye when he read that.)

"Well, tell me, Edward. Who had?"

"I never seen no cutters on no one, honest I didn't. We wasn't none of us tooled up, Mr. Rumpole."

"Come on, Eddie. Someone must have been. They say even young Noreen was brandishing a potato peeler."

"Not me, honest."

"What about your sword?"

There was one part of the prosecution evidence that I found particularly distasteful. It was agreed that on the previous Sunday morning, Eddie "Turpin" Timson had appeared on the stairs of Keir Hardie Court and flourished what appeared to be an antique cavalry saber at the assembled O'Dowds, who were just popping out to Mass.

"Me sword I bought up the Portobello? I didn't have that there, honest."

"The prosecution can't introduce evidence about the sword. It was an entirely different occasion." Mr. Barnard, my instructing solicitor who fancied himself as an infallible lawyer, spoke with a confidence which I couldn't feel. He, after all, wouldn't have to stand up on his hind legs and argue the legal toss with Mr. Justice Vosper.

"It rather depends on who's prosecuting us. I mean, if it's some fairly reasonable fellow—"

"I think," Mr. Barnard reminded me, shattering my faint optimism and ensuring that we were all in for a very rough Christmas indeed, "I think it's Mr. Wrigglesworth. Will he try to introduce the sword?"

I looked at "Turpin" Timson with a kind of pity. "If it is the Mad Monk, he undoubtedly will."

When I went into Court, Basil Wrigglesworth was standing with his shoulders hunched up round his large, red ears, his gown dropped to his elbows, his bony wrists protruding from the sleeves of his frayed jacket, his wig pushed back, and his huge hands joined on his lectern in what seemed to be an attitude of devoted prayer. A lump of cotton wool clung to his chin where he had cut himself shaving. Although well into his sixties, he preserved a look of boyish clumsiness. He appeared, as he always did when about to prosecute on a charge carrying a major punishment, radiantly happy.

"Ah, Rumpole," he said, lifting his eyes from the police verbals as though they were his breviary. "Are you defending *as usual?*"

"Yes, Wrigglesworth. And you're prosecuting *as usual?*" It wasn't much of a riposte but it was all I could think of at the time.

"Of course, I don't defend. One doesn't like to call witnesses who may not be telling the truth."

"You must have a few unhappy moments then, calling certain members of the Constabulary."

"I can honestly tell you, Rumpole—" his curiously innocent blue eyes looked at me with a sort of pain, as though I had questioned the doctrine of the immaculate conception "—I have never called a dishonest police-man."

"Yours must be a singularly simple faith, Wrigglesworth."

"As for the Detective Inspector in this case," counsel for the prosecution went on, "I've known Wainwright for years. In fact, this is his last trial before he retires. He could no more invent a verbal against a defendant than fly."

Any more on that tack, I thought, and we should soon

be debating how many angels could dance on the point of a pin.

"Look here, Wrigglesworth. That evidence about my client having a sword: it's quite irrelevent. I'm sure you'd agree."

"Why is it irrelevant?" Wrigglesworth frowned.

"Because the murder clearly wasn't done with an antique cavalry saber. It was done with a small, thin blade."

"If he's a man who carries weapons, why isn't that relevant?"

"A man? Why do you call him a man? He's a child. A boy of seventeen!"

"Man enough to commit a serious crime."

"*If* he did."

"If he didn't, he'd hardly be in the dock."

"That's the difference between us, Wrigglesworth," I told him. "I believe in the presumption of innocence. You believe in original sin. Look here, old darling." I tried to give the Mad Monk a smile of friendship and became conscious of the fact that it looked, no doubt, like an ingratiating sneer. "Give us a chance. You won't introduce the evidence of the sword, will you?"

"Why ever not?"

"Well," I told him, "the Timsons are an industrious family of criminals. They word hard, they never go on strike. If it weren't for people like the Timsons, you and I would be out of a job."

"They sound in great need of prosecution and punishment. Why shouldn't I tell the jury about your client's sword? Can you give me one good reason?"

"Yes," I said, as convincingly as possible.

"What is it?" He peered at me, I thought, unfairly.

"Well, after all," I said, doing my best, "it is Christmas."

It would be idle to pretend that the first day in Court went well, although Wrigglesworth restrained himself

from mentioning the sword in his opening speech, and
told me that he was considering whether or not to call
evidence about it the next day. I cross-examined a few
members of the clan O'Dowd on the presence of lethal
articles in the hands of the attacking force. The evidence
about this varied, and weapons came and went in the
hands of the inhabitants of Number Twelve as the witnesses were blown hither and thither in the winds of
Rumpole's cross-examination. An interested observer
from one of the other flats spoke of having seen a ma-
chete.

"Could that terrible weapon have been in the hands of
Mr. Kevin O'Dowd, the deceased in this case?"

"I don't think so."

"But can you rule out the possibility?"

"No, I can't rule it out," the witness admitted, to my
temporary delight.

"You can never rule out the possibility of anything in
this world, Mr. Rumpole. But he doesn't think so. You
have your answer."

Mr. Justice Vosper, in a voice like a splintering ice-
berg, gave me this unwelcome Christmas present. The case
wasn't going well, but at least, by the end of the first
day, the Mad Monk had kept out all mention of the
swords. The next day he was to call young Bridget
O'Dowd, fresh from her triumph in the Nativity play.

"I say, Rumpole, I'd be *so* grateful for a little help."

I was in Pommeroy's Wine Bar, drowning the sorrows
of the day in my usual bottle of the cheapest Chateau
Fleet Street (made from grapes which, judging from the
bouquet, might have been not so much trodden as kicked
to death by sturdy peasants in gum boots) when I looked
up to see Wrigglesworth, dressed in an old mackintosh,
doing business with Jack Pommeroy at the sales counter.
When I crossed to him, he was not buying the jumbo-
sized bottle of ginger beer which I imagined might be

his celebratory Christmas tipple, but a tempting and respectably aged bottle of Chateau Pichon Longueville.

"What can I do for you, Wrigglesworth?"

"Well, as you know, Rumpole, I live in Croydon."

"Happiness is given to few of us on this earth," I said piously.

"And the Anglican Sisters of St. Agnes, Croydon, are anxious to buy a present for their Bishop," Wrigglesworth explained. "A dozen bottles for Christmas. They've asked my advice, Rumpole. I know so little about wine. You wouldn't care to try this for me? I mean, if you're not especially busy."

"I should be hurrying home to dinner." My wife, Hilda (She Who Must Be Obeyed), was laying on rissoles and frozen peas, washed down by my last bottle of Pommeroy's extremely ordinary. "However, as it's Christmas, I don't mind helping you out, Wrigglesworth."

The Mad Monk was clearly quite unused to wine. As we sampled the claret together, I saw the chance of getting him to commit himself on the vital question of the evidence of the sword, as well as absorbing an unusually decent bottle. After the Pichon Longueville I was kind enough to help him by sampling a Boyd-Cantenac and then I said, "Excellent, this. But of course the Bishop might be a burgundy man. The nuns might care to invest in a decent Macon."

"Shall we try a bottle?" Wrigglesworth suggested. "I'd be grateful for your advice."

"I'll do my best to help you, my old darling. And while we're on the subject, that ridiculous bit of evidence about young Timson and the sword—"

"I remember you saying I shouldn't bring that out because it's Christmas."

"Exactly." Jack Pommeroy had uncorked the Macon and it was mingling with the claret to produce a feeling of peace and goodwill towards men. Wrigglesworth frowned, as though trying to absorb an obscure point of theology.

"I don't quite see the relevance of Christmas to the question of your man Timson threatening his neighbors with a sword."

"Surely, Wrigglesworth—" I knew my prosecutor well "—you're of a religious disposition?" The Mad Monk was the product of some bleak northern Catholic boarding school. He lived alone, and no doubt wore a hair shirt under his black waistcoat and was vowed to celibacy. The fact that he had his nose deep into a glass of burgundy at the moment was due to the benign influence of Rumpole.

"I'm a Christian, yes."

"Then practice a little Christian tolerance."

"Tolerance towards evil?"

"Evil?" I asked. "What do you mean, evil?"

"Couldn't that be your trouble, Rumpole? That you really don't recognize evil when you see it."

"I suppose," I said, "evil might be locking up a seventeen-year-old during Her Majesty's pleasure, when Her Majesty may very probably forget all about him, banging him up with a couple of hard and violent cases and their own chamber-pots for twenty-two hours a day, so he won't come out till he's a real, genuine, middle-aged murderer."

"I did hear the Reverend Mother say—" Wrigglesworth was gazing vacantly at the empty Macon bottle "—that the Bishop likes his glass of port."

"Then in the spirit of Christmas tolerance I'll help you to sample some of Pommeroy's Light and Tawny."

A little later, Wrigglesworth held up his port glass in a reverent sort of fashion.

"You're suggesting, are you, that I should make some special concession in this case because it's Christmas-time?"

"Look here, old darling." I absorbed half my glass,

relishing the gentle fruitiness and the slight tang of wood. "If you spent your whole life in that highrise hell-hole called Keir Hardie Court, if you had no fat prosecutions to occupy your attention and no prospect of any job at all, if you had no sort of occupation except war with the O'Dowds—"

"My own flat isn't particularly comfortable. I don't know a great deal about *your* home life, Rumpole, but you don't seem to be in a tearing hurry to experience it."

"Touché, Wrigglesworth, my old darling." I ordered us a couple of refills of Pommeroy's port to further postpone the encounter with She Who Must Be Obeyed and her rissoles.

"But we don't have to fight to the death on the staircase," Wrigglesworth pointed out.

"We don't have to fight at all, Wrigglesworth."

"As your client did."

"As my client *may* have done. Remember the presumption of innocence."

"This is rather funny, this is.." The prosecutor pulled back his lips to reveal strong, yellowish teeth and laughed appreciatively. "You know why your man Timson is called 'Turpin' ?"

"No." I drank port uneasily, fearing an unwelcome revelation.

"Because he's always fighting with that sword of his. He's called after Dick Turpin, you see, who's always dueling on television. Do you watch television, Rumpole?"

"Hardly at all."

"I watch a great deal of television, as I'm alone rather a lot." Wrigglesworth referred to the box as though it were a sort of penance, like fasting or flagellation. "Detective Inspector Wainwright told me about your client. Rather amusing, I thought it was. He's retiring this Christmas."

"My client?"

''No. D.I. Wainwright. Do you think we should settle on this port for the Bishop? Or would you like to try a glass of something else?''

''Christmas,'' I told Wrigglesworth severely as we sampled the Cockburn, ''is not just a material, pagan celebration. It's not just an occasion for absorbing superior vintages, old darling. It must be a time when you try to do good, spiritual good to our enemies.''

''To your client, you mean?''

''And to me.''

''To you, Rumpole?''

''For God's sake, Wrigglesworth!'' I was conscious of the fact that my appeal was growing desperate. ''I've had six losers in a row down the Old Bailey. Can't I be included in any Christmas spirit that's going around?''

''You mean, at Christmas especially it is more blessed to give than to receive?''

''I mean exactly that.'' I was glad that he seemed, at last, to be following my drift.

''And you think I might give this case to someone, like a Christmas present?''

''If you care to put it that way, yes.''

''I do not care to put it in *exactly* that way.'' He turned his pale-blue eyes on me with what I thought was genuine sympathy. ''But I shall try and do the case of R. *v.* Timson in the way most appropriate to the greatest feast of the Christian year. It is a time, I quite agree, for the giving of presents.''

When they finally threw us out of Pommeroy's, and after we had considered the possibility of buying the Bishop brandy in the Cock Tavern, and even beer in the Devereux, I let my instinct, like an aged horse, carry me on to the Underground and home to Gloucester Road, and there discovered the rissoles, like some traces of a vanished civilization, fossilized in the oven. She Who

Must Be Obeyed was already in bed, feigning sleep. When I climbed in beside her, she opened a hostile eye.

"You're drunk, Rumpole!" she said. "What on earth have you been doing?"

"I've been having a legal discussion," I told her, "on the subject of the admissibility of certain evidence. Vital, from my client's point of view. And, just for a change, Hilda, I think I've won."

"Well, you'd better try and get some sleep." And she added with a sort of satisfaction, "I'm sure you'll be feeling quite terrible in the morning."

As with all the grimmer predictions of She Who Must Be Obeyed, this one turned out to be true. I sat in the Court the next day with the wig feeling like a lead weight on the brain and the stiff collar sawing the neck like a blunt execution. My mouth tasted of matured birdcage and from a long way off I heard Wrigglesworth say to Bridget O'Dowd, who stood looking particularly saintly and virginal in the witness box, "About a week before this, did you see the defendant, Edward Timson, on your staircase flourishing any sort of weapon?"

It is no exaggeration to say that I felt deeply shocked and considerably betrayed. After his promise to me, Wrigglesworth had turned his back on the spirit of the great Christmas festival. He came not to bring peace but a sword.

I clambered with some difficulty to my feet. After my forensic efforts of the evening before, I was scarcely in the mood for a legal argument. Mr. Justice Vosper looked up in surprise and greeted me in his usual chilly fashion.

"Yes, Mr. Rumpole. Do you object to this evidence?"

Of course I object, I wanted to say. It's inhuman, unnecessary, unmerciful, and likely to lead to my losing another case. Also, it's clearly contrary to a solemn and binding contract entered into after a number of glasses

of the Bishop's putative port. All I seemed to manage
was a strangled, "Yes."

"I suppose Mr. Wrigglesworth would say—" Vosper,
J., was, as ever, anxious to supply any argument that
might not yet have occurred to the prosecution "—that
it is evidence of 'system.' "

"System?" I heard my voice faintly and from a long
way off. "It may be, I suppose. But the Court has a
discretion to omit evidence which may be irrelevant and
purely prejudicial."

"I feel sure Mr. Wrigglesworth has considered the
matter most carefully and that he would not lead this
evidence unless he considered it entirely relevant."

I looked at the Mad Monk on the seat beside me. He
was smiling at me with a mixture of hearty cheerfulness
and supreme pity, as though I were sinking rapidly and
he had come to administer supreme unction. I made a
few ill-chosen remarks to the Court, but I was in no condition, that morning, to enter into a complicated legal
argument on the admissibility of evidence.

It wasn't long before Bridget O'Dowd had told a deeply
disapproving jury all about Eddie "Turpin" Timson's
sword. "A man," the judge said later in his summing up
about young Edward, "clearly prepared to attack with
cold steel whenever it suited him."

When the trial was over, I called in for refreshment at
my favorite watering hole and there, to my surprise, was
my opponent Wrigglesworth, sharing an expensive-
looking bottle with Detective Inspector Wainwright, the
officer in charge of the case. I stood at the bar, absorbing
a consoling glass of Pommeroy's ordinary, when the D.I.
came up to the bar for cigarettes. He gave me a friendly
and maddeningly sympathetic smile.

"Sorry about that, sir. Still, win a few, lose a few.
Isn't that it?"

"In my case lately, it's been win a few, lose a lot!"

"You couldn't have this one, sir. You see, Mr. Wrigglesworth had promised it to me."

"He had *what?*"

"Well, I'm retiring, as you know. And Mr. Wrigglesworth promised me faithfully that my last case would be a win. He promised me that, in a manner of speaking, as a Christmas present. Great man is our Mr. Wrigglesworth, sir, for the spirit of Christmas."

I looked across at the Mad Monk and a terrible suspicion entered my head. What was all that about a present for the Bishop? I searched my memory and I could find no trace of our having, in fact, bought wine for any sort of cleric. And was Wrigglesworth as inexperienced as he would have had me believe in the art of selecting claret?

As I watched him pour and sniff a glass from his superior bottle and hold it critically to the light, a horrible suspicion crossed my mind. Had the whole evening's events been nothing but a deception, a sinister attempt to nobble Rumpole, to present him with such a stupendous hangover that he would stumble in his legal argument? Was it all in aid of D.I. Wainwright's Christmas present?

I looked at Wrigglesworth, and it would be no exaggeration to say the mind boggled. He was, of course, perfectly right about me. I just didn't recognize evil when I saw it.

SANTA'S WAY

by James Powell

Lieutenant Field parked behind the Animal Protective League van. The night was cold, the stars so bright he could almost taste them. Warmer constellations of tree lights decorated the dark living rooms on both sides of the street. Field turned up his coat collar. Then he followed the footprints in the snow across the lawn and up to the front door of the house where a uniformed officer stood shuffling his feet against the weather.

Captain Fountain was on the telephone in the front hallway and listening so hard he didn't notice Field come in. "Yes, Commissioner," he said. "Yes, sir, Commissioner." Then he laid a hand over the mouthpiece, looked up at a light fixture on the ceiling, and demanded, "Why me, Lord? Why me?" (The department took a dim view of men talking to themselves on duty. So Fountain always addressed furniture or fixtures. He confided much to urinals. They all knew how hard-done-by Fountain was.) Turning to repeat his question to the hatrack he saw Field. "Sorry to bring you out on this of all nights, Roy," he said. He pointed into the living room and added cryptically, "Check out the fireplace, why don't you?" Then he went back to listening.

Field crossed to the cold hearth. There were runs of blood down the sides of the flue. Large, red, star-shaped spatters decorated the ashes.

A woman's muffled voice said, "I heard somebody coming down the chimney." A blonde in her late thirties sitting in a wing chair in the corner, her face buried in a handkerchief. She looked up at Field with red-rimmed eyes. "After I called you people I even shouted up and told him you were on your way. But he kept on coming."

Captain Fountain was off the telephone. From the doorway he said, "So Miss Doreen Moore here stuck her pistol up the flue and fired away."

"Ka-pow, ka-pow, ka-pow," said the woman, making her hand into a pistol and, in Field's opinion, mimicking the recoil quite well. But he didn't quite grasp the situation until men emerged from the darkness on the other side of the picture window and reached up to steady eight tiny reindeer being lowered down from the roof in a large sling.

"Oh, no!" said Field.

"Oh, yes," said Fountain. "Come see for yourself."

Field followed him upstairs to the third-floor attic where the grim-faced Animal Protective League people, their job done, were backing down the ladder from the trap door in the roof.

Field and Fountain stood out on the sloping shingles under the stars. Christmas music came from the radio in the dashboard of the pickle-dish sleigh straddling the ridge of the roof. Close at hand was Santa, both elbows on the lip of the chimney, his body below the armpits and most of his beard out of sight down the hole. He was quite dead. The apples in his cheeks were Granny Smiths, green and hard.

Only the week before Field had watched the PBS documentary "Santa's Way." Its final minutes were still fresh in his mind. Santa in an old tweed jacket sat at his desk at the Toy Works backed by a window that looked right down onto the factory floor busy with elves. Mrs. Claus, her eyes on her knitting, smiled and nodded at his words and rocked nearby. "Starting out all we could afford to leave was a candy cane and an orange," Santa had said. "The elves made the candy canes and it was up to me to beg or borrow the oranges. Well, one day the United Fruit people said, 'Old timer, you make it a Chiquita banana and we'll supply them free and make a sizable donation to the elf scholarship fund.' But commercializing Christmas wasn't Santa's way. So we made do with the orange. And look at us now." He lowered his hairy white head modestly. "The Toy Works is running three shifts making sleds and dolls and your paint boxes with your yellows, blues, and reds. The new cargo dirigible lets us restock the sleigh in flight." Santa gave the camera a sadder look. "Mind you, there's a down side," he acknowledged. "We've strip-mined and deforested the hell out of the North Pole for the sticks and lumps of coal we give our naughty little clients. And our bond rating isn't as good as it used to be. Still, when the bankers say, 'Why not charge a little something, a token payment for each toy?' I always answer, 'That isn't Santa's way.' "

An urgent voice from the sleigh radio intruded on Field's remembering. "We interrupt this program for a news bulletin," it said. "Santa is dead. We repeat, Santa is dead. The jolly old gentleman was shot several times in the chimney earlier this evening. More details when they are available." At that late hour all good little boys and girls were in bed. Otherwise, Field knew, the announcer would've said, "Antasay is eadday," and continued in pig Latin.

Field stood there glumly watching the street below where the A.P.L. people were chasing after a tiny reindeer which had escaped while being loaded into the van. Lights had come on all over the neighborhood and faces were appearing in windows. After a moment, he turned his attention to the corpse.

But Fountain was feeling the cold. "Roy," he said impatiently, "Santa came down the wrong chimney. The woman panicked. Ka-pow, ka-pow, ka-pow! Cut and dried."

Field shook his head. "Rooftops are like finger-prints," he reminded the Captain. "No two are alike. Santa wouldn't make a mistake like—" He frowned, leaned forward, and put his face close to the corpse's.

"It wasn't just the smell of whiskey on his lips, Miss Moore," said Field. "You see, if Santa'd been going down the chimney his beard would've been pushed up over his face. But it was stuck down inside. Miss Moore, when you shot Santa he was on his way up that chimney."

The woman twisted the handkerchief between her fingers. "All right," she snapped. Then in a quieter voice she said, "All right, Nicky and I go back a long way. Right around here is end of the line for his Christmas deliveries. I'll bet you didn't know that."

Field had guessed as much. Last year when his kids wondered why the treat they left on a tray under the tree was never touched he had suggested maybe Santa was milk-and-cookied out by the time he got to their house.

"Anyway," continued Miss Moore, "Nicky'd always drop by afterwards for a drink and some laughs and one thing would lead to another. But I'm not talking one-night stands," she insisted. "We took trips. We spent time together whenever he could get away. He said he loved Mrs. Claus but she was a saint. And I wasn't a saint, he said, and he loved me for that. And I was crazy about him. But tonight he tried to walk out on me. So I shot him."

In the distance Field heard the police helicopter come to take the sleigh on the roof to Impound.

Fountain said, "Better get Miss Moore down to the station before this place is crawling with reporters. I'll wait for the boys with the flue-extractor rig."

* * *

Field turned on his car radio to catch any late-breaking developments. "O Tannenbaum, O Tannenbaum, how beautiful your branches!" sang a small choir. They drove without speaking for a while. Then out of nowhere the woman said, "You know that business about Nicky having a belly that shook like a bowl full of jelly? Well, that was just the poet going for a cheap rhyme. Nicky took care of himself. He exercised. He jogged. And he had this twinkle in his eye that'd just knock my socks off."

"I heard about the twinkle," Field admitted.

"But underneath it all there was this deep sadness,' she said. "It wasn't just the fund-raising, the making the rounds every year, hat in hand, for money to keep the North Pole going. And it wasn't the elves, although they weren't always that easy to deal with. 'They can be real short, Doreen,' he told me once. 'Hey, I know elves are short, Nicky. Give me credit for some brains,' I said. He said, 'No, Doreen, I mean abrupt.'

"One time I asked him why he got so low and he said, 'Doreen, when I look all those politicians, bankers, lawyers, and captains of industry in the eye do you know who I see staring back at me? Those same naughty little boys and girls I gave the sticks and lumps of coal to. Where did I do wrong, Doreen? How did they end up running the show?'

"Well, a while back Nicky got this great idea how he could walk away from the whole business. Mr. Santa franchises. He'd auction the whole operation off country by country. Mr. Santa U.S.A. gets exclusive rights to give free toys to American kids and so on, country by country. 'And the elves'd take care of Mrs. Claus,' he said. 'They love her. She's a saint. And with the money I'll raise you and me'll buy a boat and sail away. We'll live off my patented Mr. Santa accessories. You know, my wide belt and the metered tape recorder of my laugh at a buck a 'ho!' "

Suddenly a voice on the radio said, "We now take you

to New York where Leviathan Cribbage, elf observer to the United Nations, is about to hold a press conference.'' After the squeal of a microphone being adjusted downward a considerable distance, a high-pitched little voice said, ''The High Council of Elves has asked me to issue the following statement: 'Cast down as we are by the murder of our great leader, Santa Claus, we are prepared, as a memorial to the man and his work, to continue to manufacture and distribute toys on the night before Christmas. In return we ask that our leader's murderer, whom we know to be in police custody, be turned over to elf justice. If the murderer is not in our hands within twenty-four hours the Toy Works at the North Pole will be shut down permanently.' '' The room erupted into a hubbub of voices.

''Turn me over to elf justice?'' said Miss Moore with a shudder. ''That doesn't sound so hot.''

''It won't happen,'' Field assured her as he parked the car. ''Even a politician couldn't get away with a stunt like that.''

Four detectives were crowded around the squad room television set. Field took Miss Moore into his office. Gesturing her into a chair, he sat down at his desk and said, ''Now where were we?''

''With a buck a 'ho!' and me waiting there tonight with my bags packed,'' she said. ''And here comes Nicky down the chimney. 'Doreen,' he says. 'I've only got a minute. I've still deliveries to make. Honey, I told Mrs. Claus about us. She's forgiven me, as I knew she would. But I can't see you again.'

'' 'What about the Mr. Santa auction?' said I.

'' 'Some auction,' he said. 'Everybody wanted America or Germany. Nobody wanted to be the Bangladeshi or the Ethiopian Mr. Santa. Crazy, isn't it? Everybody wants to load up the kids who've already got everything when giving to kids with nothing is the real fun.' Then he looked at me and said, 'It got me thinking about where I went wrong, Doreen. Maybe I should have given my naughty little clients toys, too. Maybe then they wouldn't have grown up into the kinds of people they did. Anyway, I'm going to give it a try. From now on, I'll be Santa of all the children, naughty or nice. Good-bye, Doreen,' he said and turned to go.

"That's when I pulled out the revolver I keep around because I'm alone so much. I was tired of men who put their careers ahead of their women. I swore I'd kill him if he tried to leave. He went 'ho-ho-ho!' and took the gun out of my hand. He knew I couldn't shoot. I burst into tears. He gathered me in his arms and gave me a good-bye kiss. Emptying the bullets onto the rug, he tossed the pistol aside and walked over to the fireplace. 'You're a nice girl, Doreen,' he said with a twinkle in his eye. 'Don't let anybody ever tell you different.' But just before he ducked his head under the mantel I saw the twinkle flicker.''

"Flicker?'' asked Field.

"Like he was thinking maybe he'd figured me wrong,'' she explained. "Like maybe I'd reload the gun. Well, up the chimney he went, hauling ass real fast. And suddenly, I was down on my knees pushing those bullets back into that pistol, furious that I'd wasted my whole life just to be there any time that old geezer in his red wool suit with that unfashionably wide belt could slip his collar and be with me, furious that he was dumping me just so he could give toys to naughty little boys and girls. I was trembling with rage. But every bullet I dropped I picked up again. When I'd gotten them all I went over and emptied the pistol up the chimney. Then I called you people.''

Field's telephone rang. "Roy,'' said his wife, "I just heard the news about Santa. Roy, there aren't any presents under our tree. What are we going to do?''

"Lois, I can't talk now,'' said Field. "Don't worry.

I'll think of something." He hung up the phone. Maybe if he worked all night he could cobble together some toys out of that scrap lumber in the basement.

Fountain was signaling from the doorway. He had an efficient-looking young woman with him. Field stepped outside. "Roy, this is Agent Mountain, Federal Witness Protection Program," he said. "I just got off the phone with the Commissioner. We're not bringing charges."

"Captain, we could be talking premeditated murder here," insisted Field, telling the part about her putting the bullets back into the pistol.

Fountain shrugged. "You want a trial? You want all the nice little boys and girls finding out that Santa was murdered and why? No way, Roy. She walks. But we can't let those damn knee-highs get her."

"You mean elves?" asked Field, who had never heard elves referred to in that derogatory way before.

"You got it," said Fountain. "So Agent Mountain's here to relocate her, give her a whole new identity.

Agent Mountain waved through the door at Doreen Moore. "Hi, honey," she said cheerily. "It looks like it's back to being a brunette."

Field put on his overcoat and closed his office door behind him. He stopped for a moment in front of the squad room television set. Somebody from the State Department was saying, "Peter, let's clear up one misconception right now. Elves are not short genetically. Their growth has been stunted by smoking and other acts of depravity associated with a perverse lifestyle. Can we let such twisted creatures hold our children's happiness hostage? I think not. I refer the second part of your question to General Frost."

A large man in white camouflage placed a plan of the Toy Works at the North Pole on an easel. "In case of a military strike against them, the elves intend to destroy the Toy Works with explosive charges set here, here, and here," he said, tapping with a pointer. "As I speak, our airborne forces, combined with crack RCMP dogsled units, have moved to neutralize—"

Field's phone was ringing. He hurried back to his office. "Hey, Lieutenant," said Impound, "We found presents in Santa's sleigh, some with your kids' names on them. Want to come by and pick them up?"

Field came in with the presents trapped between his chin and his forearm, closing the door quietly behind him. His wife was rattling around in the kitchen. He didn't call out to her, not wanting to wake the children. The light from the kitchen would be enough to put the presents under the tree. He was halfway across the living room when the lights came on. His children were staring down at him from the top of the stairs. Zack and Lesley, the eldest, exchanged wise glances. Charlotte was seven. She'd lost her first baby tooth that afternoon and her astonished mouth had a gap in it.

Field smiled up at them. "Santa got held up in traffic," he lied. "So he deputized a bunch of us as Santa's little helpers to deliver his presents." Charlotte received this flimsy nonsense with large, perplexed eyes. It was the first time he had ever told her anything she didn't believe instantly.

Ordering the children back to bed, Field went into the kitchen. Lois was watching a round-table discussion called "Life After Santa" on the little television set. When he told her about the presents from Impound she said, "Thank God." He didn't tell her what had just happened with the kids. Maybe one of these days he'd be able to sit down and give them the straight scoop, how there really had been this nice guy called Santa Claus who went around in a sleigh pulled by reindeer giving kids presents because he loved them, so, of course, we had to shoot him.

He turned on the kettle to make himself a cup of instant coffee and sat down beside his wife. On the screen a celebrated economist was saying, "Of course, we'll have to find an alternate energy source. Our entire industrial base has always depended on Santa's sticks and lumps of coal."

"But what a golden opportunity to end our kids' dependence on free toys," observed a former National Security advisor. "That's always smelled like socialism to me. Kids have to learn there's no free lunch. We should hand the Toy Works over to private enterprise. I hear Von Clausewitz Industries are interested in getting into toys."

"What about distribution?" asked someone else.

"Maybe we could talk the department stores into selling toys for a week or two before Christmas."

"Selling toys?" asked someone in disbelief.

The National Security advisor smiled. "We can hardly expect the Von Clausewitz people to pick up the tab. No, the toys'll have to be sold. But the play of the marketplace will hold prices—"

Field heard a sound. Someone had raised an upstairs window. Footsteps headed down the hall toward the children's rooms. He took the stairs two at a time, reaching the top with his service revolver drawn. Someone was standing in the dark corner by Charlotte's door. Crouching, pistol at the ready, Field snapped on the hall light. "Freeze!" he shouted.

The woman turned and gave him a questioning look. She had immense rose-gossamer wings of a swallow-tail cut sprouting from her shoulder-blades and a gown like white enamel shimmering with jewels. He didn't recognize who it was behind the surgical mask until she tugged at the wrists of her latex gloves, took a shiny quarter from the coin dispenser at her waist and stepped into Charlotte's room.

Field came out of his crouch slowly. Returning his weapon to its holster he went back down to the kitchen. He turned off the kettle, found the whiskey bottle in the cupboard and poured himself a drink with a trembling hand. "Lois," he said, "I almost shot the Tooth Fairy."

"Oh, Roy," she scolded in a tired voice.

On the television screen someone said, "Of course, we'll need a fund to provide toys for the children of the deserving poor."

"Don't you mean 'the deserving children of the poor'?" someone asked.

" 'Deserving children of the deserving poor,' " suggested another.

Lois shook her head. "Store-bought toys, Roy?" she asked. "We've got mortgage payments, car payments, Lesley's orthodontist, and saving for the kids' college. How can we afford store-bought toys?"

It'd been a hard day. He didn't want to talk about next year's toys. "Lois, please—" he started to say a bit snappishly. But here the program broke for a commercial and a voice said, "Hey, Mom, hey, kids, is Dad getting a little short? (And we don't mean abrupt). Why not send him along to see the folks at Tannenbaum Savings and Loan. All our offices have been tastefully decorated for the season. And there's one near you. So remember—" here a choir chimed in "—Owe Tannenbaum, Owe Tannenbaum, how beautiful their branches!"

CARMINE AND THE CHRISTMAS PRESENCE

by Charles Ardai

"It is for my daughter, but it's not just for her. Do you understand what I'm telling you?" Guy Weston looked at his watch. "Hold on a sec." He pressed his intercom button. "Debbie, keep McCabe out there another minute, will you?" He released the button.

Across the desk, Carmine Turturo shifted his hands in his lap.

"I want this for her for Christmas, Carmine. But I'm not going to be here for Christmas. I leave for Tokyo on the eighteenth. And if I'm going to pay you to build the damn thing, I want to see it before I go. So be sure it's finished before the eighteenth. I'll have Martin make space for it in the living room, and you can bring it in any time after the tenth. Understand?"

Carmine nodded. "Can I ask you one thing? Was the tree your idea or your wife's?"

"What do you think?" Weston looked at his watch again. "Any other questions?"

"No," Carmine said. "No questions."

It was cold out, so Carmine pulled his coat tight around him until he was inside his apartment. Even then, he took some time to warm up, rubbing his hands together in his gloves and pressing his thighs against each other through his pants. The radiator was hissing and clanking as though the landlord had just turned on the heat, but he hadn't; the pipes were as cold as the pans in Carmine's kitchen cabinet. The clanking and hissing were only sound effects. Carmine didn't know how the landlord created them, but it certainly wasn't the ordinary way.

Carmine took down his biggest saucepan, filled it with water from the tap, and set it on top of his gas range. In a few minutes, the water started to give off steam. Carmine unbuttoned his jacket. A little later, he took it off. Then he sat on his bed and removed his shoes.

In one corner of his bedroom, Carmine had his workbench set up with all his tools. There wasn't enough room for much in the way of materials, just odds and ends of scrap wood that he had saved out from his last job. But this was enough to test out new designs or to whittle into interesting shapes on particularly cold nights. Carmine couldn't sleep when he was cold, and in Buffalo that meant lots of nights for whittling.

His newest project sat in miniature on a stack of sketches: a hollow wooden Christmas tree. The tree had a little entrance on one side of its trunk. From his bed, Carmine could look through it. Inside, a tiny human figure sat on a pedestal. This was one of the interesting shapes he had whittled one night, a project to keep his mind busy while he couldn't get to sleep. How small could you carve a human shape and still make it look like a person? Carmine had discovered the answer just before dawn: very small. With a sharp knife, very small indeed.

But small was not Carmine's worry now. Big was— big, with lots of detail. Guy Weston wanted a hollow tree for his little girl Kingsley. A life-sized wooden tree with an opening big enough for Kingsley to crawl through, and inside a life-sized wooden elf for her to fall in love with. Which would be easier than falling in love with her father, who was life-sized and wooden but not much of an elf.

Weston had come to Carmine because a friend of his wife's had had Carmine do their deck. "Carpentry with class" was apparently how Carmine had been recommended to Sophie Weston, back when the Westons had been set on adding a wing to their house. That had fallen through. But when Sophie had seen Carmine's portfolio of special projects, she had hit on the idea of having him custom-make a Christmas gift for Kingsley. She didn't know what, but something special.

That was the last he had heard of the idea, and that had been in July.

But now it was November, and he had come home one afternoon to a message from Weston's secretary, Debbie, on his answering machine. Carmine had called Weston back and heard the good news direct from the boss's mouth: the deal was on. That was how Weston had put it.

The deal was that Carmine would create a work for hire, under deadline, to Guy Weston's specifications. Which specifications were typed out in memo form with a line at the bottom for Carmine's signature. Which Carmine gave. A job was a job.

At least this was an interesting job—something special, as Sophie had put it. The specifications were clear enough: no pointy beard on the elf, no small pieces on the tree that might break off and injure Kingsley. There was nothing outrageous.

And heaven knew Kingsley Weston deserved something nice for Christmas, something to make up for not having her father around for the holiday, though Carmine imagined that not having Guy Weston around was pretty nice all by itself.

So Carmine had agreed to take the job.

And then he had gone to that awful meeting in Weston's office where Weston had carefully negotiated him down to half his fee. Which Carmine had reluctantly accepted because half was better than nothing, and nothing was what he had coming in if he turned down this job.

So he went to his sketchpad, and then to his workbench, coming up with a design that would be sturdy and safe. And he took it back to Guy Weston, who looked at it, shrugged, and said he would show it to his wife.

Today had been Carmine's fourth meeting with Guy Weston, and he found himself wishing it had been his last. Weston was a rotten father and a rotten human being, not to mention a rotten customer, and Carmine couldn't sit in the same room with him without feeling dirty. Photos of Weston's family hung behind his desk like trophies, Weston's beefy arms encircling his daughter or his wife or both at once, with an expression on his face in all the pictures that said, *Look what I've got. Good deal, huh?*

And always with the watch when you were with him, making sure that you didn't use up a minute more than he had allotted you in his schedule. The first day they had met, Weston had cut Carmine off in the middle of a sentence. ''Got to go,'' he had said. And he had gone.

Debbie had ushered Carmine out of Weston's office so quickly that time that he'd had to beg her to let him back in to get the portfolio he'd left on Weston's desk. She'd agreed, but just barely.

Carmine set his finished sketches aside and started working on enlarged details: the grooves of the trunk, the tapering branches, the arch of the opening. His pencil flew over the paper. Kingsley would get her tree, and by the deadline, too. Sophie would get the pleasure of making her daughter smile. And Weston—Weston would get the pleasure of having bought something else. That was the man's whole life as far as Carmine could tell. Buying something else.

Carmine scribbled out the design he was working on and started again on a new sheet of paper.

The pedestal inside the tree was modeled after a Doric

column—that had been Sophie's idea. Sophie was quite a creative woman, though she didn't have much of a chance to show it. Planning a party for Guy's partners seemed to be the extent of her self-expression, and she had to do that so often that she didn't have time for much else.

Once, over the summer, she had shown Carmine some sketches she'd made of the new wing they'd talked about adding. She was no architect, nor even a trained artist, but she had skill with a pen and Carmine had told her so. He had never seen her as happy as she had been when he'd said that.

Then, at the end of the summer, Sophie had called him to say that they weren't going to build the new wing after all. When she told him, she said it in her husband's words: the deal was off. She never said why, but it was clear that it had been Guy's decision.

It wasn't because they couldn't afford it—Carmine was offering the job for barely more than the cost of materials, and Guy Weston could have afforded twice that. Carmine didn't even think it was because Guy didn't want it; there's nothing a man like Guy Weston likes more than being able to tell everyone that he is adding a wing to his house.

No, Carmine felt certain that he had found out that Carmine had praised his wife's sketches. And Weston had realized that the new wing would be *her* wing, or at least her design, and he couldn't stand that. So he had said no, and then had made her call Carmine and say no herself.

When he got the call, Carmine could almost feel Weston on the other end of the phone. He could almost see Weston standing behind Sophie with his hands on her shoulders, coaxing her.

Since then Weston had evidently decided, out of whatever shred of compassion there was in him, to let her at least have her tree. That was what he had meant when

he had said that the gift was not just for his daughter. It
was also a peace offering for Sophie.

That was another reason Carmine hadn't hesitated to
take the job, and another reason that he would even put
up with more meetings with Guy Weston. Sophie Weston
would be happy, Kingsley Weston would be happy, and
as for Guy Weston—he could go to hell.

Carmine shook his head. There was a kicker. He had
caught the bastard with his secretary.

That had been the last nail in Weston's coffin as far as
Carmine was concerned. He had almost called Sophie up
and told her. She had a right to know what her husband
was doing. But Carmine had decided in the end that it
wasn't his business to tell her.

Carmine had gone by for his second meeting with
Weston on Tuesday instead of Thursday. It was an honest
mistake; Carmine had scrawled "Weston—T. 2:00" in
the notebook he carried in his pocket, but had forgotten
which "T" he had meant. So he went on Tuesday.

The door to the office was unlocked, which was a care-
less mistake on Debbie's part. Carmine went in quietly,
saw that Debbie wasn't at her desk, and walked up to
Weston's office door.

It was open a crack. Through the crack, Carmine saw
two pairs of naked legs on the carpet. He heard two
voices. One of them was Weston's, and the other one was
Debbie's.

So Carmine left. And went back on Thursday, feeling
nothing for Guy Weston but contempt.

Carmine sat back in his chair and looked at the work
he had done. In front of him were three sketches of the
elf, the wooden doll he would carve for Kingsley. The
elf's features were screwed up in an expression halfway
between disgust and anger.

That's what I get for sketching and thinking about Guy
Weston at the same time, Carmine thought. He turned

his pencil around to erase the elf's face. But he stopped himself.

On second thought, he liked the face. He could soften it a bit in the carving, but there was no reason an elf had to smile. Not much to smile about in the Weston house anyway.

Carmine worked on the sketches some more and then went to sleep when the heat finally came on. Over the following weeks, he bought wood with Weston's up-front money and started carving out the pieces that he would assemble into the tree. A week before the deadline, he took a solid block of wood and started carving the elf.

And then it was December seventeenth, and Carmine Turturo was finished.

He drove over in the early morning, the tree pieces rattling in the back of his station wagon. The elf sat on the seat next to him, strapped in with the seat belt. Its face hadn't gotten any softer, but Carmine thought the expression was the right one. The elf had one arm up, reaching over its shoulder, and in this hand it held a red cloth sack. Each morning Sophie would put a gift in the sack for Kingsley to find. Carmine wondered if she would think it was magic.

Martin was the Westons' help, a gaunt, sad-faced man with a shock of yellow-white hair that lay on his head like a bad toupee. It was his own hair, Carmine was certain, but it looked like a cheap imitation. Martin helped Carmine unload the tree and carry it into the living room, where Guy Weston waited. The two men put the tree together while Weston watched. Finally, Carmine carried the elf in and held it out for Weston's inspection.

"What's that?" Weston pointed at the elf's face. "What the hell is wrong with you? Didn't I tell you this is for my daughter? You want her to have nightmares?"

Sophie Weston stepped forward and looked over her husband's shoulder. "I think it's very interesting."

Weston reached into the breast pocket of his jacket and pulled out a folded piece of paper. He unfolded it. "This is your contract, Turturo. See your signature there at the bottom? Now look up here. Here. Where it says you'll carve an elf." He waved at the elf. "That's not an elf. That's a goddamn gnome. That's a goblin! I'm not paying you."

"Mr. Weston," Carmine said, "you didn't specify how the elf should look. You didn't say you wanted to see it beforehand. You want me to change it, it will take a few days at least."

"In one day I'll be in Japan, mister."

"Guy, it's all right." Sophie put her hands on his arm. "I think it's very beautiful."

"Thank you," Carmine said.

Guy looked at his wife, then at Carmine. Then he picked up the elf. "I'll pay you half," he said.

In the end, Carmine agreed.

Sophie helped Martin position the tree in the living room. They had to push the stereo console against the wall to do so, and that meant moving a pair of Chippendale chairs to make room. A little reshuffling was all that was necessary—the living room was enormous and could easily hold the new addition.

The bottom of the tree was covered with a thick layer of felt, so as not to scratch the hardwood floor. The trunk and branches had been left unpainted to match the room's decor. Inside, Carmine had painted the trunk wall nut brown and the pedestal leaf green. The elf's suit was stained Santa Claus red, to match the sack. The elf's face remained the natural color of the wood.

Sophie set the elf on its pedestal, the sack hanging down behind it like a cape, then crawled out of the tree backwards. Her shoulders were just narrow enough to fit through the opening. "Guy, it's wonderful."

"Certainly cost enough."

"Kingsley will love it." She kissed her husband, quickly, on the cheek.

He looked at his watch.

"What is it?"

"Got to go.'

"Wait till Kingsley has seen it," Sophie said. "Please."

"Kingsley!" Weston bellowed. "Come down here."

Kingsley sang out from her bedroom on the second floor, "Coming!" A minute later, she appeared on the stairs.

When she saw the tree, a huge smile spread over her face. She circled the trunk, found the opening, and went inside. When she came out again, she was carrying the elf in her arms. "Oh, Daddy, I love it! He's wonderful! Is he mine?"

Weston held his watch up for his wife to see.

"Yes," Sophie said. "He's yours."

"Thank you!" Kingsley spun the doll around. "I'm going to call him Ernie, Daddy!"

"Good," Weston said. "Got to run. Merry Christmas."

The tree did not fit in, not really. Not with the Mondrian hanging behind it or the Malevich on the other wall, not with the Tiffany lamp on the end table, and certainly not with the pieces in the display case by the door. The tree was too simple, too straightforward. It would fit in a poor man's apartment and put a rich man's home to shame.

But that was not particularly a bad thing. Sophie liked the effect the tree had. It stood in the middle of the room as though it had grown there overnight, pushing the ostentatious reminders of Guy's taste as a decorator off to the sides. The tree dominated the room now, as Sophie had known it would. She was glad she had talked Guy into commissioning it, and especially into hiring Carmine Turturo. She didn't think anyone else could have made it.

And the elf! The elf was so realistic it was almost unnerving. The detail work was exquisite: the little man's wrinkled cheeks and forehead, his hard fingernails just long enough to want paring, the tiny bunions pressing out at the sides of his boots. It was extraordinary, really.

Each morning when Sophie awoke, she crawled into the tree to put a gift in Ernie's sack. Then she went back to sleep and, a few hours later, was awakened by Kingsley's delighted squeal. Kingsley would run into Sophie's bedroom, all flying limbs and blonde hair, and show her mother what Ernie had brought her.

But those minutes spent in the tree were special all by themselves. Sophie grew to relish them, to wake up earlier and earlier so she would be able to spend more time sitting with her back to the pedestal, Ernie's sack behind her head, looking out at the room she lived in. She felt safe and private sitting in the tree, safe from the life she had built up with Guy and safe from her role as Guy Weston's wife.

His trip to Japan was a blessing, really. Sophie didn't mind being alone for Christmas anymore. Spending the holiday with Guy was worse. She even found herself wishing, sometimes, that Guy would never come back. Not that he would die or get lost, but that time would slow down and the days before Christmas would extend forever. Each day she would give Kingsley another gift, each day she would wake up hearing laughter, and New Year's Day, when Guy was to return, would never come.

She started to cry once when she thought of this. It was three days before Christmas and she had just put a stuffed turtle in Ernie's sack. She turned to Ernie and looked up into his face, and through her tears she thought she saw his beige face blush a pale pink. When she wiped the tears away, the blush was gone.

She didn't think about it again until the next morning when, crying once more, she looked at Ernie and saw his eyes blink shut and then open again. The wooden elf's lips trembled, as though about to speak, and then were solid and fixed when Sophie stood to look closer.

She left the tree feeling foolish and self-conscious, the stern self-control Guy preached taking hold of her.

But the day before Christmas there was no mistaking it. Sophie woke before dawn and sat in the tree facing Ernie. His body never moved, but his cheeks inflated with breath, and his eyes grew moist and dark. His voice when it came, sounded deep, like the wind blowing through a pipe or a horn.

"Your husband is not in Japan." The voice seemed to echo inside the tree. "He never got on the plane from Hawaii."

The doll's lips barely moved. But they moved.

Sophie was mute.

"He is cheating on you, Sophie."

The words could barely come out of her mouth. "With Debbie?"

Slowly and gravely, Ernie nodded.

"God!" Sophie's tears ran onto her palms as she put her head in her arms.

"Your daughter loves you very much."

"My husband hates me!"

"No," the doll said. "But you hate him."

"Yes," Sophie said. She looked up into his angry face. "Have there been other women?"

"Many," said the elf.

"And you know this? How?"

"Because you know it."

Sophie nodded. "Thank you," she said.

"Merry Christmas," said the elf.

* * *

On the first day of January, Guy Weston drove back to his house. It was already dark, though it was only the early evening, and he drove slowly to give his digestion a chance to settle. Flying gave him an upset stomach.

He was not surprised to find his house dark when he arrived. Earlier in his marriage he would have expected Sophie to wait for him and wrap him in her arms as soon as he walked through the door. But that spark had died long ago, to be replaced by an unbecoming iciness. It wasn't entirely Sophie's fault, Weston knew; he'd handled her badly, too. But she was the only one who could change it now, and from the looks of things she wasn't going to change it tonight. He'd walk into a dark house, climb into a dark bed, and wake up in a dark mood. Her own fault.

He unlocked his front door noisily. If they woke up, that was too bad. It was his house, wasn't it? No reason he should have to sneak around in the dark.

He flipped on the lights.

The living room was empty.

The walls were stark white, with squares of clean paint where the pictures had hung. The antiques were gone—it wasn't that the cabinet was empty, it wasn't there at all. The stereo, the recessed bar and projection TV console, the Tiffany lamp, the end table—all gone. A note taped to the wall began, "Guy, I'm taking Kingsley."

At the instant Guy Weston's eyes fastened, with disbelief, on the note, a single, loud knock came on Carmine's door.

He turned off the gas under the pot of soup he was stirring, put down his spoon, and went to look out the peephole. He saw no one in the hall.

Part of Carmine told him to ignore the knock, that it was either nothing or something he shouldn't open the door to, but another part of him moved his hands to turn the locks and lift the chain bolt.

Outside, silhouetted by the hallway's fluorescent light, was a three foot tall man in a parka and boots with a bulging red sack on his back. He pushed past Carmine and dropped the sack on the floor. Carmine let the door swing shut. Otherwise he couldn't move.

The little man bent over the sack and undid the tie that held it closed. Then he reached in and started pulling out item after item, filling Carmine's apartment with jewels and antiques and flatware and appliances. When, at last, the sack was empty, Ernie climbed in it and pulled it closed over his head.

Carmine didn't open the sack until days afterward and when he did, he only found his carved elf, its features locked in a blissful smile.

—*with thanks to Connie Scarborough*

THE SHAPE
OF THE NIGHTMARE

by Francis M. Nevins, Jr.

On the afternoon of the second day before Christmas, just before the terror swept the airport, Loren Mensing was studying the dispirited and weaving line in front of the ticket counter and wishing fervently that he were somewhere else.

He had turned in his exam grades at the law school, said goodbye to the handful of December graduates among his students, and wasted three days moping, with the dread of spending the holidays alone again festering inside him like an untreated wound. The high-rise apartment building he'd lived in for years was being converted to condominiums, dozens of tenants had moved out and dozens more had flown south for the holidays, and the isolation in the building reinforced his sense of being alone in the world.

He had called a travel agent and booked passage on a week-long Caribbean cruise where, if he was lucky, he might find someone as seasonally lonely as he was himself. A *Love Boat* fantasy that he tried desperately to make himself believe. He drove to the airport through swirling snow that froze to ice on the Volkswagen's windshield. He checked his bags, went through security at the lower level, and was lounging near the departure gate for Flight 317, nonstop to Miami, when he heard his name over a microphone.

And learned that he'd been bumped.

"I'm very sorry, Mr. Mensing." The passenger service rep seemed to look bored, solicitous, and in charge all at once. "We have to overbook flights because so many reserved-seat holders don't cancel but don't show up either. Today everyone showed up! You have a right to compensatory cash payment plus a half-fare coupon for the next Miami flight." His racing fingers leafed through the schedule book. "Which departs in just five hours. If you'll take this form to the counter on the upper level they'll write you a fresh ticket."

If he took the next flight he'd miss connections with the excursion ship. He kept his rage under control, detached himself from the horde of travelers at the departure gate, and stalked back upstairs to find a supervisor and demand a seat on the flight he was scheduled to take. When he saw the length of the line at the upper level he almost decided to go home and forget the cruise altogether.

A large metropolitan airport two days before Christmas. Men, women, children, bundled in overcoats and mufflers and down jackets and snowcaps, pushing and jostling and shuffling in the interminable lines that wove and shifted in front of the ticket counters like multicolored snakes. Thousands of voices merging into an earsplitting hum. View through panoramic windows of snow sifting through the gray afternoon, of autos and trucks and taxis crawling to a halt. Honeyed robot voices breaking into the recorded Christmas carols to make flight announcements no one could hear clearly.

Loren was standing apart from the line, trying to decide whether to join it or surrender his fantasy and go home, when it happened.

He heard a voice bellowing something through the wall of noise in the huge terminal. "Bon! Bonreem!" That was what it sounded like in the chaos. It was coming from a man standing to one side of the line like himself.

A short sandy-haired man wearing jeans and a down jacket and red ski cap, shouting the syllables in a kind of fury. "Bonreem!"

A man standing in the line turned his head to the right, toward the source of the shout, as if he were hearing something that related to him. A woman in a tan all-weather coat with a rain hood, just behind the man in the line, began to turn her head in the same direction.

The sandy-haired man dropped into a combat crouch, drew a pistol from the pocket of his down jacket, and fired four times at the two who were turning. In the bedlam of the airport the shots sounded no louder than coughs. The next second the face of the man in the line was blown apart. Someone screamed. Then everyone screamed. The man with the shattered face fell to the tiled floor, his fingers still moving, clutching air. The line in front of the ticket counter dissolved into a kaleidoscope of figures running, fainting, shrieking. Instinctively Loren dropped to the floor.

The killer raced for the exit doors, stumbled over Loren's outstretched feet, fell on one knee, hard, cried out in pain, picked himself up, and kept running. John Wilkes Booth flashed through Loren's mind. He saw uniformed figures racing toward them, city and airport police, pistols drawn. Two of them blocked the exit doors. The killer wheeled left, stumbled down the main concourse out of sight, police rushing after him.

In the distance Loren heard more screams, then one final shot.

The public-address system was still playing "White Christmas."

At first they put Loren in with the other witnesses, all of them herded into a large auditorium away from the public areas of the airport. Administrative people brought in doughnuts and urns of coffee on wheeled carts. The witnesses sat or stood in small knots—friends, family groups, total strangers, talking compulsively and pacing and clinging to each other. A few stood or sat alone. Loren was one of them. He was still stunned and he knew no one there to talk to.

After a while he pulled out of shock and looked around the room at the other loners. An old man with a wispy white mustache, probably a widower on his way to visit grandchildren for Christmas. A thin dour man with a cleft chin who blinked continually behind steel-rimmed glasses as if the sun were shining in his eyes. In a folding chair in a corner of the auditorium he saw the woman in the tan hooded coat, her head bowed, eyes indrawn, hugging herself and trying not to shudder. He started to get out of his chair and move toward her.

Another woman flung back the swing doors of the auditorium and stood in the entranceway, a tall fortyish woman in a pantsuit, her hair worn long and straight and liberally streaked with gray. "Loren Mensing?" she called out. Her strong voice cut through the hubbub of helpless little conversations in the vast room. "Is there a Loren Mensing here?"

Loren raised his hand and the woman came over to him. "I'm Gene Holt," she said. "Sergeant Holt, city police, Homicide. You're wanted in the conference room."

He followed her to a room down the hall with a long oak table in the center, flanked by chairs. The air was thick with smoke from cigarettes and a few pipes. He counted at least twenty men in the room—airport police, local police, several in plainclothes. The man at the head of the conference table stood up and beckoned. "Lou Belford," he introduced himself. "Special Agent in charge of the F.B.I. office for the area. The locals just told me you're a sort of detective yourself in an oddball way."

"I used to be deputy legal adviser on police matters

for the mayor's office," Loren said. "A part-time position. I teach law for a living."

"And you've helped crack some weird cases, right?"

"I've helped a few times," Loren conceded.

"Well, we've got a weird one here, Professor," Belford grunted. "And you're our star witness. Tell me what you saw."

As Loren told his story Belford scrawled notes on a pad. "It all fits," he said finally. "The guy tripped over your feet and hurt his knee. When he saw he couldn't get out the front exit he headed for the side doors that lead to the underground parking ramps. If he hadn't stumbled over you he could have made it out of the building. Bad luck for him."

"You caught him then? Who was he, and why did he kill that man?"

"We didn't catch him," Belford said. "Cornered him in the gift shop. He saw he was trapped and ate his gun. One shot, right through the mouth. Dead on the spot."

Loren clenched his teeth.

"He wasn't carrying ID," Belford went on, "but we made him a while ago. His name was Frank Wilt. Vietnam vet, unemployed for the last three years. He couldn't hold a job, claimed his head and body were all screwed up from exposure to that Agent Orange stuff they used in the war. The VA couldn't do a thing to help him."

"The man he killed worked for the Veterans Administration?" Loren guessed.

"No, no." Belford shook his head impatiently. "Wilt was obviously desperate for money. It looks as if he took a contract to waste somebody. We just learned he put twenty-five hundred dollars in a bank account Monday. That part of the case is easy. It's the other end we need help with."

"Other end? You mean the victim?" Loren's mind sped to a conclusion from the one fact he knew for certain. "So that's why the F.B.I. are involved! Murder in an airport isn't a Federal crime, and neither is murder by a veteran. So there must be something special about the victim." He leaned forward, elbows on the conference table. "Who was he?"

"The accountant who testified against Lo Scalzo and Pollin in New York last year," Belford said. "John Graham. We gave him and his family new identities under the Witness Relocation Program. They've been living in the city for eighteen months. And now, Professor, we've got an exam for you. Question one: How did the mob find out who and where Graham was? Question two: why did they hire a broken-down vet to waste him instead of sending in a professional hit man?"

Loren had a sudden memory of one of his own law-school professors who had delighted in posing impossible riddles in class. The recollection made him distinctly uncomfortable.

He stayed with the investigators well into the evening, helping Lieutenant Krauzer of Homicide and Sergeant Holt and the F.B.I. agents interrogate all the actual and possible witnesses. Shortly before midnight, bone-weary and almost numb with the cold, he excused himself, trudged out into the public area of the airport, retrieved his luggage, and grabbed a tasteless snack in the terminal coffee shop. He found his VW in the underground parking garage and drove through hard-packed snow back to his high-rise.

He was unlocking his apartment door when he heard footsteps behind him and whirled, then relaxed. It was the woman, the one in the tan hooded coat who had been standing in the line directly behind John Graham at the time of the murder. "Please let me in, Mr. Mensing," she said. Her voice was soft but filled with desperation, her face taut with tension and fatigue. Loren was afraid she'd collapse at any moment. "Come on in," he nodded. "You need a drink worse than I do."

Ten minutes later they were sitting on the low-backed blue couch, facing the night panorama of the city studded with diamond lights, a pot of coffee, a bottle of brandy, and a plate of cheese and crackers on the cocktail table in front of them. Slowly the warmth, the drinks, and the presence of someone she could trust dissipated the tightness from the woman. Loren guessed that she was about thirty, and that not too long ago she had been lovely.

"Thank you," she said. "I haven't eaten since early this morning, I mean yesterday morning."

"Let me make you a real meal." Loren got up from the couch. "I don't have much in the refrigerator but I think I could manage some scrambled eggs."

"No." She reached out with her hand to stop him. "Maybe later. I'd like to talk now if you don't mind. You may want to kick me out when I'm through." She gave a nervous high-pitched giggle, and Loren sat down again and held her hand, which still felt all but frozen.

"My name is Donna," she began. "Donna Keever. That's my maiden name. I'm married. No, I was married. My husband died just about a year ago. His name was Greene, Charles Greene." Her eyes filled with tears. "It was a year ago last week," she mumbled. "You must have read about it."

Loren groped in the tangle of his memory. Yes, that was it, last year's Christmas heartbreak story in the media. Charles Greene and his six-year-old daughter had been driving home from gift shopping, going west on U.S. 47, when a car traveling east on the same highway hit a rut. The eastbound lane at that point was slightly higher than the westbound because of the shape of a hill on which U.S. 47 was built. The eastbound auto had bounced up into the air, literally flown across the median, and landed nose first on top of Greene's car. Then it had bounced off, flown over the roofs of other passing cars, and landed in the ditch at the side of the highway. Greene, his child, and the other driver, who turned out to be driving on an expired license and with his blood full of alcohol, all died instantly. "I remember," Loren said softly.

"I was ill that day," Donna Greene said, "or I'd have been shopping with Chuck and Cindy. That's the only reason I'm still alive while my family's dead. Isn't life wonderful?"

"It was just chance," Loren told her. "You can't feel guilty about it and ruin the rest of you life."

"No!" Her voice rose to the pitch of a scream. "It wasn't chance. That accident didn't just happen. Someone wanted to kill Chuck or Cindy or me. Or all of us!"

She broke then, and Loren held her while she sobbed. When she could talk again he asked her the obvious question. "Have you told the police what you think?"

"Not the police, not the lawyer who's handling the wrongful death claim for me, not anyone. It was only last week that I knew. A burglar broke into my house a week ago Monday night, came into my bedroom. He was wearing a stocking mask and he—he put his hands on me. I screamed my head off and scared him away. The police said it was just a burglar, but I knew. That man was going to kill me! The police think I'm exaggerating, that I'm still crazy with grief because of the accident."

"How about family? Friends? Have you told them of your suspicions?"

"My parents and Chuck's are all dead. My older brother ran away from home about fifteen years ago, when I was fifteen and he was twenty, and no one's heard from him since. I don't work, I don't have a boyfriend and I just couldn't go to my women friends with something like this."

"What made you come to me?" he asked gently.

"Out at the airport auditorium, when that police-woman or whatever she was paged you, I recognized your name. I've read how you've helped people in trouble.

When they let me go I looked up where you live in the phone book and came up here to wait for you.''

"Why were you at the airport?"

"I had to get away. If I stayed here I knew that burglar would come back and kill me, if I didn't kill myself first. And I was right! You were there, you saw that man, that gunman standing a few feet from me and he called my name, Donna Greene, and I started to turn and he shot at me and hit the man next to me in the line. Oh, God, somebody, help me!'' She broke again, terror and despair poured out of her, and Loren held her and made comforting sounds while his mind raced.

Yes, the two names, John Graham and Donna Greene, sounded just enough alike that in the crowded terminal, with noises assaulting the ears from every side, both of them might have thought their name was being called and turned. To Loren, less than a dozen feet away, the name had sounded like "Bonreem." But which of the two *had* Frank Wilt been paid to kill? If Donna was right, the double-barreled question posed by Agent Belford became meaningless. And if she was the intended victim, what would the person who had hired Wilt do next?

All the time he was soothing Donna Greene he fought with himself. "Don't get involved again," something inside told him. "The last time you saved someone he went out later and killed a bunch of innocent people. This time you're already partly responsible for Wilt's death. And for all you know this woman may be a raving paranoid.''

And then all at once he knew what to do, something that would reconcile the conflicting emotions within him and make his Christmas a lot brighter too. He waited until Donna was under control again before he explained.

"I've been thinking," he said. "I don't think I'm qualified to judge whether you're right or wrong about being the target at the airport. But I knew someone who is—a woman private detective up in Capital City named Val Tremaine. She's fantastically good at her work. I'm going to ask her to come down and spend a couple of days on your case, getting to know you, talking with you, forming judgments. You'll like her. Her husband died young too and she had to start life over.'' He disengaged himself gently and rose to his feet. ''I'll make the call from my study. You'll be all right?''

''I'm better now. I just needed someone I could open up to who wouldn't treat me like a fool or a lunatic. Look, Mr. Mensing, I'm not a charity case. My lawyer is suing the estate of that other driver for three million dollars. He was rich, his attorneys already offered to settle for three-quarters of a million. I'm not asking you or your detective friend to work for nothing.''

''Don't worry about money now,'' Loren said, and went down the inner hall to the second bedroom that was fixed up as his study, closing the door behind him. He had to check his address book for the number of Val's house, the lovely house nestled on the side of a mountain forty miles from the capital's center, the house she had built as therapy after her husband had died. God, had it been that long since he'd called her? He wondered what had made their relationship taper off, his choice or hers or just the natural drifting of two people who cared deeply for each other but were hundreds of miles apart. He hoped she wouldn't mind his calling in the middle of the night. He hoped very much that she'd be alone.

On the fourth ring she answered, her voice heavy with sleep and bewilderment and a touch of anger.

''Hi, Val, it's me . . . Yes, much too long. I've missed you too. Want to make up for lost time?'' He told her about his involvement in the airport murder which she'd heard reported on the evening's TV newscasts, and about the riddle of the intended target which Donna Greene had dropped in his lap. ''So if you haven't any other plans for the holidays, why not spend Christmas here? Check her story, be her bodyguard if she needs one, help her start functioning again. Take her to the police with me if

you believe she's right." He knew better than to hold out
the prospect of a substantial fee. That wasn't the way Val
operated.

"You've got yourself a guest," she said. "You know,
I was going to invite you up to my place for Christmas
but—well, I wasn't sure you'd come."

"I'd have come," he told her softly. If she had invited
him he wouldn't have been at the airport this afternoon,
and maybe Frank Wilt would be alive and able to tell
who had hired him, and maybe Donna Greene would be
dead. Chance.

"I'll have to get someone to run the office and I'll
need an hour to pack. No way I can get a plane reser-
vation this time of year, so I'll drive. See you around,
oh, say eight in the morning if I don't get stuck in the
snow."

"I hope you like quiche for breakfast," Loren said.

A soft rapping on the front door jerked him out of a
doze on the blue couch. Sullen gray light filling the living
room told him it was morning. His watch on the end
table read 7:14. "Yes?" he called in the door's direction.

"Me." He recognized Val's voice, undid the deadbolt
and the chain lock. The second she was inside with her
suitcase he kissed her. It was their first kiss in months
and they both made it last. Then they just looked at each
other. Val's cheeks were red from the cold and her eyes
showed the strain of a long drive through snow-haunted
darkness. She was beautiful as ever.

"I missed you," he whispered. "Mrs. Greene's asleep
in the bedroom."

They talked quietly in the kitchen while they grated
some cheddar, cut a strip of pepper and an onion and
ham slices into bits, beat two eggs in cream and melted
butter, poured the ingredients into a ready-made pie
crust, seasoned them with salt and nutmeg, and popped
the quiche into the oven. Loren reported on the murder

and Donna's story as the aroma of hot melted cheese filled the kitchen.

"The first step isn't hard to figure," Val said, cutting the quiche into thirds as Loren poured orange juice and coffee. "She'll have to look at pictures of Wilt and tell us if he was her Monday-night burglar. If she identifies him we'll know she was the target at the airport."

"But if she can't identify him," Loren pointed out, "it's not conclusive the other way. Maybe two guys were after her, maybe she didn't get a good look at the burglar . . . We do make a delicious quiche, partner."

"And I'm glad we saved a third of it for our client," Val said, "because the minute she gets up I'm borrowing your bed. I can't take sleepless nights the way I used to."

They left Val asleep and drove downtown through the snow in Loren's VW and entered the office of the homicide detail a little after eleven. Lieutenant Krauzer was in his cubicle, and from his rumpled red-eyed look he'd been working through the night. He was a balding soft-spoken overweight man in his fifties who never seemed to react to anything but, like a human sponge, absorbed whatever came before him.

The lieutenant listened to Loren's story and to Donna Greene's, then picked up his phone handset, and twirled the dial. "Gene, you still have the Wilt photos? Yeah, bring them in, please."

"We've learned a bunch about Frank Wilt since you hung it up last night, Professor," Krauzer said. "He spent most of his time in bars, one joint in particular that's owned by a guy with mob connections. That could explain how he was hired for the hit if the target was John Graham, but it doesn't explain why. Damn it, the mob just doesn't pay washed-up vets to waste a top man on their hit list.

"Your story reads better on that score, Mrs. Greene.

An amateur hires Wilt for a private killing. He messes it
up at your house last week and runs. He follows you to
the airport yesterday, tries again, and messes it up again,
because the guy next to you in line happened to have a
name that sounds a little like yours, turned faster than
you did, and took the bullets meant for you. But, ma'am,
you just can't ask me to believe that there's a plot to wipe
out your family, because there's no way on earth the freak
accident that killed your husband and daughter could have
been anything but—''

A knock sounded on the cubicle door and a woman
entered. Loren recognized her as Sergeant Holt from last
night. She placed a sheaf of photos on Krauzer's desk
and left after the lieutenant thanked her. Loren handed
the pictures to Donna and watched her face as she
squinted and studied the shots with intense deliberation.
In the outer office phones were ringing constantly, voices
rising and falling, doors slamming, and in the street
Loren heard the wail of sirens. Violent crime seemed to
thrive on holidays.

There was a hunted look in Donna Greene's eyes when
she handed the photos back to Krauzer. ''I can't tell,''
she said in almost a whisper. ''I think the burglar was
taller but with that stocking mask he wore and in the dark
I couldn't see his face well enough to be sure. Oh, I'm
sorry!'' She began to cry again and Loren reached out
for her. Krauzer lifted the phone and a minute later Sergeant Holt came back in, put her arm around the other
woman, and led her away.

Leaving Loren alone with Krauzer and free to ask the
lieutenant for a large favor.

The Homicide specialist kept shaking his head sadly.
''I can't spare the personnel to put a twenty-four-hour
watch on her, Professor. Not short-handed the way we
are around Christmas. Not without more proof she's really in danger. I like the lady, I think she was totally

honest with us, and I know she's scared half to death, but—''

"But she's paranoid?" Loren broke in. "Like all the dissidents in the Sixties and Seventies who thought the government was persecuting them? Look, suppose she's right the way they were right?"

"Then you've got Val Tremaine to protect her," Krauzer said, "and we both know they don't come better." He gave Loren a bleak but knowing smile. "Go on, get out of here with your harem, and have a merry Christmas. Call me if something should happen."

If something should happen . . .

He decided to let Val sleep at the apartment and take Donna shopping so that he and his unexpected guests could have some sort of Christmas. After weaving through downtown streets in a crazy-quilt pattern to throw off any possible followers, he swung the VW onto the Interstate and drove out to the tri-leveled Cherrywood Mall. On the day before Christmas there was more safety among the crowds of frantic last-minute shoppers than behind fortress walls.

The excursion seemed to take Donna out of herself, erase some of the hunted look from her eyes. It was after four and their arms were full of brightly wrapped packages when they slipped into a dark quiet bar on the mall's third level.

"Feeling better?" Loren asked as they sipped Alexanders.

"Much." She smiled hesitantly in the dimness. "Mr. Mensing, these are the happiest few hours I've had since, well, since last year. I can never repay you. You've even made me begin to feel different about everything that's happened to me."

"Different how?"

"I've decided it wasn't just blind chance that I didn't go in the car with Chuck and Cindy that day and that the man next to me was shot and not me. I think I'm meant to live awhile yet. And, oh, God, there's so much I've got to do after the holidays to put my life back in order. The house is a hopeless mess and the tires on my car are getting bald and I need a new will—Chuck and I had mutual wills, we each left everything to the other—and, you know, I may start dating again." She looked into her glass and then into Loren's eyes. "You're, ah, not available, right?"

"I'm honestly not sure," Loren said. "Val and I have been out of touch for months and we've been sort of preoccupied since she got in this morning." He paused, blinked behind his glasses, bewildered as he habitually was by the thought that any young woman could find a bear-bodied, unaggressive, overly learned intellectual in his late thirties even slightly desirable. "But look. However that turns out, I'm your friend. Val and I both are."

"To friendship," she said as they touched glasses. "To a new life."

It was the strangest Christmas Eve he'd ever spent. To an outsider it would have seemed that an exotic fantasy had become real—a man and two lovely women, a high-rise well stocked with food and drink. As night fell and with it fresh snow, Loren made a bowl of hot mulled wine and played the new recording of the Dvorak Piano Quintet No. 5 that he'd bought as his Christmas present to himself. Later he turned on the radio to an FM station and they listened to traditional carols as he gave Val and Donna the gifts he'd purchased at Cherrywood. Their squeals of delight warmed him more than the wine.

Part of him felt relaxed and at peace and part of him stayed alert like an animal in fear of predators. But as midnight approached he found it harder and harder to believe there was danger. Not with the snow outside turning to ice as it fell, not behind the deadbolt and chain lock in a haven twenty stories high.

A little after 12:30 they exchanged good-night kisses and Loren surrendered his bedroom to the women. When they'd closed the door behind them he made a last ritual concession to security by tugging the massive blue couch over against the front door before arranging its cushions on the living-room rug in a makeshift bed.

He was fitting a spare sheet over the couch cushions when Val came back, her blonde hair falling soft and loose over the shoulders of the floor-length caftan he'd given her for Christmas. She smiled and helped him smooth the sheets. "Now you'll sleep better," she said. "I feel like a toad kicking you out of your bed on Christmas Eve."

"Can't be helped. Donna's asleep?"

"Out like a light. You were right to serve decaffeinated coffee." She sat on a sheet-draped cushion. "And thanks to that nap I had before the sergeant dropped by, I'm not tired in the least—"

"Sergeant?" Loren asked. He was suddenly alert.

Her face dropped slightly. "Oh, rats, I wasn't supposed to tell you. Lieutenant Krauzer sent a man over this afternoon just in case Donna was in danger. He came while you were shopping, showed me his ID, looked this place over, and set up a stakeout in 20-B, the vacant apartment across the hall. He said not to tell you and Donna so you'd act natural and not scare any suspects away. But it's good to know Sergeant Holt is standing guard."

Loren leaped to his feet. "Sergeant *who?*" he shouted.

"Gene Holt, Lieutenant Krauzer's assistant. He's been in 20-B since midafternoon. The couple that lives there is in Florida—"

"Describe him." Loren's face was white, and wet fear crawled down his spine.

"A tall man in his middle thirties, thin face, cleft chin. He wears glasses and blinks a lot as if his eyes were weak."

In that moment Loren saw the shape of the nightmare. "That's it," he muttered, and stood there frozen with understanding. He could hear clocks ticking, the night stirrings of the building, the plock-plock of icy snow falling on the outdoor furniture on his balcony. Every sound was magnified now, transformed into menace.

Val shook his shoulders, fear twisting her own face. "Loren, what in God's name is the matter?"

"Sergeant Gene Holt," Loren told her, "is a woman. And now I know who Weak Eyes is too."

"He had a badge and identification!" she protested.

"And if you know the right document forger you can have stuff like that made to order while you wait." He pushed her aside, headed for the phone on a stand in the corner. "I'm calling Krauzer and getting some real cops here.

The phone exploded into sound before he'd crossed the room and he jumped as if shot. A second ring, a third. He picked it up as if it were a cobra, forced it to his ear. Silence. Then a voice, smooth, low, calm. "Unfortunately, Professor, I can't let you call for reinforcements," it said.

Loren slammed the phone down, held it in its cradle for a count of ten, then lifted the handset. He didn't hear a dial tone. He punched the hook furiously. Still no dial tone. He whirled to Val. "Him," he whispered. "He must have planted a bug here while he was pretending to check the place out for security. He heard every word we said all evening and was just waiting for all of us to go to bed. We can't phone outside—he's tying up the line by keeping the phone in 20-B off the hook."

"We can phone for help from one of the other apartments on this floor!"

"We can't. 20-C moved out when the building converted to condo and 20-D's out of town. Besides, he's at the front door of 20-B. If you try to go out in the hall he's got you."

''Let's get out on the balcony and scream for help!''

''Who'd hear us in that storm?''

Val swung around, raced down the inner hall to the bedroom. Loren knew why. To throw on street clothes and get her gun. If she'd brought one with her. Loren hadn't asked.

The phone shrilled again. Loren stared at it as if hypnotized. He let it ring six times, nine. Over the rings he heard Donna's sobs of terror from the bedroom. Oh, God, if only it were Krauzer on the other end, or Belford the F.B.I. man, or anyone in the world except Weak Eyes, anyone Loren could ask to call the police! On the twelfth ring he picked up the receiver.

''Mensing,'' the low calm voice said, ''I have just placed a charge of plastic explosive on the outside of your door. You have two minutes to take down that barricade I heard you put up and send Donna across the hall. Do that and you and Tremaine live.''

Loren slammed the phone down. Val in a dark gray jumpsuit ran back into the living room. There was no gun in her hand. Loren almost cried out with frustration. ''Donna's in your closet,'' she whispered. ''I pushed the dresser against the door.''

Loren nodded, held her close, and spoke feverishly into her ear. Time slipped away into nothingness. Val went down the inner hall, turning off lights, opened the fusebox, and cut the master switch. The apartment was pitch-dark now. Loren found the hall closet, put on rubbers, and his heaviest overcoat. Then he tugged the couch away from the front door, undid the deadbolt and chain, and ran across the room.

He slipped on the couch cushions in the middle of the floor and pain shot through his ankle. He bit down on his lower lip, hobbled the rest of the way across the room, threw open the door leading to his balcony. Sudden cold stunned him, made him shake uncontrollably as he stood outside, behind the curtained balcony door, and watched through the thin elongated crack.

The front door was flung back and Weak Eyes leaped in, using a combat crouch like Wilt at the airport. In his hand there was a gun. His eyes focused on the patch of light across the dark room, the light coming from the balcony. He stalked across the room like a wolf. Loren tensed, waiting. Yes, he was close enough to the balcony now, time for Val to make her move.

There she went, crawling across the wall-to-wall carpet in the dark, all but invisible in her jumpsuit, making the front door and then for the firestairs.

Weak Eyes heard nothing, didn't turn. He kicked the balcony door all the way open, looked down the long balcony. There was nothing to see but a white-painted cast-iron outdoor table and three matching chairs. He took a cautious step out onto the balcony, his eyes trying to pierce the deeper shadows at the far end.

Loren brought the fourth iron chair down hard on the back of the killer's neck. Weak Eyes howled, flung his arms up for balance. The gun flew out of his hand into the slush. He skidded halfway down the balcony, his belly slammed into the outdoor table.

Loren kept hitting him with the chair until Weak Eyes wasn't moving. It was all Loren could do to keep from hurling him over the balcony rail and down twenty stories to the street.

Loren was still standing there, his teeth chattering in the cold, his ankle throbbing, sweat pouring down him, when a few minutes later Val and two uniformed patrolmen rushed out to the balcony.

"What a world," Lieutenant Krauzer grunted eight hours later. "Her own brother."

Weak Eyes was in a cell, Donna had been taken to the hospital under sedation, and they were gathered in Loren's apartment. He sat on the blue couch with his right leg raised on a kitchen chair and the ankle bandaged tightly. Val sat on a hassock at his side, refilling his coffee cup, handing him tissues when he sneezed. Outside, Christmas morning dawned in shades of smoky gray.

"It had to be her brother," Loren said. "Once Val described the fake Gene Holt it all clicked, because I remembered seeing a man of that exact description in the airport auditorium after the Graham murder. And then I remembered three things Donna had mentioned in passing: that she and her late husband had had mutual wills, that she hadn't gotten around to making a new will yet, and that her wrongful-death suit against the driver of the car that killed her family was going to net her a lot of money.

"Now suppose she'd been killed by that burglar, or at the airport? Who would have wound up with that money? Obviously if she died intestate it would go to her next of kin. Who's her next of kin? Her parents are dead, her only child is dead—*but she had a brother who dropped out of sight fifteen years ago.*

"Now the picture clears up," he went on. "Charles and Cindy Greene die in a tragic accident that gets heavy coverage in the media. Wherever he was at the time, Donna's brother hears of it, sees huge financial possibilities, comes to the city quietly, and begins shadowing her. He satisfied himself that the wrongful-death action is going to produce big money and that his sister hasn't made out a new will. He had to get rid of her before she does. He looks around—the forged ID and bugging equipment and plastique show he has underworld connections—and hires Frank Wilt for the hit.

"Wilt breaks into her house a week ago Monday night and bungles the job. Brother gives him another chance. Wilt follows her to the airport, makes his move—and by blind chance a man with a name similar to Donna's is next to her in line, turns faster than she does, and dies instead of her.

"Brother has gone to the airport too, as a backup in case Wilt blew it again. He and Donna are both rounded up as witnesses and taken to the auditorium but either she doesn't see him in the crowd or just doesn't recognize him after fifteen years. When she's let go he follows her to my place and works out a plan to kill her here, doing the job himself this time. He reads the newspaper stories about the airport murder, picks up the name of Sergeant Gene Holt, and uses it as his cover identity but makes the big mistake of assuming from the name that the sergeant is a man."

"And that bit of chauvinism's going to cost him twenty years in the slam." Krauzer yawned and lumbered wearily to his feet. "Well, if you'll excuse me it's Christmas morning and I've got grandkids to play Santy for." He winked broadly at Val. "Remember he's a sick man and needs his rest."

When he had let himself out Val slid off the hassock to sit on the floor. "Funny," Loren said as he ran his hand through her hair. "The way Christmas turned out isn't anything like what I either was afraid of or hoping for. I can't walk, I haven't slept in two nights, I've got the chills, but all in all I feel good. The crazy way this world goes, I'll be damned if I know if it's all chance or if it's meant."

"I'll take the world either way if you're part of it," Val told him softly.

CHRISTMAS PARTY

by Martin Werner

People in the advertising business said the Christmas party at French & Saunders was the social event of the year. For it wasn't your ordinary holiday office party. Not the kind where the staff gets together for a few mild drinks out of paper cups, some sandwiches sent in from the local deli, and a long boring speech by the company president. At F&S it was all very different: just what you'd expect from New York's hottest advertising agency.

The salaries there were the highest in town, the accounts were strictly blue chip, and the awards the agency won over the years filled an entire boardroom. And the people, of course, were the best, brightest, and most creative that money could buy.

With that reputation to uphold, the French & Saunders Christmas party naturally had to be the biggest and splashiest in the entire industry.

Year after year, that's the way it was. Back in the late Seventies, when discos were all the rage, the company took over Numero Uno, the club people actually fought over to get in. Another year, F&S hired half the New York Philharmonic to provide entertainment. And in 1989, the guest bartenders were Mel Gibson, Madonna, and the cast of *L.A. Law*.

There was one serious side to the party. That's when the president reviewed the year's business, announced how much the annual bonus would be, and then named the Board's choices for People of the Year, the five lucky

employees who made the most significant contributions
to the agency's success during the past twelve months.

The unwritten part to this latter (although everyone
knew it, anyway) was that each one of the five would
receive a very special individual bonus—some said as
high as $50,000 apiece.

Then French & Saunders bought fifteen floors in the
tallest, shiniest new office tower on Broadway, the one
that had actually been praised by the *N.Y. Times* archi-
tecture critic.

The original plan was to hold the party in the brand-
new offices that were to be ready just before Christmas.
A foolish idea, as it turned out, because nothing in New
York is ever finished when it's promised. The delay meant
the agency had to scramble and find a new party site—
either that, or make do in the half finished building itself.

Amazingly—cleverly?—enough, that was the game
plan the party committee decided to follow. Give the biggest, glitziest party in agency history amid half finished
offices in which paneless windows looked out to the open
skies, where debris and building supplies stood piled up
in every corner, and where doors opened on nothing but
a web of steel girders and the sidewalk seventy floors
below.

Charlie Evanston, one of the company's senior vice-
presidents (he had just reached the ripe old of age of
fifty), was chosen to be party chairman. He couldn't have
been happier. For Charlie had a deepdown feeling that
this was finally going to be his year. After being passed
over time and again for one of those five special Christmas bonuses, he just knew he was going to go home a
winner.

Poor Charlie.

In mid-November—the plans for the party proceeding
on schedule—the agency suddenly lost their multi-

million-dollar Daisy Fresh Soap account, no reason given. Charlie had been the supervisor on the account for years, and although he couldn't be held personally responsible for the loss a few people (enemies!) shook their heads and wondered if maybe someone else, someone a little stronger—and younger—couldn't have held on to the business.

Two weeks later, another showpiece account—the prestigious Maximus Computer Systems—left the agency. Unheard of.

The trade papers gave away the reason in the one dreaded word "kickbacks." Two French & Saunders television producers who had worked on the account had been skimming it for years.

Again, Charlie's name came up. Not that he had anything remotely to do with the scandal. The trouble was that he personally had hired both offenders. And people remembered.

There's a superstition that events like these happen in threes, so it was only a question of time before the next blow. And, sure enough, two weeks before Christmas, it happened. A murder, no less. A F&S writer shot his wife, her lover, and himself.

With that, French & Saunders moved from front-page sidelines in the trade papers straight to screaming headlines in every tabloid in town. In less than a month, it had been seriously downgraded from one of New York's proudest enterprises to that most dreaded of advertising fates—an agency "in trouble."

It was now a week before Christmas and every F&S employee was carrying around his or her own personal lump of cold, clammy fear. The telltale signs were everywhere. People making secret telephone calls to headhunters and getting their resumes in order. Bitter jokes about the cold winter and selling apples on street corners told in the elevators and washrooms. Rumors that a buy-out was in the making and *nobody* was safe.

And yet, strange as it sounds, there were those who still thought there would be a happy ending. At the Christmas party, perhaps. A last-minute announcement that everything was as before—the agency was in good shape and, just like always, everyone would get that Christmas bonus.

Charlie was one of the most optimistic. He didn't know why. Just a gut feeling that the world was still full of Christmas miracles and, bad times or not, he was going to be one of F&S's five magical People of the Year.

Poor Charlie.

A few days before the party, his phone rang. It was the voice of J. Stewart French, president and chairman of the board.

"Hi, Charlie. Got a minute?"

"Sure."

"I wonder if you'd mind coming up to my office. I've got a couple of things I'd like to talk to you about."

Nothing menacing about that, thought Charlie. J probably wants to discuss the party. The food. The caterers. The security measures that would be needed so that no one would be in any danger in those half finished offices.

Very neatly, very efficiently, Charlie got out his files and headed upstairs. When he arrived in the president's office—it was the only one that had been completely finished (vulgar but expensive, thought Charlie)—J was on the phone, his face pale and drawn, nothing like the way he usually looked, with that twelve-months-a-year suntan he was so proud of. He nodded over the phone. "Sit down, Charlie, sit down."

Charlie sank into one of the comfortable $12,000 chairs beside the desk and waited. After a minute the conversation ended and J turned to give him his full attention. Charlie had known J for fifteen years and had never seen him so nervous and ill at ease.

Then he spoke.

"Charlie, they tell me you've really got the Christmas party all together. Looks like it'll be a smash."

"We're hoping so, J."

"Well, we can certainly use some good times around here. I don't have to tell *you* that. It's been a bad, *bad* year."

"Things'll be better. I know it."

"Do you really think so, Charlie? Do you? I'd like to believe that, too. That's why this party means so much to me. To all of us. Morale—"

"I know."

"Well, you've certainly done your part. More than your part. That's why I called you in."

Here it comes, thought Charlie, here comes my special Christmas bonus! Ahead of time, before anyone else hears about it!

"I wanted you to be one of the first to know. The Board and I have agreed that, even with all our troubles, there'll be something extra in everybody's paycheck again this year. Nothing like before, of course, but it will be something."

"That's wonderful."

"Yeah. Wonderful. We monkeyed around with the budget and found we could come up with a few bucks. The *problem* is, we'll have to make some cuts here and there."

"Cuts?"

"Well, for one thing, I'm afraid there won't be any of those special bonuses this year, Charlie. And I'll level with you—you were down for one. After all these years, you had really earned it. I can't tell you how sorry—"

Sure, thought Charlie. "It's not the end of the world, J," he said. "Maybe next year."

"No, Charlie, that's not all. With our losses and the

cost of moving—I don't know how to tell you this, but we're doing something else. We're cutting back—some of our best people. I've never had to do anything like that in my life.''

You bastard, Charlie thought. "Go on, J," he said. "I think I know what you're going to say.''

J looked at him miserably. "You're one of the people we'll have to lose, Charlie. Wait a minute, please hear me out—it's nothing personal. I wanted to save you. After all, we've been together fifteen years. I talked and talked, I even threatened to resign myself. But no one wanted to listen.''

Sure, Charlie thought.

"They said you hadn't produced anything worthwhile in years. And there was the business of those two crazies you hired. And—''

"Is that it?'' Charlie asked.

"Don't get me wrong, Charlie. Please, let's do the Christmas party as we planned, just as if nothing happened. As for leaving, take your time. I got you a year's severance. And you can use your office to make calls, look around, and—''

"No problem, J.'' Charlie was moving to the door. "I understand. And don't worry about the party. Everything's all taken care of.''

Not even a handshake.

Many people at some time or other have fantasized about killing the boss. In Charlie's case, it was different. From the minute he heard the bad news from J, he became a changed man. Not outwardly, of course. He wasn't about to become an overnight monster, buy a gun, make a bomb, sharpen an axe. No, he would be the same Charlie Evanston. Friendly. Smiling. Efficient. But now that he knew the worst, he began piling up all the long-suppressed injustices he had collected from J for fifteen years. The conversations that stopped abruptly when he entered an executive meeting. The intimate dinners at J's that he and his wife were never invited to. The countless other little slights. And, finally, this.

December 20. Party time! Everyone agreed it was the best bash French & Saunders had ever thrown.

The day was fair and warm. The milling crowds that drifted from the well stocked bars and refreshment tables didn't even notice there wasn't a heating system. The lack of carpets, the wide-open window spaces, the empty offices—it all added to the fun.

Carefully groomed waiters in white gloves and hard hats pressed their way from room to room, carrying silver trays laden with drinks and hors d'oeuvres. A heavy metal band blared somewhere. A troupe of strolling violinists pressed in and out. From the happy faces, laughter, and noise, you'd never know the agency had a care in the world.

But Charlie Evanston knew. He pushed his way over to a small crowd pressing around J. All of them were drunk, or on the way, and J, drink in hand, was swaying slightly. His laugh was louder than anybody's whenever one of the clients told a funny story. He spotted Charlie and shouted to him. "Charlie, c'mere a minute! Folks, you all know my old pal Charlie Evanston. We've been together since this place opened its doors. He's the guy who put this whole great party together."

There were murmurs of approval as J drew Charlie into his embrace.

'J," Charlie said, "I just came to ask you to come over here and let me show you something."

"Oh, Charlie, always business. Can't it wait till next week? After the holidays?"

"No, I think it's important. Please come over here. Let me show you."

"Oh, for Chrissakes, Charlie. What *is* it?"

"Just follow me. Won't take long."

J pulled away from the group with a back-in-a-minute wave of his hand and followed Charlie down a narrow hall to a room that would one day become the heart of the agency's computer operation.

It was empty. Even the floors hadn't been finished. Just some wooden planks, a few steel beams—and the sidewalk below. J glanced around the room and turned to Charlie. "So? What's the problem?"

"Don't you get it, J? There isn't a single Keep Out sign on that outside door. The workmen even forgot to lock it. Someone could walk in here and fall straight down to Broadway!"

"Oh, come on, Charlie, this place is off the beaten path—no one's going to be coming this way. Stop worrying."

"Yes, but—"

"No buts, Charlie. Just tell one of the security guards. My God, you drag me all the way out here just to see this. Jesus Christ, I'll bet I could even *walk* across one of these steel beams. The workmen do it every day."

It was uncanny. Charlie knew that was exactly what J would say. It was part of the macho, daredevil reputation he had cultivated so carefully. "Hey, wait a minute, J," he said.

"No. Serious. Watch me walk across this beam right here. It can't be more than twenty feet long. And I'll do it with a drink in each hand."

"Come on, J, don't be crazy."

But J had already taken his first tentative step on the beam—with Charlie directly behind him.

It was all so simple. Now all Charlie had to do was give J the tiniest of shoves in the back, watch him stagger and plunge over the side, and it would be all over.

As J continued to move along the beam, he seemed to grow more confident. Charlie continued to follow a few steps behind, his right arm outstretched. It was now or never. Suddenly he made his move. But J moved a couple of quick steps faster and Charlie missed J's back by an inch. Instead, he felt himself slipping over the side. He gasped. Then all he remembered was falling.

The hospital room was so quiet you could barely hear a murmur from the corridor outside.

On the single bed there lay what looked like a dead body. Every inch was covered in a rubbery casing and yards and yards of white gauze. All you could see of what was underneath was a little round hole where the mouth was supposed to be and another opening where a blood-shot blue eye stared up at the ceiling. Charlie Evanston.

The door opened slightly, admitting J, followed by one of Charlie's doctors.

J shuddered. He always did, every time he'd visited over the past six months. He turned to the doctor. "How's he doing today?"

"About the same. He tries to talk a little now and then."

"Can he hear me yet? Can he understand?"

"We think so. But don't try and get anything out of him."

"Yes. I know." He bent over the bed. "Charlie. Charlie. It's me, J. I just wanted you to know I'm here. And I want to thank you again—I guess I'll be thanking you for the rest of my life—for reaching out and trying to save me at that damn Christmas party."

The blue eye blinked. A tear began to tremble on the edge.

"I was a fool. Only a fool would have tried to do what I did. And you tried to stop me. I felt you grab my jacket and try to hold me back. Then you took the fall for me."

The blue eye stared.

"So what I came to say—what I hope you can under-stand—is that no matter how long it takes you're going to get the best care we can find. Just get well. Every-thing's going to be okay."

The blue eye continued to look at J without blinking.

"And, Charlie, here's the best news of all. The agency's just picked up three big accounts. Over a hundred million."

A light breeze blew the curtains from the window.

"So today the Board asked me to come up here and give you a special bonus. Not a Christmas bonus—more like Purple Heart. You deserve it, Charlie. You saved the old man's life, you bastard!"

Charlie tried to nod, but it was impossible.

"And just wait till you come back," J said enthusiastically. "You're a hero, Charlie! We've got all kinds of great things waiting for you. All kinds of plans. It's going to be a whole new ballgame, Charlie! Imagine!"

Yeah, thought Charlie. Imagine.

SUPPER WITH MISS SHIVERS

By Peter Lovesey

The door was stuck. Something inside was stopping it from opening, and Fran was numb with cold. School had broken up for Christmas that afternoon—"Lord dismiss us with Thy blessing"—and the jubilant kids had given her a blinding headache. She'd wobbled on her bike through the London traffic, two carriers filled with books suspended from the handlebars. She'd endured exhaust fumes and maniac motorists, and now she couldn't get into her own flat. She cursed, let the bike rest against her hip, and attacked the door with both hands.

"It was quite scary, actually," she told Jim when he got in later. "I mean, the door opened perfectly well when we left this morning. We could have been burgled. Or it could have been a body lying in the hall."

Jim, who worked as a systems analyst, didn't have the kind of imagination that expected bodies behind doors. "So what was it—the doormat?"

"Get knotted. It was a great bundle of Christmas cards wedged under the door. Look at them. I blame you for this, James Palmer."

"Me?"

Now that she was over the headache and warm again, she enjoyed poking gentle fun at Jim. "Putting our address book on your computer and running the envelopes through the printer. This is the result. We're going to be up to our eyeballs in cards. I don't know how many you sent, but we've heard from the plumber, the dentist, the television repairman, and the people who moved us in, apart from family and friends. You must have gone straight through the address book. I won't even ask how many stamps you used.''

"What an idiot," Jim admitted. "I forgot to use the sorting function."

"I left some for you to open."

"I bet you've opened all the ones with checks inside," said Jim. "I'd rather eat first."

"I'm slightly mystified by one," said Fran. "Do you remember sending to someone called Miss Shivers?"

"No. I'll check if you like. Curious name."

"It means nothing to me, but she's invited us to a meal."

Fran handed him the card—one of those desolate, old-fashioned snow scenes of someone dragging home a log. Inside, under the printed greetings, was the signature *E. Shivers (Miss)* followed by *Please make my Christmas—come for supper seven next Sunday, 23rd.* In the corner was an address label.

"Never heard of her," said Jim. "Must be a mistake."

"Maybe she sends her cards by computer," said Fran, and added, before he waded in, "I don't think it's a mistake, Jim. She named us on the envelope. I'd like to go."

"For crying out loud—Didmarsh is miles away. Berkshire or somewhere. We're far too busy."

"Thanks to your computer, we've got time in hand," Fran told him with a smile.

The moment she'd seen the invitation, she'd known she would accept. Three or four times in her life she'd felt a similar impulse and each time she had been right. She didn't think of herself as psychic or telepathic, but sometimes she felt guided by some force that couldn't be explained scientifically. A good force, she was certain. It had convinced her that she should marry no one else but Jim, and after three years together she had no doubts.

Their love was unshakable. And because he loved her, he would take her to supper with Miss Shivers. He wouldn't understand *why* she was so keen to go, but he would see that she was in earnest, and that would be enough . . .

"By the way, I checked the computer," he told her in front of the destinations board on Paddington Station next Sunday. "We definitely didn't send a card to anyone called Shivers."

"Makes it all the more exciting, doesn't it?" Fran said, squeezing his arm.

Jim was the first man she had trusted. Trust was her top requirement of the opposite sex. It didn't matter that he wasn't particularly tall and that his nose came to a point. He was loyal. And didn't Clint Eastwood have a pointed nose?

She'd learned from her mother's three disastrous marriages to be ultra-wary of men. The first—Fran's father, Harry—had started the rot. He'd died in a train crash just a few days before Fran was born. You'd think he couldn't be blamed for that, but he could. Fran's mother had been admitted to hospital with complications in the eighth month, and Harry, the rat, had found someone else within a week. On the night of the crash he'd been in London with his mistress, buying her expensive clothes. He'd even lied to his pregnant wife, stuck in hospital, about working overtime.

For years Fran's mother had fended off the questions any child asks about a father she has never seen, telling Fran to forget him and love her stepfather instead. Stepfather the First had turned into a violent alcoholic. The divorce had taken nine years to achieve. Stepfather the Second—a Finn called Bengt (Fran called him Bent)— had treated their Wimbledon terraced house as if it were a sauna, insisting on communal baths and parading naked around the place. When Fran was reaching puberty, there were terrible rows because she wanted privacy. Her mother had sided with Bengt until one terrible night when he'd crept into Fran's bedroom and groped her. Bengt walked out of their lives the next day, but, incredibly to Fran, a lot of the blame seemed to be heaped on her, and her relationship with her mother had been damaged forever. At forty-three, her mother, deeply depressed, had taken a fatal overdose.

The hurts and horrors of those years had not disappeared, but marriage to Jim had provided a fresh start. Fran nestled against him in the carriage and he fingered a strand of her dark hair. It was supposed to be an Intercity train, but B.R. were using old rolling-stock for some of the Christmas period and Fran and Jim had this compartment to themselves.

"Did you let this Shivers woman know we're coming?"

She nodded. "I phoned. She's over the moon that I answered. She's going to meet us at the station."

"What's it all about, then?"

"She didn't say, and I didn't ask."

"You didn't? Why not, for God's sake?"

"It's a mystery trip—a Christmas mystery. I'd rather keep it that way."

"Sometimes, Fran, you leave me speechless."

"Kiss me instead, then."

A whistle blew somewhere and the line of taxis beside the platform appeared to be moving forward. Fran saw no more of the illusion because Jim had put his lips to hers.

Somewhere beyond Westbourne Park Station, they noticed how foggy the late afternoon had become. After days of mild, damp weather, a proper December chill had set in. The heating in the carriage was working only in fits and starts and Fran was beginning to wish she'd worn trousers instead of opting decorously for her corduroy skirt and boots.

"Do you think it's warmer farther up the train?"

"Want me to look?"

Jim slid aside the door. Before starting along the corridor, he joked, "If I'm not back in half an hour, send for Miss Marple."

"No need," said Fran. "I'll find you in the bar and mine's a hot cuppa."

She pressed herself into the warm space Jim had left in the corner and rubbed a spy-hole in the condensation. There wasn't anything to spy. She shivered and wondered if she'd been right to trust her hunch and come on this trip. It was more than a hunch, she told herself. It was intuition.

It wasn't long before she heard the door pulled back. She expected to see Jim, or perhaps the man who checked the tickets. Instead, there was a fellow about her own age, twenty-five, with a pink carrier bag containing something about the size of a box file. "Do you mind?" he asked. "The heating's given up altogether next door."

Fran gave a shrug. "I've got my doubts about the whole carriage."

He took the corner seat by the door and placed the bag beside him. Fran took stock of him rapidly, hoping Jim would soon return. She didn't feel threatened, but she wasn't used to these old-fashioned compartments. She rarely used the trains these days except the tube occasionally.

She decided the young man must have kitted himself in an Oxfam shop. He had a dark-blue car coat, black trousers with flares, and crepe-soled ankle boots. Around his neck was one of those striped scarves that college students wore in the sixties, one end slung over his left shoulder. And his thick, dark hair matched the image. Fran guessed he was unemployed. She wondered if he was going to ask her for money.

But he said, "Been up to town for the day?"

"I live there." She added quickly, "With my husband. He'll be back presently."

"I'm married, too," he said, and there was a chink of amusement in his eyes that Fran found reassuring. "I'm up from the country, smelling the wellies and cowdung. Don't care much for London. It's crazy in Bond Street this time of year."

"Bond Street?" repeated Fran. She hadn't got him down as a big spender.

"This once," he explained. "It's special, this Christmas. We're expecting our first, my wife and I."

"Congratulations."

He smiled. A self-conscious smile. "My wife, Pearlie—that's my name for her—Pearlie made all her own maternity clothes, but she's really looking forward to being slim again. She calls herself the frump with a lump. After the baby arrives, I want her to have something glamorous, really special. She deserves it. I've been putting money aside for months. Do you want to see what I got? I found it in Elaine Ducharme."

"I don't know it."

"It's a very posh shop. I found the advert in some fashion magazine." He had already taken the box from the carrier and was unwrapping the pink ribbon.

"You'd better not. It's gift-wrapped."

"Tell me what you think," he insisted, as he raised the lid, parted the tissue, and lifted out the gift for his wife. It was a nightdress, the sort of nightdress, Fran privately reflected, that men misguidedly buy for the women they adore. Pale-blue, in fine silk, styled in the empire line, gathered at the bodice, with masses of lace interwoven with yellow ribbons. Gorgeous to look at and hopelessly impractical to wash and use again. Not even comfortable to sleep in. His wife, she guessed, would wear it once and pack it away with her wedding veil and her love letters.

"It's exquisite."

"I'm glad I showed it to you." He stated to replace it clumsily in the box.

"Let me," said Fran, leaning across to take it from him. The silk was irresistible. "I know she'll love it."

"It's not so much the gift," he said as if he sensed her thoughts. "It's what lies behind it. Pearlie would tell you I'm useless at romantic speeches. You should have seen me blushing in that shop. Frilly knickers on every side. The girls there had a right game with me, holding these nighties against themselves and asking what I thought."

Fran felt privileged. She doubted if Pearlie would ever be told of the gauntlet her young husband had run to acquire the nightdress. She warmed to him. He was fun in a way that Jim couldn't be. Not that she felt disloyal to Jim, but this guy was devoted to his Pearlie, and that made him easy to relax with. She talked to him some more, telling him about the teaching and some of the sweet things the kids had said at the end of the term.

"They value you," he said. "They should."

She reddened and said, "It's about time my husband came back." Switching the conversation away from herself, she told the story of the mysterious invitation from Miss Shivers.

"You're doing the right thing," he said. "Believe me, you are."

Suddenly uneasy for no reason she could name, Fran said, "I'd better look for my husband. He said I'd find him in the bar."

"Take care, then."

As she progressed along the corridor, rocked by the speeding train, she debated with herself whether to tell Jim about the young man. It would be difficult without risking upsetting him. Still, there was no cause really.

The next carriage was of the standard Intercity type. Teetering toward her along the center aisle was Jim, bearing two beakers of tea, fortunately capped with lids. He'd queued for ten minutes, he said. And he'd found two spare seats.

They claimed the places and sipped the tea. Fran decided to tell Jim what had happened. "While you were getting these," she began—and then stopped, for the carriage was plunged into darkness.

Often on a long train journey, there are unexplained breaks in the power supply. Normally, Fran wouldn't have been troubled. This time, she had a horrible sense of disaster, a vision of the carriage rearing up, thrusting her sideways. The sides seemed to buckle, shattered glass rained on her, and people were shrieking. Choking fumes. Searing pain in her legs. Dimly, she discerned a pair of legs to her right, dressed in dark trousers. Boots with crepe soles. And blood. A pool of blood.

"You've spilt tea all over your skirt!" Jim said.

The lights came on again, and the carriage was just as it had been. People were reading the evening paper as if nothing at all had occurred. But Fran had crushed the beaker in her hand—no wonder her legs had smarted.

The thickness of the corduroy skirt had prevented her from being badly scalded. She mopped it with a tissue. "I don't know what's wrong with me—I had a nightmare, except that I wasn't asleep. Where are we?"

"We went through Reading twenty minutes ago. I'd say we're almost there. Are you going to be okay?"

Over the public-address system came the announcement that the next station stop would be Didmarsh Halt.

So far as they could tell in the thick mist, they were the only people to leave the train at Didmarsh.

Miss Shivers was in the booking hall, a gaunt-faced, tense woman of about fifty, with cropped silver hair and red-framed glasses. Her hand was cold, but she shook Fran's firmly and lingered before letting it go.

She drove them in an old Maxi Estate to a cottage set back from the road not more than five minutes from the station. Christmas-tree lights were visible through the leaded window. The smell of roast turkey wafted from the door when she opened it. Jim handed across the bottle of wine he had thoughtfully brought.

"We're wondering how you heard of us."

"Yes, I'm sure you are," the woman answered, addressing herself more to Fran than Jim. "My name is Edith. I was your mother's best friend for ten years, but we fell out over a misunderstanding. You see, Fran, I loved your father."

Fran stiffened and turned to Jim. "I don't think we should stay."

"Please," said the woman, and she sounded close to desperation, "we did nothing wrong. I have something on my conscience, but it isn't adultery, whatever you were led to believe."

They consented to stay and eat the meal. Conversation was strained, but the food was superb. And when at last they sat in front of the fire sipping coffee, Edith Shivers explained why she had invited them. "As I said, I loved your father Harry. A crush, we called it in those days when it wasn't mutual. He was kind to me, took me out, kissed me sometimes, but that was all. He really loved your mother. Adored her."

"You've got to be kidding," said Fran grimly.

"No, your mother was mistaken. Tragically mistaken. I know what she believed, and nothing I could say or do would shake her. I tried writing, phoning, calling personally. She shut me out of her life completely."

"That much I can accept," said Fran. "She never mentioned you to me."

"Did she never talk about the train crash—the night your father was killed, just down the line from here?"

"Just once. After that it was a closed book. He betrayed her dreadfully. She was pregnant, expecting me.

It was traumatic. She hardly ever mentioned my father after that. She didn't even keep a photograph.''

Miss Shivers put out her hand and pressed it over Fran's. "My dear, for both their sakes I want you to know the truth. Thirty-seven people died in that crash, twenty-five years ago this very evening. Your mother was shocked to learn that he was on the train, because he'd said nothing whatsoever to her about it. He'd told her he was working late. She read about the crash without supposing for a moment that Harry was one of the dead. When she was given the news, just a day or two before you were born, the grief was worse because he'd lied to her. Then she learned that I'd been a passenger on the same train, as indeed I had, and escaped unhurt. Fran, that was chance—pure chance. I happened to work in the City. My name was published in the press, and your mother saw it and came to a totally wrong conclusion.''

"That my father and you—"

"Yes. And that wasn't all. Some days after the accident, Harry's personal effects were returned to her, and in the pocket of his jacket they found a receipt from a Bond Street shop for a nightdress.''

"Elaine Ducharme," said Fran in a flat voice.

"You *know?*''

"Yes.''

"The shop was very famous. They went out of business in 1969. You see—''

"He'd bought it for her," said Fran, "as a surprise.''

Edith Shivers withdrew her hand from Fran's and put it to her mouth. "Then you know about me?''

"No.''

Their hostess drew herself up in her chair. "I must tell you. Quite by chance on that night twenty-five years ago, I saw him getting on the train. I still loved him and he was alone, so I walked along the corridor and joined him. He was carrying a bag containing the nightdress. In the course of the journey he showed it to me, not realizing that it wounded me to see how much he loved her still. He told me how he'd gone into the shop—''

''Yes,'' said Fran expressionlessly. ''And after Reading, the train crashed.''

''He was killed instantly. The side of the carriage crushed him. But I was flung clear—bruised, cut in the forehead, but really unhurt. I could see that Harry was dead. Amazingly, the box with the nightdress wasn't damaged.'' Miss Shivers stared into the fire. ''I coveted it. I told myself if I left it, someone would pick it up and steal it. Instead, I did. *I* stole it. And it's been on my conscience ever since.''

Fran had listened in a trancelike way, thinking all the time about her meeting in the train.

Miss Shivers was saying, ''If you hate me for what I did, I understand. You see, your mother assumed that Harry bought the nightdress for me. Whatever I said to the contrary, she wouldn't have believed me.''

''Probably not,'' said Fran. ''What happened to it?''

Miss Shivers got up and crossed the room to a sideboard, opened a drawer, and withdrew a box—the box Fran had handled only an hour or two previously. ''I never wore it. It was never meant for me. I want you to have it, Fran. He would have wished that.''

Fran's hands trembled as she opened the box and laid aside the tissue. She stroked the silk. She thought of what had happened, how she hadn't for a moment suspected that she had seen a ghost. She refused to think of him as that. She rejoiced in the miracle that she had met her own father, who had died before she was born—met him in the prime of his young life, when he was her own age.

Still holding the box, she got up and kissed Edith Shivers on the forehead. ''My parents are at peace now, I'm sure of it. This is a wonderful Christmas present,'' she said.

NOEL, NOEL

by Barry Perowne

It was on a gray December morning, under a sky threatening snow, that I called by request at the Colonial Office (Pacific Section) in the matter of my brother, recently deceased. As his only relative surviving in England, I was handed a letter written by the Resident Commissioner of the remote archipelago where my brother's life had come to an end. The letter was accompanied by a photograph of his grave, and I was given also a small box or chest, carved with strange island designs, which had been found in his palm-thatched house and contained, I was told, a manuscript he had left, of an autobiographical nature.

The official who interviewed me was a young-old individual, impeccably dressed in black jacket and striped trousers, and of great urbanity. When I took my leave, he helped me into my tweed overcoat, handed me my gray bowler hat and my cane. No doubt in deference to my frailty and my silver hair, he insisted on carrying the chest out to the waiting taxi.

The snow had set in by now, in earnest.

"Christmas in a few days," said my official, as we shook hands through the taxi window. "It'll be a white one."

He gave me a rather odd look, and I had no doubt, as the taxi set off for Victoria Station, that he was thinking about my brother, who had been born on a Christmas Day and named, accordingly, Noel.

I lived in the country, and returning home in the train, I had a first-class compartment to myself. Prior to opening the chest on the seat beside me, I studied again the photograph of my brother's far-off memorial. A small obelisk of what looked like white coral, it bore the curious epitaph "1°.58′ N., 157°.27′ W.," together with two sets of initials, my brother's and, I had been told, those of the woman to whom he had been for a great many years (though today was the first I had heard of it) most happily married.

Touching those years, the terms used by the Resident Commissioner to describe them, filled me with astonishment as I glanced over his letter again: "Beloved by this small community of forty-two souls—a source of comfort—sage in council—kind, courageous, selfless—"

With the best will in the world, I could not recognize in this picture my brother as I had known him. I turned for enlightenment to the chest on the seat beside me. I studied the carving for a moment—designs of outrigger canoes, paddles, coconut palms, turtles, and land crabs; and when, with an uncomfortable sense of intrusion, I lifted the lid, there came from the chest a subtle aroma that suggested to my imagination palm fibre and seashells, sunshine and coral grottoes, baked breadfruit and petals of frangipani. I breathed again, it seemed to me—in that train rocking through the December snowfall—the trade winds which had blown from the pages of my boyhood reading, which was as near as I had ever got to the Pacific.

I took from the chest my brother's manuscript book, ran my fingers over its frayed binding, turned the yellowed leaves at random. They were covered with faded writing in a hand which, even after all the long years, I recognized as my brother's. And at the opening sentence, simple and conventional—*My earliest memory is of Christmas in the year 1880*—I nodded to myself, remembering that and many another Christmas at home.

I was five years older than Noel. We were a large family, living in a rambling country house, and our father, an awesome man normally, was always rollicking and jovial at Christmastime. For us, his eight children, it was always, outstandingly, the happiest time of the year. Especially was it so, in boyhood and adolescence, for Noel, the youngest of us, being his birthday as well as the season for which he was named. For Noel it was a time of pure magic. His eyes shone with excitement. He was a handsome boy, sensitive and imaginative, not a bit like the rest of us, who were rather homely looking and stodgy. Yes, at Yuletide my brother Noel, as a boy, was always at his best—though later, in young manhood, by a kind of reaction to a most unfortunate circumstance, he was to be always at his disastrous worst.

My sister Emily once remarked, ''I suppose it's natural that Christmas should mean even more to Noel than to the rest of us, but, you know, I wonder at times if his excitement is quite healthy. His anxiety that we should all be here together, his intense preoccupation with whether it will snow at just the right time, the utter extravagance with which he'd reward the waits if we didn't restrain him—it all makes me wonder if there's not perhaps a slight instability in him somewhere. Really, I tremble at times to think of his future.''

She had good reason. At sixteen he began to get into scrapes. At eighteen his behavior gave rise to a deeper disquiet. At twenty, while articled to an estate agent in Shropshire, he kicked over the traces so seriously that my father told him never to show his face at home again.

Poor Noel. Christmas was not the same for him without us—or for us without him. Some of us were married by then, but we always foregathered in the old home in deference to our father. Our natural stodginess, lacking the inspiration of Noel's presence, was quite stupefying.

As for Noel, the very next Christmas season after he had been cast out, he was brought before a London magistrate and charged with drunkenness and insulting behavior. We heard about it later. Asked if he had anything to say, he blamed his misdemeanor on the need he had felt to drown the memory of past joyous Christmases in the home from which his own folly had barred him forever.

''Young man,'' said the magistrate, ''your trouble is less unique than you fancy. We are all prone to self-pity at this season. We all have memories and regrets. We are all sensitive at Christmastime, but it is a sign of immaturity in you that you have allowed such a universal feeling to become, in your case, morbidly developed. Case dismissed, but don't leave the court. I haven't finished with you.''

What followed was surprising. The magistrate, moved perhaps by Noel's good looks and charm of manner, and by a certain pathos in his aberration, invited him into his own home as a guest over Christmas. The visit grew extended. Long after the holly had been taken down, my brother continued to loll in the magistrate's house. Instead of resenting this, the magistrate and his good lady felt a growing affection for him. In a sense, they adopted him; but, not liking to see him idle, they found him a sound position in a South Coast town.

The following Christmas found Noel in trouble again. It was so serious that, instead of returning ''home'' to the magistrate's house, where he was expected on Christmas Eve, he sent the unfortunate man a telegram announcing his intention of throwing himself from Beachy Head at midnight.

The harassed magistrate caused police to be rushed to the spot. Noel, however, having sent his telegram, had succumbed to drink and was later found insensible in a snow-covered beach shelter. The magistrate, though furious, yielded to his wife's insistence that he smooth over the trouble Noel was in; but he told my brother that thenceforth he could go to the devil in his own way.

The magistrate and his wife, on the other hand, went to Aix-les-Bains to recuperate from their undeserved anxieties. One morning, as they were walking from their hotel to the curative baths, in the pleasant winter sunshine, a man darted out from behind a date palm and planted himself squarely in their path.

It was my brother Noel, handsome as ever, but much disheveled and in that state of excitement, peculiar to himself, which my sister Emily had once described as "unhealthy."

"Go to the devil, can I?" he shouted at the magistrate. "In my own way? All right, watch me! *This* is my way!"

His hand flashed to his mouth. A cloaked gendarme came running towards the scene, blowing his whistle. My brother Noel lurched heavily to the left. He lurched heavily to the right. His knees buckled. The magistrate's good lady screamed. My brother Noel fell contorted at her feet with a white froth on his lips.

It was proved afterward that he had eaten soap.

His object had been to frighten the couple into taking him back into their good graces. The extraordinary thing was that the magistrate did not have him jailed. He was eager to do so, but his good lady took the view that it was no good sending Noel to prison, since he would be out in a month or two, and free to plague them again. She would be terrified to put a foot outside her house, she said, for fear he might spring at her from the shrubbery and open his veins with a razor before her very eyes. He must be sent, she insisted, somewhere very far away.

The magistrate provided funds for Noel's emigration to Australia.

At home, we of his family heard of all this later. Our father had passed away in the interim—our sister Emily too—and those of us who were still living in the family home had resolved to let bygones be bygones and to make Noel welcome among us, should he ever show up.

But we heard nothing from him, and it was only now,

as I sat in the train reading his manuscript, that I came to that part of it which dealt with adventures of which I had had no previous inkling.

I laid down the book on my knees for a moment. The lights had come on in the compartment. Outside, the snow was falling thickly, and the woods and fields glimmered under their mantle of white as the December evening drew in.

Poor Noel, I thought again; he had been worthless through and through when he had left England. I marveled again at the letter, so full of praise of my brother, which I had been handed at the Colonial Office. What experience had befallen him, I wondered, to have changed him so greatly?

I picked up the book again, to read of a continuing succession of disasters and infamies. Within a year, he had made Australia too hot to hold him. He was compelled to leave clandestinely aboard a trading schooner, the *Ellis P. Harkness,* skippered by a toothless Cockney named Larkin, as incorrigible a scoundrel as my brother.

The third member of the schooner's company was a slim, brown, silent, smiling boy, a native of Tokelau, called Rahpi. He was far too good for the precious pair he sailed with, but through months of their hucksterings and rogueries among the archipelagos he served them loyally, and for my brother the boy conceived an inexplicable devotion.

One day, as the two men were drinking morosely in the cabin, an excited hail from Rahpi, at the wheel, sent them staggering up the companionway. The boy pointed off to starboard. Far across the shining water, under the blue Pacific sky, was an open boat. The prevailing easterly blew light and fitful; the boat's sail trembled, in irons. It was clear there was no hand at the helm.

By mid-afternoon the schooner came up with the boat. There lay in it the sun-blackened body of a man. My brother Noel dropped down into the boat to examine the corpse. Clutched in its brittle fingers was a wash-leather bag. Noel loosed it from the dead man's grip and shook the contents onto his palm. His heart gave a great thud.

Pearls!

He felt the boat rock as Larkin leaped down into it.

"Halves, mate!" Larkin said. "How about it, mate?"

Noel looked at him. Larkin's eyes were narrowed, his tongue moved round over his toothless gums, his right hand rested tensely on the bulge of the revolver in the pocket of his tattered ducks.

My brother smiled. "Halves it is," he said.

Larkin looked with sly gloating at the pearls on Noel's palm. "What a Christmas present, mate!" Larkin said. "Eh, mate?"

The bright day seemed to my brother Noel suddenly, strangely to darken. He said slowly, "Christmas present?"

Larkin flared up. It was as though, all at once, he were anxious to find cause for offense, an excuse for a fight.

"Why, you lowdown, busted boozer," he shouted, "ain't you got a spark of decency left in you? Ain't you got a family back home to bow your head in shame to think of at a time like this? Don't you know tomorrow's Christmas Eve?"

The pearls spilled unheeded from my brother's hand to the bottom of the boat. Larkin plunged to his knees, pouring curses on the corpse as he shoved it aside to get at the boat's bilges. Noel swung himself back to the schooner's deck. He thrust past the staring Rahpi and went below. He flung his broken-peaked cap across the cabin and reached for a bottle.

That night, swaying on his feet as he stood his trick at the wheel, he brooded alcoholically, heedless of the starbright sky. More acutely than ever before, the memory of long-lost happy Yuletides returned to plague him. He could neither relive them nor forget them. That nostalgia known to all men—but developed in my brother Noel to a destructive morbidity—made him as desperate as a trapped animal. He had a blind urge to flight, which in his befuddled mind shaped itself into a plan to seize the schooner and the pearls and *be rid of Larkin—*

Suddenly, leaving the wheel spokes spinning aimlessly, he lurched down the companion into the cabin. The lamp there, swaying in gimbals, cast an oily yellow gleam that made the shadows move. Larkin lay on his back in his bunk, snoring, his toothless mouth agape, his gums glistening pink in a tangle of beard.

My brother, holding his breath, slid a hand under the man's pillow. He felt the wash-leather bag, the butt of the revolver. He drew them out cautiously. He raised the revolver to Larkin's head, but then the thought of the boy Rahpi flashed into his mind. The Tokelau boy was asleep in the forepeak. He would hear a shot. My brother stood biting his lips. His rage flamed up again. Kill one, kill both! Rahpi must go, too. He must be hounded out and ruthlessly shot down.

Again my brother raised the revolver to Larkin's head. But now the schooner, to a sudden freshening of the wind, and with the wheel spinning free, broached-to with a jerk that sent Noel staggering. Before he could recover himself, the squall struck—one of those Pacific squalls which an alert wheelsman could see coming from afar, in good time to reef down and make all snug. But there was no wheelsman, and with a rush and hiss of rain, a screaming wind, the squall was on them. Larkin woke with a shout as the schooner was lifted high on the first of the rollers, then dropped dizzily into its trough. Glass crashed as the lamp blacked out.

The two men were flung together, struggling, fighting with each other to be first up the companion. Finally both gained the deck and clung where they could as a sea swept over them. Through the tumult about them sounded a deeper, more distant note, a rumbling note like thunder.

"Breakers!" Larkin yelled.

After that, according to the account in the manuscript, my brother Noel had no clear idea of what happened, no recollection of clawing a handhold on the reef as the schooner struck. He did not know how many hours passed before he regained consciousness. His whole body stung from the cruel abrasions of the coral. His head seemed to weigh a ton as he raised it.

He struggled to his knees. The vast sky of morning was sheened over with radiant tints of pearl. The passing of the squall had left the sea shining and level to the horizon, though here and there along the curve of the reef spray leaped with a white flash against the blue. At some distance from him, two figures were picking their way along the reef, slowly and painfully, sometimes stumbling.

Noel watched them, conscious of the heavy, measured thumping in his chest. Larkin and Rahpi! Alive! With a creeping horror he remembered how a few hours before, in his madness, he had stood at the very brink of murder. Mere chance had plucked him back from that awful precipice. They were alive, and he drew in his breath, deeply, in relief and gratitude.

A shout reached him, not from the men on the reef, but from the lagoon within its shelter. Noel got to his feet with difficulty, his salt-soaked body smarting, and turned. The lagoon lay tranquil, edged in the distance by a white beach and leaning palms. A canoe, driven swiftly by paddles that flashed as they rose and fell, was coming towards him. There were two people in it, a young man and a girl. The *pareus* they wore were gaily colored, and the girl's shining dark hair streamed over her brown shoulders

"Hello?" the young man called to Noel. "All right, there? Hello?"

My brother lifted a hand slowly in reply. He wondered where he was. The young man had spoken in English.

Nearing the reef, the couple, obviously brother and sister, and Tahitian in appearance, backed with their paddles, and beached the canoe.

The girl looked up at my brother with dark, gentle eyes that seemed to hold a puzzled look. She was very beautiful. My brother had a strange feeling that this meeting between them had been inevitable—that he had come to the one place in the world where he could find peace—that before him, here, lay the beginning of his real life.

There had been nobody here to greet Captain Cook when he had discovered the island on December 24, 1777, at precisely 1°.58′ N., 157°.27′ W. But for my brother Noel there was this girl, and she smiled at him gravely, yet with a kind of wonder in her eyes, as though she had been waiting for him for a long time and could not quite believe that he had come, at last.

"Welcome," she said, "to Christmas Island."

THE EMBEZZLER'S CHRISTMAS PRESENT

by Ennis Duling

Entire mornings could pass at the First National Bank without anyone speaking to Herb Cubbey about anything that wasn't business. Checks were cashed, and money was entered in personal accounts at the window where Herb worked. Customers were rewarded with a nod and a barely audible thank you. At the end of the day his records were always in perfect order.

Twenty-five-year-old Sue Rigney, who worked two windows away, thought that Herb moved around the bank as if he were a frightened herbivore (she liked the pun) in a jungle of meateaters. He might have blended into a paneled wall, his brown bow tie and the pattern of his remaining hair serving as protective coloration. Like a mouse at the cat's water dish, he poured water for tea, allowed it to steep weakly, and then darted away, leaving only the spore of the tea bag. Sue noticed that he used a tea bag more than once.

Sue had heard the other tellers and the secretaries discussing Herb's personal life. He spent his evenings at home with his widowed mother, and that was the sum of his life. Probably he kept a goldfish, watched the same television shows each week, and made his mother breakfast in bed on Sundays.

The secretaries made occasional jokes about Herb's saintly mother, but he was such little game that they usually found other targets such as the newly appointed assistant manager, Edward Bridgewright, who at thirty-three was exactly Herb's age. In fact, they had both entered the bank's employ at the same time, and while Herb remained at his original position, Bridgewright had risen to better things.

One morning before opening, a group of secretaries and tellers gathered near the coffee machine and talked about the Christmas presents they were giving their boyfriends and husbands. When Herb appeared, Sue, who at the moment had no boyfriend and wanted to keep the fact a secret, said, "What are you giving your mother for Christmas, Herb?"

Herb squeezed his tea bag between two spoons. "I really shouldn't say."

"Aw, come on, Herb," Dot Levin said. After twenty years at the bank, she liked to play mother to the younger employees. "Your mother is such a wonderful woman." Sue wished she hadn't said anything.

"I know I shouldn't tell you this," Herb said, "but I'm giving her ten thousand dollars." The water in his cup had turned a light amber. "Merry Christmas to you all." He looked down at his cup as he balanced it in retreat.

"Did he say ten thousand?" Dot asked.

"Where would the little man get that kind of money?" said Jan Washington, a strikingly beautiful black woman.

At that moment Mr. Bridgewright stepped out of the elevator and marched toward the conversation. "Girls, girls, girls, this is no time to stand around and talk. Back to work!"

"This is my break time, Mr. Bridgewright," Sue said.

He gave her one of his sincere smiles, the type she always saw before he asked her for a date.

"And Herb Cubbey has lots of money," Paula Kimble said.

"No, he doesn't. Work!"

Sue slipped away with the rest of them.

In the parking lot after closing, Herb's money was again the topic of conversation. "Maybe the man lied," Jan suggested.

"No!" Sue insisted. She thought that Herb deserved his privacy as much as anyone. She hated it when the others started to pry into her life.

"Herbert has never told a lie since he was born," Paula said. "He's afraid his mommy might slap his hand."

"Then he inherited it," Sue said.

John Franks from the trust department said, "I drove him home two years ago during the bus strike. He lives over in Bultman Village. You know those little bungalows built back in the Roaring Twenties. They looked better then, I imagine. He asked me in, and the old lady served me tea and biscuits. She looked like she was posing for a painting with her knitting. She kept telling me how hard it was to make ends meet and how her husband had been a wonderful man but didn't have a head for money. No, Herb didn't have any money then."

"A rich uncle," Sue said.

"A man like that with no idea in the world of how to spend money would be lucky enough to have an uncle leave him a bundle," Dot said.

"Worry not, ladies," John said. "I see Herb coming now. I'll just ask him."

As Herb walked by, he touched his hat. John said, "Sorry to hear about your relative dying like that, Mr. Cubbey. Your uncle, wasn't it?"

Herb glanced down. "You must be mistaken, Mr. Franks. My family has excellent health, except for my father, of course, and that was years ago. Good night all."

John watched him until he was out of sight and then he said, "He's a sly one. If he inherited the money, he's not telling."

"He seems to be a very private sort of person," Sue said.

"He has responsibilities," Jan said.

"He's not shy; he's just a Scrooge," Paula said.

"Goes home and counts it at night," Jan agreed. "Won't let anyone get any use out of it except his mother and what's she need with the cash?"

"Maybe he just saved that much and decided to give it to his mother," Sue suggested.

The next morning John steered Sue into Mr. Bridgewright's office. "Ed, I just want you to know how poorly trained your employee is," he said grinning.

"What?" Mr. Bridgewright gave his supervisor's frown.

"I was trying to explain to Susie here that Herb Cubbey could no more save up enough money to give his mom ten thousand dollars than I could convince the trust department to play the ponies. Now I don't want you giving away any state secrets, but let us put down a round figure for Herb's salary." He switched on a calculator and pushed Sue in front. "Look about right, Ed? Now let's subtract food and clothing for two, house maintenance, and taxes. We can multiply the small remainder by fifty-two weeks in a year. He could save that much, but the canary would have to go hungry. Women just don't have a head for money. That's one of the things that's so charming about them."

She twisted out of John's grasp and hurried to the door. "Maybe he made it on Wall Street!"

There was a long silence. "Maybe he did," Mr. Bridgewright said.

"Several hundred thousand," John added with awe in his voice.

At the coffee machine that noon Paula touched Herb's arm. "Would you be willing to give a poor girl like me a little advice, Herb?"

"I beg your pardon?"

"Advice. You know—good ideas from your storehouse of wisdom."

"Certainly," he said doubtfully.

"What percent of a portfolio should a small investor have in stocks?"

Herb backed away as if she had been making demands on him in a foreign language. "I don't understand."

By Christmas Eve most people had concluded that there had been a misunderstanding. Dot said that Herb was probably giving his mother "ten towels and a dollar."

"Weird present!" Jan said.

"But he can afford it," Dot said.

But Paula, who wouldn't let go, cornered him by the drinking fountain. "Is your mother's present all ready, Herb?" she said.

"All but the signature."

"Won't she be surprised by such a large sum of money?"

"Oh, I don't think so. She's used to it." And then Herb smiled. Nobody had seen him really smile before, but they were sure it made him look roguish.

So as Christmas passed, Sue noticed that people's attitude toward Herb had begun to change. His fearful movements around the bank were clear signs of the secretiveness that had made him his money. His near baldness reminded them of the complete baldness of a TV star. His bow tie was like that of a famous lawyer who had been in the news. His tea drinking was a sign of international tastes.

"How are you doing today, Herb honey?" Paula said each morning.

Jan put forward the theory that Herb was a gambler. "He couldn't admit to it and still work in a bank, could he?"

Once Sue met Herb by the candy machine in the basement. "I'm sorry for how the others are treating you," she said. "I feel like I started all this."

"I don't mind really, Sue, although I don't understand a lot that they say to me. John asked me today what I thought of a copper kettle in the third. I don't know anything about kettles."

"I wish I could make it up to you in some way," she said. "Maybe dinner. How about New Year's?" Then she realized that she was doing exactly what she was apologizing for.

"I appreciate the offer, but I'll have to check with my mother. She usually has some friends over, and she might need me." He had a surprised, cornered look on his face.

Sue wasn't sure she wanted to go out with Herb—she was certain she wasn't going to mention the possibility to anyone—but he was kind and polite, characteristics that made him a good deal more attractive than John Franks or Mr. Bridgewright.

Instead of the gambler's image fading, it grew, along with that of the Wizard of Wall Street and the fortunate heir. Only Mr. Bridgewright scoffed at the entire question. Later Sue figured that he would have continued to pay no attention if it hadn't been for her.

"I just want to give you one last opportunity to go out with me on New Year's, Susie," he said after calling her into his office.

"No, thank you. I have a date already." And then before she could clamp her mouth shut, she said, "With Herb!"

The word got around the bank fast. Paula said that Herb might not be much to look at and that his mother might be a millstone, but money made up for a lot of faults.

"We never took you for the greedy type," Dot teased.

"I'm not going out with him for his money."

"With a man like him, what else is there?" Paula said.

''I kind of feel sorry for him.''

''You'll feel sorry for him all right when he starts giving you diamonds.''

For the next two days, Sue noticed Mr. Bridgewright standing at the door to his office watching Herb. When Herb left his window for the men's room, Bridgewright would make a mark in a notebook. Jan noticed, too. ''The man goes to the john more than anyone I've ever seen.''

John whispered the conclusion first: ''Embezzlement!''

''What an awful thing to say,'' Sue said.

''First thing you know he'll figure out a way to steal thousands at once, and he'll be off to South America,'' Paula said.

John laughed. ''I can just picture him in a hotel room in Rio wishing he could understand what they were saying on TV.''

''Are you serious?'' Sue demanded.

''Bridgewright is,'' John said.

''He can't be.''

''I expect the examiners to swoop down at any moment.''

The next afternoon, December 31st, Bridgewright stepped over to Herb's cash drawer at the end of the day. ''We're going to have someone else check your drawer tonight, Mr. Cubbey,'' he said. A grim-faced young man in a gray suit stood at his elbow.

''Certainly,'' Herb said in a voice filled with surprise.

''And Mr. Hamilton wants to see you in his office immediately.'' Mr. Hamilton was the bank president.

''Yes, sir.'' Herb walked a few steps away and stood looking out the plate glass window at the bustle on Main Street. Sue could see his shoulders slump in defeat.

Mr. Bridgewright came over to her. ''Well, Miss Rigney, we're going to be at the bottom of the Herbert Cubbey case soon enough. Mr. Hamilton has been informed. We've played games far too long.''

"I don't think Herb even knows what game we're playing," Sue said.

She went to where Herb stood and squeezed his arm. "Whatever happens, Herb, I know you're innocent.''

"Am I in some sort of trouble?'' He seemed terribly afraid, and she wanted to mother him.

"They say you stole the money.''

"What money?''

"The ten thousand dollars you gave your mother for Christmas.''

He swallowed hard. "You didn't really think I had all that money?''

"You said you did.''

"If I did have that much, I'd take you out on New Year's to the best restaurant in town. You'd have flowers, and we'd drink champagne and dance all night.''

"It doesn't take that much money to have a good time,'' Sue said. "I already lied and told Mr. Bridgewright we were going out.''

"All right then,'' he said, straightening his shoulders. "We'll make some plans when we get back from talking to Mr. Hamilton. Will you come along with me?''

Sue followed him to the elevator.

"Could I have the opportunity to explain?'' Herb said to President Hamilton.

"I expect you'd like one, Cubbey,'' Hamilton said. He was a short, heavy man with bushy eyebrows. "You should anyway! I'm an old man, so I don't need to be subtle. No time for it. So let's hear it. Bridgewright tells me you've been giving away thousands of dollars and the only explanation is you've got your hand in the till.''

"I've honestly accounted for every cent that I've handled.''

"Thought so. What about the gift?''

"I wrote my mother a check for ten thousand dollars at Christmas. I never should have told anyone."

"How's that again?"

"We haven't had much since my father passed away, so we pretend. Every year we write each other large checks. This year she gave me a check for two thousand. The year before I wrote one for five thousand, and she gave me one for eight thousand. *Checks* that is. We sit around and talk about what we'd like to buy until midnight, and then we burn the checks in the fireplace. We've always had a good time doing it. It must sound strange to outsiders."

Mr. Hamilton chuckled. "It's unusual, that's for sure, but not a bad idea. You get the pleasure of the money without the cost, which is not bad management at all. Not bad at all. Shows a good deal more sense than Mr. Bridgewright just exhibited."

"Do you have any further questions, sir?"

"Why hasn't an honest, imaginative young man like you received a promotion recently? Who's running this bank anyway? That's what I'd like to know."

THE CHRISTMAS SPIRIT
by Thomasina Weber

I didn't realize anything was wrong until the little old lady in front of me in line began to cry.

"What were you doing while the boy bagged your groceries?" asked the cashier.

"I was getting my money together," said the customer, her voice quavery with tears as she nervously snapped and unsnapped the catch of her shabby pocketbook.

"Can't you see this poor woman is upset?" I demanded. "Do you have to be so rude?"

"Look behind you, sonny," said the cashier. "The line is backed up into pickles already. Go talk to the manager."

I am a journalism major here in Florida, and this little lady intrigued me because, based upon my skill in judging character, I plan to specialize in the real people behind the headlines.

"Come along," I said, leading the woman to the manger's booth, where he invited her to tell her story.

"After putting my change away," she finished. "I found that my groceries were gone. The bag boy said my husband took them out." I had seen the man—tall, thin, elderly, with an outstandingly hooked nose.

"And you don't have a husband," said the manger. I thought I detected a note of weariness in his tone.

"He died of consumption ten years ago, bless him." I had never heard of consumption, but I could readily see it might be a result of consumer frustration, which is certainly reaching epidemic proportions these days.

"It happens all the time," said the manger. "Husband waits outside while the wife shops and then comes in and grabs the wrong bag. Take a cart and refill your order."

"But I can't afford—"

"You already paid. Merry Christmas."

"Oh, thank you," she said, "and thank you, young man."

"For what?" I asked.

"For caring."

Well, after that, I could hardly walk out and leave her, so I helped her fill her cart. "You must eat an awful lot," I observed.

"I'm having a guest for dinner."

"I'll load the groceries in your car," I said.

"I didn't bring the car. I'm staying in the trailer park next door."

Over her protests, I drove her home. Her small travel trailer was old, but it looked sturdy and the tires were new. "Do you pull your trailer down here every winter?"

"Oh, heavens no! This trailer hasn't been moved in years."

"That's funny," I said. "The undercarriage is caked with road dirt."

She bent down to look. "Well, isn't that strange? I'll have to speak to the manager about that. I certainly wouldn't want anyone using my trailer when I'm up north. You know, I don't think he's the most honest person in the world." I got the shopping bags from the car.

"Just set them down, dear."

"I can carry them inside for you, Mrs.—"

"Posey."

"I'm Melvin Slater. I'd be glad to—"

She smiled at me sheepishly. "I didn't have time to tidy up this morning."

I left, wishing her a merry Christmas. It wasn't until

I got back to my room that I realized there had been no car in her carport.

This is not the happiest day of my life, I thought the next morning as I rode the creaky elevator up to the seventh floor of the old building where my dentist has his office. If there is anything harder to do than winning a sweepstakes, it is getting a dental appointment at a time convenient to you, which is why I was still on campus while nearly everyone else had gone home for the holidays.

But I believe that everything happens for a reason, and it looked as though I was here to champion Mrs. Posey. There was a warm glow in the region of my heart.

Until I was sitting in That Chair waiting for the novocaine to take effect. The chair faced the window, permitting its occupant to gaze down at the main street below. I wondered how many others had sat here and contemplated jumping.

Suddenly a yellow pickup truck swerved to the curb and who should get out but Mr. Hooknose. He came up behind a girl in a blue pantsuit. After a short conversation, she entered the bank on the corner. Anyone who could steal food from a little old lady would not stop at anything, I thought. What was he planning now?

I was considering leaping out of the chair and dashing downstairs—white bib and deadened jaw notwithstanding—when the man returned to his truck and drove away. The dentist chose that moment to enter the room.

When he finally finished with me, I hurried to the bank in the hope that someone would recall seeing the girl and could identify her for me.

I got the shock of my life when I saw her in a teller's cage. "Who was the man in the yellow pickup truck that you were speaking to?" I asked.

Her eyebrows rose. She was a well-preserved thirty,

but I didn't hold her age against her. "You must have the wrong person," she said, smiling.

"Oh, no, it was you." I returned her smile.

"Why do you ask?"

"I—uh—I thought I recognized him."

She straightened a stack of currency. "I speak to a lot of people." Then, her glance going beyond me, "May I help you, sir?"

Her character wasn't hard to read, I mused as I left the bank. A beautiful face, a sweet smile, and a gentle, considerate way of telling me to mind my own business. Perhaps I had been too forthright.

I drove to the trailer park and knocked on Mrs. Posey's door, but there was no answer. The adjacent window was open and a small gust of wind lifted the curtain. I saw a pipe in an ashtray on the table.

"Melvin?"

I turned guiltily to see Mrs. Posey holding a basketful of wet laundry. She set it down and seated herself on a deck chair, motioning for me to do the same. I was going to mention the pipe, but actually, it could belong to anyone—a friend, a neighbor—who knows, even to Mrs. Posey herself, what with woman's lib and all.

"I thought you'd like to know that I saw the man who stole your groceries."

"Oh?"

"He was talking to a teller at the bank."

"The poor man probably needed those groceries."

"His truck is practically new."

"Maybe that's all he owns."

"Speaking of trucks, Mrs. Posey, where's your car?"

"My car? Why, it's in the repair shop." She tucked a stray hair behind her ear. "Melvin, please forget about the groceries. It's the Christmas season and we should be charitable."

My admiration for her altruistic attitude battled with

my love of justice. "But people who get away with petty thievery go on to bigger crimes," I said.

"I don't feel I have the right to pass judgment on anyone, Melvin."

Something in her tone made me bite back my reply. Her dress was faded, her shoes, rundown. A picture was beginning to form, and I did not like it one bit. How could I have been so wrong about her?

"Mrs. Posey, through your window, I saw a pipe." She averted her eyes and I knew I was on the right track. "You do have a husband, and he drives a yellow pickup truck." I waited for a denial, but none came. "The two of you have found a way to beat the high cost of living."

She raised teary eyes. I felt like a rat. "We don't have much money, Melvin. We scrimp all year so that we can come to Florida to spend Christmas with our daughter."

"The bank teller."

"Yes. She had no idea what a financial hardship it is for us."

"Why doesn't she go up north to be with you?"

"She doesn't care that much."

Another misjudgment: daughter was not sweet and gentle at all. I sighed. "But, about the groceries—"

"That little ruse keeps us alive while we're here. The supermarkets can afford it." She must have sensed my thoughts. "We don't eat very much, and we'll be leaving the day after Christmas."

I went back to my room, wishing I had never met Mrs. Posey. She had no right to leave it up to me whether to report her or not. I vacillated between pride at having figured out their racket and disappointment at my failure to read her character correctly, a fact that could threaten my entire career.

I felt sorry for them, yet they were breaking the law. But if I reported them, I would ruin all their Christmases as well as my own. After much soul-searching, I finally decided just to go home tomorrow, as planned.

The next morning I headed for the trailer park to give Mrs. Posey the good news about my decision.

Her trailer was gone. I looked at the empty space in disbelief and barely heard a neighbor telling me they had pulled out the previous evening.

The guilt came while I was filling my gas tank. Worried over whether I would turn them in, they had hitched up and left, foregoing Christmas with their daughter, the whole purpose of it all. Much as I hated the thought of facing their daughter, I felt obligated to apologize.

There was an empty space in front of the bank, and as I drew abreast of the car parked ahead of it, the driver turned to look at me, her engine idling. It was the Posey's daughter. I was so surprised to see her that I had to make a second attempt at parking.

Just as I opened my door, two figures in stocking masks dashed out of the bank and into her car, their arms loaded with bags. Stunned, I watched as the car screeched away from the curb. One figure was tall and thin and its stocking mask did not fit flat against the face as did the mask of the short, dumpy robber. Mr. Hooknose and Mrs. Posey; and, of course, daughter Posey. Helpless little old lady and sweet gentle daughter—some judge of character I am! I stared glumly at the steering wheel, picturing my career as an in-depth journalist in ruins. This was surely the lowest point in my whole life.

"Hey, buddy, open up!"

I looked up to see a policeman at the window. I had not even heard the cops arrive.

"Did you see anything!" he asked.

Suddenly the sun came out. Of course! My reason for staying here was not to help Mrs. Posey with her Christmas plans, but to show me where my *real* talent lay—not in personalities, but in detection! *Melvin Slater, Ace Crime Reporter.*

"Yes, officer, I saw the robbers. I'll give you their complete descriptions—"

THE SPY AND
THE CHRISTMAS CIPHER

by Edward D. Hoch

It was just a few days before the Christmas recess at the University of Reading when Rand's wife Leila said to him over dinner, "Come and speak to my class on Wednesday, Jeffrey."

"What? Are you serious?" He put down his fork and stared at her. "I know nothing about archaeology."

"You don't have to. I just want you to tell them a Christmas story of some sort. Remember last year? The Canadian writer Robertson Davies was over here on a visit and he told one of his ghost stories."

"I don't know any good ghost stories."

"Then tell them a cipher story from before you retired. Tell them about the time you worked through Christmas Eve trying to crack the St. Ives cipher."

Ivan St. Ives. Rand hadn't thought of him in years.

Yes, he supposed it was a Christmas story of sorts.

It was Christmas Eve morning in 1974, when Rand was still head of Concealed Communications, operating out of the big old building overlooking the Thames. He remembered his superior, Hastings, making the rounds of the offices with an open bottle of sherry and a stack of paper cups, a tradition that no one but Hastings ever looked forward to. A cup of government sherry before

noon was not something to warm the heart or put one in
the Christmas spirit.

"It promises to be a quiet day," Hastings said, pouring the ritual drink. "You should be able to leave early
and finish up your Christmas shopping."

"It's finished. I have no one but Leila to buy for."
Rand accepted the cup and took a small sip.

"Sometimes I wish I was as well organized as you,
Rand." Hastings seemed almost disappointed as he sat
down in the worn leather chair opposite Rand's desk. "I
was going to ask you to pick up something for me."

"On the day before Christmas? The stores will be
crowded."

Hastings decided to abandon the pretense. "They say
Ivan St. Ives is back in town."

"Oh? Surely you weren't planning to send him a
Christmas gift?"

St. Ives was a double agent who'd worked for the British, the Russians, and anyone else willing to pay his
price. There were too many like him in the modern world
of espionage, where national loyalties counted for nothing against the lure of easy money.

"He's back in town and he's not working for us."

"Who, then?" Rand asked. "The Russians?"

"Perkins and Simplex, actually."

"Perkins and Simplex is a department store."

"Exactly. Ivan St. Ives has been employed over the
Christmas season as their Father Christmas—red suit,
white beard, and all. He holds little children on his knee
and asks them what they want for Christmas."

Rand laughed. "Is the spying business in some sort of
depression we don't know about? St. Ives could always
pick up money from the Irish if nobody else would pay
him."

"I just found out about it last evening, almost by accident. I ran into St. Ives's old girlfriend, Daphne Sollis,
at the Crown and Piper. There's no love lost between the

two of them and she was quite eager to tell me of his hard times.''

"It's one of his ruses, Hastings. If Ivan St. Ives is sitting in Perkins and Simplex wearing a red suit and a beard it's part of some much more complex scheme.''

"Maybe, maybe not. Anyway, this is his last day on the job. Why don't you drop by and take a look for yourself?''

"Is that what this business about last-minute shopping has been leading up to? What about young Parkinson—isn't this more his sort of errand?''

"Parkinson doesn't know St. Ives. You do.''

There was no disputing the logic of that. Rand drank the rest of his sherry and stood up. "Do I have to sit on his lap?''

Hastings sighed. "Just find out what he's up to, Jeff.''

The day was unseasonably warm, and as Rand crossed Oxford Street toward the main entrance of Perkins and Simplex he was aware that many in the lunchtime crowd had shed their coats or left them back at the office. The department store itself was a big old building that covered an entire block facing Oxford Street. It dated from Edwardian times, prior to World War I, and was a true relic of its age. Great care had been taken to maintain the exterior just as it had been, though the demands of modern merchandising had taken their toll with the interior. During the previous decade the first two floors had been gutted and transformed into a pseudo-atrium, surrounded by a balcony on which some of the store's regular departments had become little shops. The ceiling was frosted glass, lit from above by fluorescent tubes to give the appearance of daylight.

It was in this main atrium, near the escalators, that Father Christmas had been installed on his throne amidst sparkly white mountains of ersatz snow that was hardly in keeping with the outdoor temperature. The man himself was stout, but not as fat as American Santa Clauses. His white beard and the white-trimmed cowl of his red robe effectively hid his identity. It might have been Ivan St. Ives, but Rand wasn't prepared to swear to it. He had to get much closer if he wanted to be sure.

He watched for a time from the terrace level as a line of parents and tots wound its way up the carpeted ramp to Father Christmas's chair. There he listened carefully to each child's request, sometimes boosting the smallest of them to his knee and patting their heads, handing each one a small brightly wrapped gift box from a pile at his elbow.

After observing this for ten or fifteen minutes, Rand descended to the main floor and found a young mother approaching the end of the line with her little boy. "Pardon me, ma'am," Rand said. "I wonder if I might borrow your son and take him up to see Father Christmas."

She stared at him as if she hadn't heard him correctly. "No, I can take him myself."

Rand showed his identity card. "It's official business."

The woman hesitated, then stood firm. "I'm sorry. Roger would be terrified if I left him."

"Could I come along, then, as your husband?"

She stared at the card again, as if memorizing the name. "I suppose so, if it's official business. No violence or anything, though?"

"I promise."

They stood in line together and Rand took the little boy's hand. Roger stared up at him with his big brown eyes, but his mother was there to give him confidence. "I hate shopping on Christmas Eve," she told Rand. "I always spend too much when I wait until the last minute."

"I think most of us do that." He smiled at the boy. "Are you ready, Roger? We're getting closer to Father Christmas."

In a moment the boy was on the bearded man's knee, having his head patted as he told him what he wanted to find under the tree next day. Then he received his brightly wrapped gift box and they were on their way back down the ramp.

"Thank you," Rand told the woman. "You've been a big help." He went back up to the terrace level and spent the next hour watching Ivan St. Ives, double agent, passing out gifts to a long line of little children.

"It's St. Ives," Rand told Hastings when he returned to the office. "No doubt of it."

"Did he recognize you?"

"I doubt it." He explained how he'd accompanied himself with the woman and child. "If he did, he might have assumed I was with my family."

"So he's just making a little extra Christmas money?"

"I'm afraid it's more than that."

"You spotted something."

"A great deal, but I don't know what it means. I watched him for more than an hour in all. After he listened to each child, he handed them a small gift. I watched one little girl opening hers. It was a clear plastic ball to hang on a Christmas tree, with figures of cartoon characters inside."

"Seems harmless enough."

"I'm sure the store wouldn't be giving out anything that wasn't. The trouble is, while I watched him I noticed a slight deviation from his routine on three different occasions. In these cases, he chose the gift box from a separate pile, and handed it to the parent rather than the child."

"Well, some of the children are quite small, I imagine."

"In those three cases, none of the boxes were opened in the store. They were stowed away in shopping bags by the mother or father. One little boy started crying for his gift, but he didn't get it.''

Hastings thought about it.

''Do you think an agent would take a position as a department store Father Christmas to distribute some sort of message to his network?''

''I think we should see one of those boxes, Hastings.''

''If there *is* a message, it probably says 'Merry Christmas.' ''

''St. Ives has worked for some odd people in the past, including terrorists. When I left the store, there were still seven or eight boxes left on his special pile. If I went back there now with a couple of men—''

''Very well,'' Hastings said. ''But please be discreet, Rand. It's the day before Christmas.''

It's not easy to be discreet when seizing a suspected spy in the midst of a crowd of Christmas shoppers. Rand finally decided he wanted one of the free gifts more than he wanted the agents at this point, so he took only Parkinson with him. As they passed through the Oxford Street entrance of Perkins and Simplex, the younger man asked, ''Is this case likely to run through the holidays? I was hoping to spend Christmas and Boxing Day with the family.''

''I hope there won't even be a case,'' Rand told him. ''Hastings heard Ivan St. Ives was back in the city, working as Father Christmas for the holidays. I confirmed the fact and that's why we're here.''

''To steal a child's gift?''

''Not exactly steal, Parkinson. I have another idea.''

They encountered a woman and child about to leave the store with the familiar square box. ''Pardon me, but is that a gift from Father Christmas?'' Rand asked her.

''Yes, it is.''

''Then this is your lucky day. As a special holiday treat, Perkins and Simplex is paying every tenth person ten pounds for their gift.'' He held up a crisp new bill. ''Would you like to exchange yours for a tenner?''

''I sure would!'' The woman handed over the opened box and accepted the ten-pound note.

''That was easy,'' Parkinson commented when the woman and child were gone. ''What next?''

''This might be a bit more difficult,'' Rand admitted. They retreated to a men's room where Rand fastened the festive paper around the gift box once more, resticking the piece of tape that held it together. ''There, looks as good as new.''

Parkinson got the point. ''You're going to substitute this for one of the special ones.''

''Exactly. And you're going to help.''

They resumed Rand's earlier position on the terrace level, where he observed that the previous stack of boxes had dwindled to three. If he was right, they would be gone shortly, too. ''How about that man?'' Parkinson pointed out. ''The one with the little boy.''

''Why him?''

''He doesn't look that fatherly to me. And the boy seems a bit old to believe in Father Christmas.''

''You're right,'' Rand said a moment later. ''He's getting one of the special boxes. Come on!''

As the man and the boy came down off the ramp and mingled with the crowd, Rand moved in. The man was clutching the box just as the others had when Rand managed to jostle him. The box didn't come loose, so Rand jostled again with his elbow, this time using his other hand to yank it free. The man, in his twenties with black hair and a vaguely foreign look, muttered something in a language Rand didn't understand. There was a trace of panic in his face as he bent to retrieve the box. Rand pretended to lose his footing then, and came down on top of the man. The crowd of shoppers parted as they tumbled to the floor.

"Terribly sorry," Rand muttered, helping the man to his feet.

At the same moment, Parkinson held out the brightly wrapped package. "I believe you dropped this, sir."

Anyone else might have cursed Rand and made a scene, but this strange man merely grasped the box and hurried away without a word, the small boy trailing along behind. "Good work," Rand said, brushing off his jacket. "Let's get this back to the office."

"Aren't we going to open it?"

"Not here."

Thirty minutes later, Rand was carefully unwrapping the gift on Hastings' desk. Both Parkinson and Hastings were watching apprehensively, as if expecting a snake to spring out like a jack-in-the-box. "My money's on drugs," Parkinson said. "What else could it be?"

"Is the box exactly the same as the others?" Hastings asked.

"Just a bit heavier," Rand decided. "A few ounces."

But inside there seemed to be nothing but the same plastic tree ornament. Rand removed the tissue paper and stared at the bottom of the box.

"Nothing," Parkinson said.

"Wait a minute. Something had to make it heavier." Rand reached in and pried up the bottom piece of cardboard with his fingernails. It was a snugly fitted false bottom. Beneath it was a thin layer of a grey puttylike substance. "Better not touch it," Hastings cautioned. "That's plastique—plastic explosive."

The man from the bomb squad explained that it was harmless without a detonator of some sort, but they were still relieved when he removed it from the office. "How much damage would that much plastic explosive do?" Rand wanted to know.

"It would make a mess of this room. That's about all."

"What about twelve or fifteen times that much?"

''Molded together into one bomb? It could take out a house or a small building.''

They looked at each other glumly. ''It's a pretty bizarre method for distributing explosives,'' Parkinson said.

''It has its advantages,'' Hastings said. ''The bomb is of little use until enough of the explosive is gathered together. If one small box falls into government hands, as this one did, the rest is still safe. No doubt it was delivered to St. Ives only recently, and this served as the perfect method for getting it to his network—certainly better than the mails during the Christmas rush.''

''Then you think it's to be reassembled into one bomb?'' Rand asked.

''Of course. And it's to be used sometime soon.''

''The IRA? Russians? Arabs?''

Hastings shrugged. ''Take your pick. St. Ives has worked for all of them.''

Rand held the box up to the light, studying the bottom. ''This may be some writing, some sort of invisible ink that's beginning to become visible. Get one of the technicians up here to see if we can bring it out.''

Heating the bottom of the box to bring out the message proved an easy task, but the letters that appeared were anything but easy to read: MPPMP MBSHG OEXAS-EWHMR AWPGG GBEBH PMBWE ALGHQ.

''A substitution cipher,'' Parkinson decided at once. ''We'll get to work on it.''

''Forty letters,'' Rand observed, ''in the usual five-letter groups. There are five Ms, five Ps, and five Gs. Using letter frequencies, one of them could be E, but in such a short message you can't be sure.''

''GHQ at the end could stand for General Headquarters,'' Hastings suggested.

Rand shook his head. ''The entire message would be enciphered. Chances are that's just a coincidence.''

Parkinson took the message off to the deciphering room

and Rand confidently predicted he'd have the answer within an hour.

He didn't.

"It's tougher than it looks," Parkinson told them. "There may not be any Es at all."

"Run it through the computer," Rand suggested. "Use a program that substitutes various frequently used letters for the most frequently used letters in the message. See if you hit on anything."

Hastings glanced at the clock. "It's after six and my niece has invited me for Christmas Eve. Can you manage without me?"

"Of course. Merry Christmas."

After he'd gone, Rand picked up the phone and told Leila he'd be late. She was living in England now, and he'd planned to spend the holiday with her.

"How late?" she asked.

"These things have been known to last all night."

"Oh, Jeffrey. On Christmas Eve?"

"I'll call you later if I can," Rand promised. "It might not take that long."

He went down the hall and stood for a time watching the computer experts work on the message. They seemed to be having no better luck than Parkinson's people. "How long?" he asked one.

"In the worst possible case it could take us until morning to run all the combinations."

Rand nodded. "I'll be back."

They had to know what the message said, but they also had to find Ivan St. Ives. The employment office at Perkins and Simplex would be closed now. His only chance was that pub where Hastings had spoken with Daphne Sollis. The Crown and Piper.

It was on a corner, as London pubs often are, and the night before Christmas didn't seem to have made much of a dent in the early-evening business. The bar was crowded and all the tables and booths were occupied. Rand let his eyes wander over the faces, seeking out either St. Ives or Daphne, but neither one seemed to be there. He didn't know either of them well, though he thought he would recognize St. Ives out of his Father Christmas garb. He was less certain about recognizing Daphne Sollis.

"Seen Daphne around?" he asked the bartender as he ordered a pint.

"Daphne Jenkins?"

"Daphne Sollis."

"Do I know her?"

"She was in here last night, talking to a grey-haired man wearing rimless glasses. He was probably dressed in a plaid topcoat."

"I don't—Wait a minute, you must mean Rusty. Does she have red hair?"

"Not the last time I knew her, but these things change."

"Well, if it's Rusty she comes in a couple of nights a week, usually alone. Once recently she was with a creepy-looking gent who kept laughing like Father Christmas. I sure wouldn't want *him* bringing gifts to my kids. He'd scare 'em half to death."

"Does she live around here?"

"No idea, mate." He went off to wait on another customer.

So whatever Daphne had told Hastings about her relationship with Ivan St. Ives, they were hardly enemies. He'd been with her recently in the Crown and Piper, apparently since he took on the job as Father Christmas.

Rand thought it unlikely that Daphne would visit the pub two nights in a row, but on the other hand she might stop by if she was lonely on Christmas Eve. He decided to linger over his pint and see if she appeared. Thirty minutes later he was about to give it up and head for

Leila's flat when he heard the bartender say, "Hey, Rusty! Fellow here's been askin' after you."

Rand turned and saw Daphne Sollis standing not five feet behind him, unwrapping a scarf to reveal a tousled head of red hair. "Daphne!" She looked puzzled for a moment and he identified himself. "Ivan St. Ives introduced us a year or so back. He did some work for me."

She nodded slowly as it came back to her. "Oh, yes— Mr. Rand. I remember you now. Is this some sort of setup? The other one, Hastings, was here just last night."

"No setup, but I *would* like to talk with you, away from this noise. How about the lobby of the hotel next door?"

"Well—all right."

The hotel lobby was much quieter. They sat beneath a large potted palm and no one disturbed them. "What do you want?" she asked. "What did your friend Hastings want last night?"

"It was only happenstance that he met you, though I'll admit I came to the Crown and Piper looking for you. I need to locate Ivan St. Ives."

"I told Hastings we're on the outs."

"I saw him at Perkins and Simplex earlier today."

"Then you've already located him."

"No," Rand explained. "His Christmas job would have ended today. I need to know where he's living."

"I said we're on the outs."

"You were drinking with him at the Crown and Piper just a week or two ago."

She bit her lip and stared off into space. "I don't know where he's living. He rang me up and we had a drink for old times' sake. That's when he told me about the Christmas job. He talked about getting back together again, but I don't know. He works for a lot of shady people."

"Who's he working for now?"

"Just the store, so far as I know. He said he'd fallen on hard times."

Rand leaned forward. "It could be worth some money if you located him for us, told us who he's palling around with."

She seemed to consider the idea. "I could tell you plenty about who he's palled around with in the past. It wasn't just our side, you know."

"I know."

"But it would have to be after New Year's. I'm going to visit a girlfriend in Hastings, on the coast. Is your friend Hastings from there?"

"From Leeds, actually." Rand was frowning. "I need St. Ives now."

"I'm sorry, I can't help you. Perhaps the store has his address."

"I'll have to ask them." Rand stood up. "Can I buy you a pint back at the pub?"

"I'd better skip it now," she said, glancing at her watch. "I want to get home and change. I'm going to Midnight Mass with some friends."

"If you'll jot down your phone number I'd like to ring you up after New Year's."

"Fine," she agreed.

He'd intended to phone Leila after he left Daphne, but back at the Double-C office, Parkinson was in a state of dejection. "We've run every possible substitution of the letter E and there's still nothing. We're going down the letter-frequency list now, working on T, A, O, and N."

"Forty characters without a single E. Unusual, certainly."

"Any luck locating St. Ives?"

"Not yet."

Rand worked with them for a time and then dozed on his office couch. It was long after midnight when Parkinson shook him awake. "I think we've got part of it."

''Let me see.''

The younger man produced long folds of computer printout. ''On this one we concentrated on the first six characters—the repetitive MPPMPM. We got nowhere substituting E, T, or A, but when we tried the next letters on the frequency list, O and N, look what came up.''

Rand focused his sleepy eyes and read NOONON. ''Noon on?''

''Exactly. And there's another ON combination later in the message.''

''Just a simple substitution cipher after all,'' Rand marveled. ''School children make them up all the time.''

''And it took us all these hours to get this far.''

''St. Ives didn't worry about making the cipher too complex because he was writing it in invisible ink. It was our good luck that the box warmed enough so that some of the message began to appear.''

''A terrorist network armed with plastic explosives, and St. Ives is telling them when and where to set off the bomb. Do you think we should phone Hastings?''

Rand glanced at the clock. It was almost dawn on Christmas morning. ''Let's wait till we get the rest of it.''

He followed Parkinson down the hall to the computer room where the others were at work. Not bothering with the machines, he went straight to the old blackboard at the far end of the room. ''Look here, all of you. The group of letters following *noon on* is probably a day of the week, or a date if it's spelled out. If it's a day of the week, three of these letters have to stand for *day.*''

As he worked, he became aware that someone had chalked the most common letter-frequency list down the left side of the board, starting with E, T, A, O, N, and continuing down to Q, X, Z. It was the list from David Kahn's massive 1967 book, *The Codebreakers*, which everyone in the department had on their shelves. He stared at it and noticed that M and P came together about halfway down the list. Together, just like N and O in the regular alphabet. Quickly he chalked the letters A to Z next to the frequency list. "Look here! The key is the standard letter-frequency list. ABCDE is enciphered as ETAON. There are no Ns in the message we found, so there are no Es in the plaintext."

The message became clear at once: NOONO NTHIS DAYCH ARING CROSS STATI ONTRA CKSIX. "Noon on this day, Charing Cross Station, track six," Rand read.

"Noon on which day?" Parkinson questioned. "It was after noon yesterday before he distributed most of the boxes."

"He must mean today. Christmas Day. A Christmas Day explosion at Charing Cross Station."

"I'll phone Hastings," Parkinson decided. "We can catch them in the act."

Police and Scotland Yard detectives converged on the station shortly after dawn. Staying as unobtrusive as possible, they searched the entire area around track six. No bomb was found.

Noon came and went, and no bomb exploded.

Rand turned up at Leila's flat late that afternoon. "Only twenty-four hours late," she commented drily, holding the door open for him.

"And not in a good mood."

"You mean you didn't crack it after all this time?"

"We cracked it, but that didn't do us much good. We don't have the man who sent it, and we may be unable to prevent a terrorist bombing."

"Here in London?"

"Yes, right here in London." He knew a few police were still at Charing Cross Station, but he also knew it was quite easy to smuggle plastic explosives past the tightest security. They could be molded into any shape, and metal detectors were of no use against them.

He tried to put his mind at ease during dinner with Leila, and later when she asked if he'd be spending the night he readily agreed. But he awakened before dawn and walked restlessly to the window, looking out at the glistening streets where rain had started to fall. It would be colder today, more like winter.

The bomb hadn't gone off at Charing Cross Station yesterday. Either the time or the place was wrong.

But it hadn't gone off anywhere else in London, so he could assume the place was correct. It was the time that was off.

The time, or the day.

This day.

Noon on this day.

He went to Leila's telephone and called Parkinson at home. When he heard his sleepy voice answer, he said, "This is Rand. Meet me at the office in an hour."

"It's only six o'clock," Parkinson muttered. "And a holiday."

"I know. I'm sorry. But I'm calling Hastings, too. It's important."

He leaned over the bed to kiss Leila but left without awakening her.

An hour later, with Hastings and Parkinson seated before him in the office, Rand picked up a piece of chalk. "You see, we assumed the wrong meaning for the word 'this.' If someone wants to indicate 'today,' they say it—they don't say 'this day.' On the other hand, if I write the word 'this' on the desk in front of me—" he did so with the piece of chalk "—what am I referring to?"

"The desk," Parkinson replied.

"Right. If I wrote the word on a box, what would I be referring to?"

"The box."

"When St. Ives's message said, 'this day,' he wasn't referring to Christmas Eve or Christmas Day. He was telling them Boxing Day. Even if they were foreign, they'd know it was the day after Christmas here and a national holiday.''

"That's today," Hastings said.

"Exactly. We need to get the men back to Charing Cross Station."

The station was almost deserted. The holiday travelers were at their destinations, and it was too soon for anyone to have started home yet. Rand stood near one of the newsstands looking through a paper while the detectives again searched unobtrusively around track six. It was nearly noon and time was running out.

"No luck," Hastings told him. "They can't find a thing."

"Plastique." Rand shook his head. "It could be molded around a girder and painted most any color. We'd better keep everyone clear from now until after noon." It was six minutes to twelve.

"Are you sure about this, Rand? St. Ives is using a dozen or more people. Perhaps they all didn't understand his message."

"They had to come together to assemble the small portions of explosive into a deadly whole. Most of them would understand the message even if a few didn't. I'm sure St. Ives trained them well."

"It's not a busy day. He's not trying to kill a great many people or he'd have waited until a daily rush hour."

"No," Rand agreed. "I think he's content to—" He froze, staring toward the street entrance to the station. A man and a woman had entered and were walking toward track six. The man was Ivan St. Ives and the woman was Daphne Sollis.

Rand had forgotten that the train to Hastings left from Charing Cross Station.

He ran across the station floor, through the beams of sunlight that had suddenly brightened it from the glass-enclosed roof. "St. Ives!" he shouted.

Ivan St. Ives had just bent to give Daphne a good-bye kiss. He turned suddenly at the sound of his name and saw Rand approaching. "What *is* this?" he asked.

"Get away from him, Daphne!" Rand warned.

"He just came to see me off. I told you I was visiting—"

"Get away from him!" Rand repeated more urgently.

St. Ives met his eyes, and glanced quickly away, as if seeking a safe exit. But already the others were moving in. His eyes came back to Rand, recognizing him. "You were at the store, in line for Father Christmas! I knew I'd seen you before!"

"We broke the cipher, St. Ives. We know everything."

St. Ives turned and ran, not toward the street from where the men were coming but through the gate to track six. A police constable blew his whistle, and the sound merged with the chiming of the station clock. St. Ives had gone about fifty feet when the railway car to his left seemed to come apart with a blinding flash and roar of sound that sent waves of dust and debris billowing back toward Rand and the others. Daphne screamed and covered her face.

When the smoke cleared, Ivan St. Ives was gone. It was some time later before they found his remains among the wreckage that had been blown onto the adjoining track. By then, Rand had explained it to Hastings and Parkinson. "Ivan St. Ives was a truly evil man. When he was hired to plan and carry out a terrorist bombing in London over the Christmas holidays, he decided quite literally to kill two birds with one stone. He planned the bombing for the exact time and place where his old girlfriend Daphne Sollis would be. To make certain she didn't arrive too early or too late, he even escorted her to the station himself. She knew too much about his past associations, and he wanted her out of his life for good. I imagine one of his men must have ridden the train into Charing Cross Station and hidden the bomb on board before he left."

But he didn't tell any of this to Daphne. She only knew that they'd come to arrest St. Ives and he'd been killed by a bomb while trying to flee. A tragic coincidence, nothing more. She never knew St. Ives had tried to kill her.

In a way Rand felt it was a Christmas gift to her.

BUT ONCE A YEAR
... THANK GOD!

by Joyce Porter

Nobody, with one glittering exception, ever enjoyed the Christmas party which the Totterbridge & District Conservative & Unionist Club traditionally gave every year for the children of its members. The ladies who organised and ran the party naturally hated every minute of it, while the guests (all under the age of ten) invariably professed themselves bored out of their tiny minds by the lousy tea, the lousy entertainment, and the even lousier presents. Only the Honourable Constance Morrison-Burke stood up to be counted when it came to asserting that the kiddies' Christmas party was a simply spiffing "do" and well worth all the trouble and heartbreak.

The Honourable Constance's enthusiasm might ring strange in the ears of those aware of her intense dislike of small children and her vehement objection to lavishing on them vast sums of money which might be better spent on comforts for Britain's impoverished aristocracy. The explanation is, however, quite simple: it was only at the Conservative Club's Christmas party that the Honourable Constance got the chance to play Father Christmas, all the Conservative menfolk having chickened out of this particular privilege many years ago.

The Honourable Constance (or the Hon. Con as she was generally known in the small provincial town in which she lived) was famous for always wearing the trousers, literally and figuratively, so that yet another breeches role was in itself no great attraction for her. What did draw her irresistably to the part were those bushy white whiskers. To tell the truth, the Hon. Con rather fancied herself in a moustache and full beard, claiming that it brought out the colour of her eyes, and she spent the fortnight before the party swaggering around her house in Upper Waxwing Drive arrayed in the complete get-up. Her ho-ho-hoing was so exuberant that Miss Jones went down daily with one of her sick headaches. Miss Jones, who also lived in the house in Upper Waxwing Drive, was the Hon. Con's dearest chum, confidante, dogsbody, doormat, better half, and who knows what else besides. It was she who had extracted a solemn promise from the Hon. Con (''see that wet, see that dry, cross my heart and hope to die'') that she wouldn't wear her Santa Claus whiskers out in the street, no matter how much breaking in they required.

The Hon. Con was not of course so bedazzled that she overlooked the grimmer side of the picture. Bringing good will and Christmas cheer to a pack of some seventy-five infant savages is no joking matter, and the Hon. Con took every reasonable precaution for her own protection. She would like to have equipped herself with an electric cattle prod or a lion-tamer's whip and a kitchen chair, but she knew the Ladies' Organising Committee would never stand for that so she settled for something less exotic. Like heavy boots with reinforced toe-caps, a pair of cricket pads to protect the old shins, and a small rubber truncheon stuffed down the leg of her red trousers just in case she was obliged to move on to the offensive.

On the day of the party the Hon. Con and Miss Jones set off in good time. This was partly because the Hon. Con, arrayed in full festive rig, had trouble even getting into the Mini, never mind actually driving it, and partly because they had to attend a final briefing in the main or Margaret Thatcher Hall of the Conservative Club.

The lady helpers were all somewhat anxious and on edge as they gathered round their leader, Mrs. Rose Johnson, Chairperson of the Ladies' Organising Committee. Mrs. Johnson, however, rattled through the battle orders with an air of quiet confidence which, though completely spurious, did help to steady the troops. Indeed, some of the ladies felt so much better that they even started grumbling about the allocation of duties. Mrs. Johnson sighed. This happened every year, no matter how often she reminded them that all the various jobs were distributed strictly by lot. She knew as well as anybody that some posts were more, well, dangerous than others, but what could she or anybody else do about it? Trying to keep track of what people had done in previous years was simply too complicated, and considerable concessions had already been made in respect of the so-called latrine fatigues. Nowadays only bona fide mothers were stationed in the cloakrooms as, when it came to over-excited kids and the undoing of buttons, a certain deftness had been found essential if disasters were to be avoided.

Taking everything into consideration, Mrs. Johnson felt that everybody should be reasonably satisfied with the arrangements, but it came as no very great surprise that one person in particular wasn't. As the meeting came to an end and the ladies, with exhortations to stand firm and unflinching ringing in their ears, began dispersing to their battle lines, the imposing figure of Lady Fowler could be seen swimming doughtily against the stream. She trapped Mrs. Johnson by the platform.

"God damn and blast it, Rose," she exclaimed—her husband had been knighted for services to the fish-paste and tinned pilchard industry which may account for the forcefulness of her language—"you've bloody well done it again!"

Mrs. Johnson tried, and failed, to move what was obviously going to be a bruising encounter away from the platform on which a dejected group of total strangers was huddled, listening gloomily to every word. "Done what, dear?"

"Given that bloody Lyonelle Lawn bitch the best goddamn job again! That's three bloody years on the trot!"

Mrs. Johnson ruffled unhappily through her sheaf of papers. "The best job, dear? Oh, I'd hardly call being stuck by the fire exit at the end of that draughty old corridor 'the best job,' would you?"

"Compared with being stuck for two solid hours in the middle of World War Three," snarled Lady Fowler, "yes, I damned well would! Last year I was on serving bloody teas and this year I've copped marshalling the little bastards up to collect their presents—and that's in addition to being on sentry-go out here all the time the entertainment's going on. I suppose you know one of the little sods bit me last time? Why the hell don't I ever get one of these cushy jobs where—with luck—you don't even see a blasted kid from start to finish?"

"The Committee draw the names out of a hat, dear," protested Mrs. Johnson feebly, noting with chagrin that the Hon. Con and that peculiar little woman of hers had moved up and were now avidly eavesdropping on the other side. "It's all absolutely fair and aboveboard."

Lady Fowler blew heavily down her nose. "Damned funny it's always Lyonelle Lawn who comes up smelling of roses!"

Mrs. Johnson bridled. "I hope you are not accusing me of indulging in some kind of favouritism, Felicity!" she snapped. "I can't think why you should imagine that I would do Lyonelle Lawn, of all people, any favours. You know she's definitely got planning permission to build that bungalow at the bottom of their garden, in spite of our objections? It'll ruin our view of the river and knock thousands off the price of our house." Mrs.

Johnson gave a bitter laugh. "Lyonelle Lawn is hardly *my* blue-eyed girl."

"Maybe you're over-compensating," suggested Lady Fowler unkindly. "You know, being especially bloody kind to the cow because you hate her so much. Understandable, but damned tough luck on your friends."

"Oh, don't be so ridiculous!" Mrs. Johnson looked round for something or somebody upon which to vent her pent-up irritation. She found it on the platform where those peculiar-looking folk were still hanging aimlessly around. Mrs. Johnson pounced on them with relief. "I say, isn't it about time you people were getting yourselves ready?" she called. "You know—make-up and costumes and things? The kiddies will be here any minute now and we don't want to start running late."

Silently, sullenly, and led, somewhat improbably, by a midget, the group began shuffling off backstage.

Lady Fowler watched them go before awarding herself the last word. "I don't know why we bother hiring outside entertainers, Rose," she observed. "Your pet, Lyonelle Lawn, is supposed to have been an actress of sorts, isn't she? I'm sure she'd be delighted to put on a show for us. Belly dancing, was it? Or striptease? Anyhow, something frightfully artistic, I'm sure. I hear they loved her in those ghastly workingmen's clubs up North."

The Hon. Con looked at her watch as Lady Fowler and Mrs. Johnson went somewhat icily their separate ways. "Oh, well, suppose it's time I went and sorted those dratted old presents out."

Miss Jones, who didn't approve of eavesdropping—at least not in such a blatant manner—thought it was more than time. She would like to have chided the Hon. Con for such ill-bred behaviour, but she knew what the answer would be so she saved her breath.

The Hon. Con, being the daughter of a peer of the realm as well as the finest private detective in Totterbridge, was naturally a law unto herself. What in common people like you and me would have been idle curiosity was in her case a serious, in-depth research project into behavioural patterns. Private detectives were by definition great students of human nature and everything was grist to their mill.

Untrammelled by the demands of husband and children, blessed with a considerable independent income and spared even from having to bother with all those time-consuming little domestic chores by the selfless devotion of Miss Jones, the Hon. Con did occasionally find it hard to fill up her day. At first she had thrown herself into charitable work, until the protests from the poor, the sick and the deprived became too vociferous to be ignored. Then she had gone in for sport, demolishing two tennis clubs, wrecking the entire local league for crown green bowling, and implanting the kiss of death on mixed hockey. Her sallies into the world of art fared little better, though the charge that she set back the cause of modern music in Totterbridge by fifty years is exaggerated.

It came, therefore, as a great relief all round (except to the police) when the Hon. Con discovered, almost by chance, that she was a natural private detective. Her progress to the very heights of her chosen profession would have been meteoric had it not been for some petty jealousy on the part of the official forces of law and order, and for the acute shortage of really juicy crimes in the Totterbridge area. Had there been even a modest sufficiency of spy rings, mass murders, kidnapings, and bank robberies to keep her going, you wouldn't have found the Hon. Con pottering around in a blooming old Santa Claus outfit, oh dear me, no! However, there wasn't so she was.

"Were that mangey crew hanging about on the stage really the entertainers?" asked the Hon. Con.

Miss Jones nodded. Although laying no claims to being either a master private detective or even a student of human nature, Miss Jones always seemed to know what was going on.

"Thought we were going to have a film show this year."

"You have to have the lights out for a film show, dear. Mrs. Johnson felt we just daren't risk it."

"What happened to that conjuror fellow?"

"He refused to come again, dear. After what they did to his rabbit."

The Hon. Con jerked her head in the direction of the stage. "So what are this lot supposed to be doing?"

"They're a kind of mini-circus, dear. You know, clowns and a juggler and a tightrope walker, I think. And that midget, of course."

"No animals?"

"They apparently have a performing dog, dear, but Mrs. Johnson thought we hadn't better tempt fate."

The Hon. Con pondered the situation and pronounced her verdict. "The kids'll eat 'em alive." She looked at her watch again. "You'd better be getting your skates on, Bones. It's only five minutes to D-day."

Miss Jones managed a brave little smile before trotting off to her post. She was on duty by the door which led from the Margaret Thatcher Hall to the corridor in which the two cloakrooms were located. It was her job to ensure that no more children at any one time passed through those portals than the facilities could cope with. It was no sinecure as almost everything seemed to get those Conservative toddlers right in the bladder.

Two o'clock struck like a death knell and the Totter-bridge & District Conservative & Unionist Club's annual Christmas party got under way with both bangs and whimpers. Viewed as a whole, this year's effort was better than some but worse than most.

It was unfortunate that the proceedings opened with the professional entertainers. They were not a success and the Hon. Con, tucked away in the manager's office, listened to the howls and cat-calls coming from the Margaret Thatcher Hall with gloomy satisfaction. Her predictions were coming true and she could only hope that the little swine would have run out of steam by the time it came to distribute the presents.

The trouble was that the children, reared on a healthy diet of slick TV sex and violence, just couldn't take a real man tossing three colored balls in the air while balancing a plate on his nose. The contortionist came on, received several suggestions as to how he might enliven his act, and switched frantically into his fire-eating routine. This did cause a momentary lull but, when it became apparent that he wasn't about to set himself on fire and burn to death, the hostilities were resumed. The midget fared no better, being told by one juvenile wit that he ought to be in a preserving bottle at the Royal College of Surgeons. But it was the lady tightrope walker who really whipped things up. Her appearance was greeted by a hail of shoes, the only offensive weapons that the mites could lay their tiny paws on, thanks to the foresight of the Ladies' Organising Committee, who had frisked every child on arrival.

The lady tightrope walker, having been given the bird in better places than Totterbridge and being in any case well insulated from the slings and arrows by gin, would probably have weathered the storm if the midget hadn't tried to come to the rescue. He rushed onstage lugging a large packing case stuffed with cheap animal masks made of paper which he proceeded to fling out at the audience by the handful. It was reminiscent of some ignoble savage attempting to placate his gods, and about as successful.

True, the children ceased baying for the lady tightrope walker's blood but only in order to husband their strength for the furious internecine struggle which now flared up over items so abysmally undesirable that, in calmer times, they wouldn't even have been removed from the corn-flakes box.

Mrs. Johnson viewed the melee with resignation and a faint touch of hope that it might die down of its own accord. Only when blood began to flow and some of the smaller children had gone not so much to the wall as halfway through it did she acknowledge that the moment for desperate measures had arrived.

"Plan B, ladies!" she screamed. "Plan B! Quickly, now!"

The ladies took a deep breath, squared their shoulders, clenched their fists, and dived in.

Plan B was simple and consisted only of taking the cheap paper masks away from the little kids and giving them to the big kids, who were going to get them anyhow in the end. It merely speeded up the natural order of things and was justified only by the fact that it worked. Gradually the turmoil quietened. The circus performers had long ago beaten a cowardly retreat and so it was, as ever, to Mrs. Carmichael that Mrs. Johnson turned in her hour of need. Mrs. Carmichael was a pianist with an inexhaustible repertoire of your old favourites and mine, and the touch of a baby elephant. But she was used to soothing the savage beast and the children were ready for a change. In a matter of seconds they were gleefully bawling out highly obscene versions to the stream of popular songs which flowed from Mrs. Carmichael's leaden fingers.

Over by the door, Miss Jones put away her smelling salts. Plan B had not involved her, of course. She was required to stick resolutely to her post at all times, but even watching the struggle to save civilisation as we know it had been alarming enough. Now that the community singing was in full swing, more children than ever were hearkening to the calls of Nature and Miss Jones had her hands full regulating the flow. Some of the tougher kids predictably began trying to buck the system but fortunately

tea was announced before that appalling blond-haired
boy—son of the town's leading Baptist minister—got a
chance to demonstrate whether or not he was man enough
to carry out the threats he'd been uttering in respect of
Miss Jones's virtue.

For tea the children were herded into the adjoining Sir
Winston Churchill Salon where a veritable feast had been
laid out for them. Almost before the last child had been
seated the walls were thick with jelly and trifle, and the
sausage rolls were zooming through the air like missiles
in an interplanetary war. Even the gorgeous cream cakes
were deemed too good to eat and were squashed flat instead upon the heads of unsuspecting neighbours.

For the twenty minutes allotted to the pleasures of the
table, Mrs. Johnson and her cohorts battled to maintain
some semblance of order, but their task was made even
more difficult by the animal masks that some of the children were still wearing. The masks hindered one of the
most effective ploys for riot control—that of actually
recognising a youngster, addressing it by name and
threatening to report its unspeakable behaviour to its parents. Not that these brats gave a damn for their parents,
but the experience of being publicly identified did seem
to unnerve them for a moment or two.

When the tea party was over, it was time for the Hon.
Con to hog the limelight. The children were driven back
into the Margaret Thatcher Hall and grouped around the
platform which, by means of some old army blankets and
a few strips of silver paper, had now been transformed
into a magic cave. In the middle, surrounded by heaps
of exciting-looking parcels, sat the Hon. Con, beaming
benevolently and not relaxing her guard for one second.

At the side of the platform, Mrs. Johnson read the
names out from her list in alphabetical order. Each child
then, theoretically, came forward in turn, shook hands
with Father Christmas, received its present, and said
thank you for it. In practice, any child that could break

through the protective barrier of lady helpers made a dive and grabbed what it could.

Personation was rife.

"Here," demanded the Hon. Con of a rather rotund frog in striped trousers and bovver boots whom, she could swear, she'd seen twice already before, "you sure you're little Gwendoline Roberts, aged six?"

"You sure you're Father Christmas, missus?" retorted the frog, tearing the parcel wrapped in pink paper out of the Hon. Con's hands. "And not some nosy old judy called Burke?"

A sweet little girl in pigtails ducked back through the phalanx of lady helpers and thrust the battered remnants of her present into the Hon. Con's hands. "I don't want no lousy farmyard animals!" she shrilled, her blue eyes flashing. " 'Sides, they're all broke. Haven't you got a knuckle duster or a horse whip or something?"

The Hon. Con tried, but failed, to give back as good as she got. All around her the Margaret Thatcher Hall was knee-deep in discarded wrapping paper, crushed cardboard boxes and broken toys—all watered by infantile tears of rage and disappointment.

Still, all good things come to an end and four o'clock struck. Mrs. Johnson and her gallant band girded up their loins for one final effort and at five past four Lady Fowler proclaimed the glad tidings in stentorian tones.

"All right, girls!" she roared. "You can relax! I counted seventy-three of the little buggers in and seventy-three of them out! They've gone. It's over for another bloody year!"

The news ran round like wildfire and most of the ladies dropped where they stood. Oh, the blessed peace and quiet! Shoes were slipped off, clothing loosened, and foreheads dabbed with eau-de-cologne. But the human frame is amazingly resilient and before too long everybody was gathering in the kitchens for a cup of tea which, it was hoped, would give them enough strength to go home. Those ladies who had given up smoking cadged cigarettes off their less strong-willed sisters and before long the air was thick with tobacco smoke and recriminations.

Everybody had her complaints, but none was more vociferous than Mrs. Hinchliffe. "Somebody," she announced, trying to ease her aching back, "is going to have to do something about that cloakroom duty. It's too much."

"We did give you those fresh air sprays, dear," Mrs. Johnson reminded her.

"It's not the pong, Rose, it's the sheer hard work. Two people aren't enough. We need at least three."

"Hear, hear!" agreed the other ladies who had been relentlessly dressing and undressing children all afternoon.

Mrs. Johnson sighed. "There isn't room for three, dear. You yourself said that."

"Two on and one off!" declared Mrs. Hinchliffe. "So we can at least take a bit of a breather. Do you realise neither Clarice nor I so much as got our noses out of that damned boys' loo all afternoon?"

"Irene and I were just the same with the girls," chimed in one of her equally aggrieved colleagues. "I'd thought one of us would be able to take a break while the other held the fort, but no such luck. We were both of us slogging away the whole time."

"We'll look into it next time," promised Mrs. Johnson blandly. "Now," she looked round brightly, "is everybody here?" It was getting time for her little speech of thanks and appreciation.

The Hon. Con was reaching for the sugar bowl. "All present and correct, old fruit! I say," she addressed the company at large, "anybody see a pork pie lying around that hasn't actually been violated? I'm feeling dashed peckish."

Miss Jones, one of whose duties was to keep the Hon. Con's waist-line within bounds, endeavoured to divert the conversation from the topic of food. "Actually, Mrs. Johnson," she twittered helpfully, "I don't think we are quite all gathered together yet, are we? There's Mrs. Lawn, for example."

"Oh, she'll have sneaked off hours ago," said Lady Fowler with her usual snort. "Bloody idle cow!"

Mrs. Johnson, who'd had enough of Lady Fowler for one afternoon, pretended not to have heard and, since she had Miss Jones there, she decided she might as well make use of her. "I wonder, Miss—er . . . would you mind just popping along and seeing what's happened to her? Remind her that we're all waiting, would you? Perhaps her watch has stopped."

"Why not just leave her there to bloody rot?" enquired Lady Fowler charitably. "Serve her damned well right if she gets locked in."

But Miss Jones was already scurrying away. After long association with the Hon. Con, it was not in her nature to question orders, however dog-tired she might be.

In a remarkably short space of time she came scurrying back, ashen-faced and trembling like a leaf.

Even the Hon. Con noticed that she wasn't quite herself. "Something up, Bones?" she asked, pausing with her second vol-au-vent of the afternoon halfway to her lips.

Miss Jones had worked out how she was going to break the news. "Mrs. Lawn is sitting on her chair by the fire exit, dear," she said with chilling composure, "quite dead and with a large knife sticking out of her chest."

"Holy cats!" breathed the Hon. Con. She tossed the unconsumed portion of the vol-au-vent heedlessly aside and leaped to her feet. "Nobody move!" she bawled. "This sounds like murder, and I don't want you lot trampling all over the clues. Everybody stay here while I go and have a look!"

"Hadn't we better phone the police, Constance?"

There's always some clever devil, isn't there? Luckily, the Hon. Con's thought processes were now rattling along at the speed of light. "Better let me check first, old bean," she advised solemnly. "It may be a false alarm."

"It's no false alarm dear," moaned Miss Jones, her handkerchief pressed to her lips. "She is quite, quite dead, I do—"

The Hon. Con regarded her chum with exasperation. "Do button it, Bones!" she growled.

Still in her Father Christmas outfit, the Hon. Con strode off masterfully towards the scene of the crime. Chin up, stomach in, white whiskers fluttering importantly in the breeze of her passage, she thudded across the Margaret Thatcher Hall, through the door by which Miss Jones had stood on duty all afternoon, down the corridor past the two cloakrooms (one on either side), round the corner at the end and—

"Golly!" said the Hon. Con.

Lyonelle Lawn was certainly as dead as a doornail.

The Hon. Con leaned forward for a close look. The knife sticking out of Lyonelle Lawn's chest seemed ordinary enough. Sort of kitchen knife you could get anywhere. Fingerprints? Grudgingly the Hon. Con acknowledged that that was one she'd have to leave to the boys in blue. Not much blood and it didn't seem as though she'd put up much of a fight. Taken unawares, perhaps? And robbery wasn't the motive because there was her handbag, still standing on the floor under her chair.

The Hon. Con straightened up. Bit creepy down there, actually, right at the end of the corridor and with nobody about. She turned her attention to the emergency door which Lyonelle Lawn had been guarding against anyone trying to break in or break out. They had experienced both gate-crashers and escapees in previous years. No,

the door was still securely fastened. And there were no
windows or—

Somebody was tiptoeing down the corridor!

The Hon. Con's hand closed round the rubber truncheon as she prepared to sell her life dearly.

"Blimey-O'Riley, Bones, I do wish you'd stop pussy-
footing about!" Sheer relief that it wasn't a maniac killer
with slavering jaws made the Hon. Con's tones unnec-
essarily sharp.

"I'm sorry, dear, but I thought you'd like to know that
Lady Fowler went to phone the police."

"She-Judas!" spat the Hon. Con. "She might have
given me a few minutes. I haven't had a decent murder
for months."

"Well, you're all right for the moment, dear, because
somebody's disconnected the telephone and jammed up
all the doors so that we can't get out. Miss Kingston
thinks it's super-glue in the locks."

The Hon. Con frowned. This was getting serious.
"The murderer, eh?" she mused aloud.

"More likely the children, dear," said Miss Jones with
a sigh. She'd always been so fond of kiddies—before she'd
been enrolled as a helper at the Totterbridge & District
Conservative & Unionist Club's annual Christmas party,
of course. "I left them trying to push little Mrs. Bellamy
through the skylight over the front door. If she doesn't
break a leg or anything, she's going to ring the police
from the call box on the corner." Miss Jones glanced
involuntarily at the corpse and regretted, not for the first
time, that dear Constance hadn't managed to find a nicer
hobby. Still, Miss Jones always felt it was up to her to
take an intelligent interest. "Have you worked out any
theories yet, dear?"

The Hon. Con emitted a rich chuckle. "Dozens, old
girl! How does Felicity Fowler grab you, for a start?"

"Oh, Constance!"

"She was being deuced catty about Lyonelle Lawn

earlier on,'' grunted the Hon. Con, ever ready to take any hasty word for the foulest deed. ''Vicious, really. Or there's Rose Johnson.''

''Mrs. Johnson is Chairperson of the Organising Committee, dear!''

''So who was in a better position to set the whole thing up? Who was it who stuck La Lawn down here all on her lonesome where she could be knocked off without anybody noticing? La Lawn's job this afternoon was precisely what Felicity Fowler was griping about, wasn't it? Well, come on, Bones, you heard her.''

''Yes, I did hear her, dear,'' said Miss Jones with dignity, ''and I think it highly improbable that Mrs. Johnson deliberately murdered Mrs. Lawn just because the extension to Mrs. Lawn's house was going to ruin Mrs. Johnson's view of the river.''

The Hon. Con scowled. ''People can get jolly steamed up about that sort of thing. And then there's the depreciation in the value of the Johnsons' house. Don't forget that.''

But Miss Jones was determined to take a more socially acceptable line. ''Surely it's the work of an outsider, isn't it, dear? A burglar or a tramp or some sort of gibbering maniac who just happened to be passing?''

'' 'Fraid that rabbit won't run, old girl,'' said the Hon. Con with evident relish. ''No outsider could infiltrate this blooming building—you know that. We've had every door manned all afternoon to keep gate-crashers out and our dratted brats in. Nor,'' the Hon. Con raised a lordly hand before Miss Jones could voice the theory that the killer might have concealed himself in the Club earlier on, ''is it any good you thinking of that door where Lyonelle Lawn was sitting. That's a proper emergency exit, you see. You can only open or close it from the inside with that bar thing. Well, the late lamented might possibly have opened it up and let her murderer in, but she jolly well didn't close it behind him after he'd gone out.

No, we've just got to face facts, Bones. It was one of us. And my money's on Rose Johnson—with Felicity Fowler a good each-way bet.''

Miss Jones was reluctant to be the hand that threw the spanner, but she had no choice. ''I'm afraid it can't be one of us, dear.''

''Why not?''

''There are only two ways of reaching the spot where Mrs. Lawn was killed, dear. You have demonstrated that we can forget about the emergency door. Well, that only leaves the route from the Margaret Thatcher Hall, along the corridor past the cloakrooms.''

''So?''

''I was on duty on the door from the Margaret Thatcher Hall, dear, all afternoon, without a second's break. After Mrs. Lawn and the four ladies on duty in the cloakrooms went through, nobody else did—apart from the kiddies, of course.''

The Hon. Con didn't look best pleased. ''You prepared to swear that on a stack of Bibles, Bones?''

Miss Jones shuddered. ''I should hope that wouldn't be necessary, Constance dear,'' she said reproachfully.

''All right,'' said the Hon. Con, whose thought processes under pressure frequently achieved the velocity of light, ''somebody sneaked through after the party was over and you'd gone to the kitchen for a cup of tea.''

Miss Jones was no slouch when it came to spiking the Hon. Con's guns. ''I was the last person to arrive in the kitchen, dear. Or almost the last. Certainly both Mrs. Johnson and Lady Fowler were already there. Besides, if poor Mrs. Lawn was killed after I left my post by the door, that would mean she had only died a matter of moments before I found her.'' Miss Jones swallowed hard as she recalled the scene. ''I don't think that was the case, dear. The blood seemed to be quite—''

The Hon. Con was growing impatient. ''Then it was one of the four lassies on duty in the cloakrooms. One of them could have sloped off any old time, nipped round the corner, stuck the knife in La Lawn, and Bob's your uncle!''

Miss Jones's head was already shaking. ''But you heard them yourself, dear, complaining that they'd never had a moment's relaxation and that they never left their cloak-rooms all afternoon. They'll be able to give each other alibis, won't they? I mean, each couple will be able to—''

If there was anything that got right up the Hon. Con's nose it was hearing blessed amateurs using technical terms like ''alibi.'' ''There's such a thing as collusion!'' she snapped. ''Or conspiracy! Two of 'em could be in it together.''

''Now don't be silly, dear!''

Miss Jones's reproof was feather-light and her smile indulgent, but the Hon. Con was never one to take criticism lying down. ''Hope you're in the clear, Bones,'' she said nastily. ''Because, if anybody could have slipped away during the afternoon and done Lyonelle Lawn in, it was *you!*''

The idea was so absurd that Miss Jones even managed a little laugh, though with a fresh corpse only a few feet away laughter was neither very easy nor appropriate.

''Then it's one of the kids,'' said the Hon. Con indifferently, as though Miss Jones was in some way to blame for this conclusion. ''It's the only answer—and it's not beyond the bounds of possibility, is it? I wouldn't put anything past those evil-minded little horrors. Do you know, I didn't get a thank you out of more than a couple of 'em all afternoon? Talk about manners! Yes, one of 'em could have come out to the cloakroom and popped round here to kill Lyonelle as easy as pie, having first nicked a knife at teatime, I shouldn't wonder. That explains why she didn't put up a struggle or anything. I mean, who expects getting knocked off by a nine-year-old, eh?''

Miss Jones had had a pretty gruelling day so far, what

with the children's party and finding a dead body and
everything, but it was all as nothing compared with the
crisis she now faced. She would like to have fainted, but
she daren't. Oh, why, oh, why hadn't she just let dear
Constance pin the murder on whomever it was she wanted
to pin it on in the first place? There would have been a
little unpleasantness, no doubt, but it would be as nothing to the storm of fury and outrage that was going to
erupt when the Hon. Con started pointing the finger of
suspicion at a group of innocent children and innocent
Conservative children, at that. Even Labor-voting parents would have been horrified, but the parents of this
lot—well, running amuck and foaming at the mouth
would just be for starters. Miss Jones's mind shied at the
possibilities: tarring and feathering? Being ridden out of
Totterbridge on a rail? Lynching?

Miss Jones moistened arid lips. "Constance, dear—"

"You know my methods, Bones," said the Hon. Con
grandly. "When you've eliminated the impossible, what
you've got left is it—however improbable. And you're the
one," she added, turning the knife, "who did most of
the eliminating for me."

"Constance, dear, you can't go around making wild
accusations against some poor child who—"

"I know that, Bones! Drat it all, I haven't had more
than five minutes to get to the bottom of things, have I?
I shall have to leave it to the cops to tie up a few loose
ends and pinpoint the actual murderous little thug who
did it. I am well used," the Hon. Con laughed bitterly,
"to having my case snatched out of my hands by so-
called professionals the minute I've cracked it. I gave up
expecting any credit for my achievements a long time
ago."

"In that case, dear," suggested Miss Jones with a cunning born of panic, "why not leave the whole thing to
the police? Let them solve it themselves. Why should you
help them? They never help you."

The Hon. Con thought a minute and then drew herself up proudly. She made a striking figure in her red Father Christmas suit and her flowing white whiskers. "Not in my nature to be a dog in the manger, Bones," she said modestly. "Now, while we're waiting, why don't you improve the shining hour by making a list for the cops of all the kids who went past you this afternoon on their way to the cloakrooms? Better stick 'em in chronological order with an indication of the times where you can."

"A list, dear?" bleated Miss Jones. "How can I possible make a list? Every child at the party went out to the toilets at some time in the afternoon, and most of them more than once. You know what a shambles it was. Besides, I don't know more than a handful of them by name. How could I?"

The Hon. Con shrugged a pair of shoulders which would have looked better in the front row of a rugby scrum. "Hope the cops don't think you're trying to obstruct the course of justice," she rumbled with sham concern. " 'Praps they'll try and make you do it with photographs. You know, one of each kid so you can shuffle 'em around like a pack of cards till you get 'em in the right order."

"But, Constance," wailed Miss Jones, ever prey to her own sense of inadequacy, "half the time I didn't even see the children's faces! They were wearing those stupid animal masks. You can vouch for that, dear. Those who'd got them wore them the entire afternoon and—"

But the Hon. Con was no longer listening. Her somewhat protuberant eyes glazed over as they always did when sheer, undiluted inspiration was about to strike. "Golly!" she breathed in an awed voice. "I've got it! I've blooming well got it!"

"Got what, dear?"

"The solution, Bones! I know who done it!"

"Again, dear?" The words were unworthy, and Miss Jones was ashamed of herself for uttering them.

Luckily the Hon. Con was still up there on Cloud Nine. "It stands out a mile. It was that dwarf!"

"Dwarf, dear?"

"That midget who was with the circus entertainers. Oh, come on, Bones, rattle the old brain-box! You can't have forgotten that crummy bunch."

"I haven't forgotten, dear," said Miss Jones, who could sometimes turn the other cheek almost audibly. "It's just that—"

"He put on an animal mask and walked right past you," explained the Hon. Con jubilantly. "Twice. Both ways. Coming and going. You just took him for one of the kids and didn't give him a second thought. Deuced cunning, eh? And he was the one who dished out the animal masks in the first place, wasn't he? You all thought he'd gone potty, but it was part of his sinister plan. Premeditated, see!"

Miss Jones took one of her deep breaths. "Constance, dear—"

"Now don't start nitpicking, Bones! Because it all fits. He knew where Lyonelle Lawn was going to be on duty and that she would be tucked away all on her own because he overheard Rose Johnson and Felicity Fowler having an argy-bargy about it. Remember? He and the rest of that grotty crew were standing there lapping up every word—and there can't be many Lyonelle Lawns kicking around, can there? Oh, *heck!*" The Hon. Con's lynx-like ears had caught the distant wail of a police siren. Little Mrs. Bellamy must have made it to the phone box in spite of some fervent prayers to the contrary. "Listen, Bones, are those circus people still in the Club?"

"Oh, I shouldn't think so, dear. They must have gone ages ago. You could check with Miss Simpson. She was on the front door and would have let them out."

"Curses!" The Hon. Con had been picturing herself tossing the miniature miscreant bodily into the arms of the Totterbridge Constabulary. That would have caused a few astounded jaws to drop, all rightie!

Miss Jones's mind meanwhile had been running on more mundane lines—such as slander and criminal libel and the bearing of false witness and what sort of damages a court might award to an outraged and injured midget against the rambunctious and wealthy daughter of a peer. Dear Constance never appeared to her best advantage in a court of law. She would keep telling the judge how to run the case and—''Constance, dear!''

The Hon. Con hitched up her Father Christmas trousers impatiently. ''What now?''

Miss Jones put it as simply as she could. ''Why should this midget have killed poor Mrs. Lawn!''

''Good grief, Bones, detectives don't have to prove motive. Thought everybody knew that. All you need do is establish means and opportunity. Well, that's what I've done. And I'll bet he nicked the knife from the kitchens here.''

''But he must have had some reason, dear.''

''The stage!'' The Hon. Con's imagination always worked best under pressure. ''Lyonelle Lawn used to be on the stage, didn't she? Well, so's that midget. They probably met up somewhere. You know what theatricals are like—all nerves and tension and things. There'd be a feud, I expect, or maybe she spurned his lascivious advances, or—''

But the time for leisurely speculation was past. Masculine voices and the tramp of heavy feet could be heard coming from the direction of the Margaret Thatcher Hall. The Hon. Con prepared herself for the encounter, smoothing down her scarlet tunic and fluffing up her white whiskers. ''It's all a question of psychology, really,'' she whispered in an attempt to allay her chum's only too evident distress. ''I'm deliberately leaving this motive question for the police to solve for the sake of their morale. You follow me? It'll give them the chance to make a contribution and earn a bit of kudos—and it'll stop 'em getting too shirty over the indisputable fact that I've unravelled the mystery and tied the whole blooming case up for 'em before they even got here.''

THE CAROL SINGERS

by Josephine Bell

Old Mrs. Fairlands stepped carefully off the low chair she had pulled close to the fireplace. She was very conscious of her eighty-one years every time she performed these mild acrobatics. Conscious of it and determined to have no humiliating, potentially dangerous mishap. But obstinate, in her persistent routine of dusting her own mantelpiece, where a great many too many photographs and small ornaments daily gathered a film of greasy London dust.

Mrs. Fairlands lived in the ground floor flat of a converted house in a once fashionable row of early Victorian family homes. The house had been in her family for three generations before her, and she herself had been born and brought up there. In those faroff days of her childhood, the whole house was filled with a busy throng of people, from the top floor where the nurseries housed the noisiest and liveliest group, through the dignified, low-voiced activities of her parents and resident aunt on the first and ground floors, to the basement haunts of the domestic staff, the kitchens and the cellars.

Too many young men of the family had died in two world wars and too many young women had married and left the house to make its original use in the late 1940's any longer possible. Mrs. Fairlands, long a widow, had inherited the property when the last of her brothers died. She had let it for a while, but even that failed. A conversion was the obvious answer. She was a vigorous seventy at the time, fully determined, since her only child, a married daughter, lived in the to her barbarous wastes of the Devon moors, to continue to live alone with her much-loved familiar possessions about her.

The conversion was a great success and was made without very much structural alteration to the house. The basement, which had an entrance by the former back door, was shut off and was let to a businessman who spent only three days a week in London and preferred not to use an hotel. The original hall remained as a common entrance to the other three flats. The ground floor provided Mrs. Fairlands with three large rooms, one of which was divided into a kitchen and bathroom. Her own front door was the original dining room door from the hall. It led now into a narrow passage, also chopped off from the room that made the bathroom and kitchen. At the end of the passage two new doors led into the former morning room, her drawing room as she liked to call it, and her bedroom, which had been the study.

This drawing room of hers was at the front of the house, overlooking the road. It had a square bay window that gave her a good view of the main front door and the steps leading up to it, the narrow front garden, now a paved forecourt, and from the opposite window of the bay, the front door and steps of the house next door, divided from her by a low wall.

Mrs. Fairlands, with characteristic obstinacy, strength of character, integrity, or whatever other description her forceful personality drew from those about her, had lived in her flat for eleven years, telling everyone that it suited her perfectly and feeling, as the years went by, progressively more lonely, more deeply bored, and more consciously apprehensive. Her daily came for four hours three times a week. It was enough to keep the place in good order. On those days the admirable woman cooked Mrs. Fairlands a good solid English dinner, which she shared, and also constructed several more main meals

that could be eaten cold or warmed up. But three half
days of cleaning and cooking left four whole days in each
week when Mrs. Fairlands must provide for herself or go
out to the High Street to a restaurant. After her eightieth
birthday she became more and more reluctant to make
the effort. But every week she wrote to her daughter Dorothy to say how well she felt and how much she would
detest leaving London, where she had lived all her life
except when she was evacuated to Wiltshire in the second
war.

She was sincere in writing thus. The letters were true
as far as they went, but they did not go the whole distance. They did not say that it took Mrs. Fairlands nearly
an hour to wash and dress in the morning. They did not
say she was sometimes too tired to bother with supper
and then had to get up in the night, feeling faint and
thirsty, to heat herself some milk. They did not say that
although she stuck to her routine of dusting the whole
flat every morning, she never mounted her low chair
without a secret terror that she might fall and break her
hip and perhaps be unable to reach the heavy stick she
kept beside her armchair to use as a signal to the flat
above.

On this particular occasion, soon after her eighty-first
birthday, she had deferred the dusting until late in the
day, because it was Christmas Eve and in addition to
cleaning the mantelpiece she had arranged on it a pile of
Christmas cards from her few remaining friends and her
many younger relations.

This year, she thought sadly, there was not really much
point in making the display. Dorothy and Hugh and the
children could not come to her as usual, nor could she
go to them. The tiresome creatures had chicken pox, in
their late teens, too, except for Bobbie, the afterthought,
who was only ten. They should all have had it years ago,
when they first went to school. So the visit was can-
celed, and though she offered to go to Devon instead,

they told her she might get shingles from the same infection and refused to expose her to the risk. Apart altogether from the danger to her of traveling at that particular time of the year, the weather and the holiday crowds combined, Dorothy had written.

Mrs. Fairlands turned sadly from the fireplace and walked slowly to the window. A black Christmas this year, the wireless report had promised. As black as the prospect of two whole days of isolation at a time when the whole western world was celebrating its midwinter festival and Christians were remembering the birth of their faith.

She turned from the bleak prospect outside her window, a little chilled by the downdraft seeping through its closed edges. Near the fire she had felt almost too hot, but then she needed to keep it well stocked up for such a large room. In the old days there had been logs, but she could no longer lift or carry logs. Everyone told her she ought to have a cosy stove or even do away with solid fuel altogether, install central heating and perhaps an electric fire to make a pleasant glow. But Mrs. Fairlands considered these suggestions defeatist, an almost insulting reference to her age. Secretly she now thought of her life as a gamble with time. She was prepared to take risks for the sake of defeating them. There were few pleasures left to her. Defiance was one of them.

When she left the window, she moved to the far corner of the room, near the fireplace. Here a small table, usually covered, like the mantelpiece, with a multitude of objects, had been cleared to make room for a Christmas tree. It was mounted in a large bowl reserved for this annual purpose. The daily had set it up for her and wrapped the bowl round with crinkly red paper, fastened with safety pins. But the tree was not yet decorated.

Mrs. Fairlands got to work upon it. She knew that it would be more difficult by artificial light to tie the knots in the black cotton she used for the dangling glass balls.

Dorothy had provided her with some newfangled strips of pliable metal that needed only to be threaded through the rings on the glass balls and wrapped round the branches of the tree. But she had tried these strips only once. The metal had slipped from her hands and the ball had fallen and shattered. She went back to her long practiced method with black cotton, leaving the strips in the box for her grandchildren to use, which they always did with ferocious speed and efficiency.

She sighed as she worked. It was not much fun decorating the tree by herself. No one would see it until the day after Boxing Day when the daily would be back. If only her tenants had not gone away she could have invited them in for some small celebration. But the basement man was in his own home in Essex, and the first floor couple always went to an hotel for Christmas, allowing her to use their flat for Dorothy and Hugh and the children. And this year the top floor, three girl students, had joined a college group to go skiing. So the house was quite empty. There was no one left to invite, except perhaps her next door neighbors. But that would be impossible. They had detestable children, rude, destructive, uncontrolled brats. She had already complained about broken glass and dirty sweet papers thrown into her forecourt. She could not possibly ask them to enjoy her Christmas tree with her. They might damage it. Perhaps she ought to have agreed to go to May, or let her come to her. She was one of the last of her friends, but never an intimate one. And such a chatterer. Nonstop, as Hugh would say.

By the time Mrs. Fairlands had fastened the last golden ball and draped the last glittering piece of tinsel and tied the crowning piece, the six-pronged shining silver star, to the topmost twig and fixed the candles upright in their socket clips, dusk had fallen. She had been obliged to turn on all her lights some time before she had done. Now she moved again to her windows, drew the curtains, turned off all the wall lights, and with one reading lamp beside her chair sat down near the glowing fire.

It was nearly an hour after her usual teatime, she noticed. But she was tired. Pleasantly tired, satisfied with her work, shining quietly in its dark corner, bringing back so many memories of her childhood in this house, of her brief marriage, cut off by the battle of the Marne, of Dorothy, her only child, brought up here, too, since there was nowhere for them to live except with the parents she had so recently left. Mrs. Fairlands decided to skip tea and have an early supper with a boiled egg and cake.

She dozed, snoring gently, her ancient, wrinkled hand twitching from time to time as her head lolled on and off the cushion behind it.

She woke with a start, confused, trembling. There was a ringing in her head that resolved, as full consciousness returned to her, into a ringing of bells, not only her own, just inside her front door, but those of the other two flats, shrilling and buzzing in the background.

Still trembling, her mouth dry with fright and open-mouthed sleep, she sat up, trying to think. What time was it? The clock on the mantelpiece told her it was nearly seven. Could she really have slept for two whole hours? There was silence now. Could it really have been the bell, all the bells, that had woken her? If so, it was a very good thing. She had no business to be asleep in the afternoon, in a chair of all places.

Mrs. Fairlands got to her feet, shakily. Whoever it was at the door must have given up and gone away. Standing still, she began to tremble again. For she remembered things Dorothy and Hugh and her very few remaining friends said to her from time to time. "Aren't you afraid of burglars?" "I wouldn't have the nerve to live alone!" "They ring you up, and if there is no answer, they know you're out, so they come and break in."

Well, there had been no answer to this bell ringing, so whoever it was, if ill-intentioned, might even now be forcing the door or prowling round the house, looking for an open window.

While she stood there in the middle of her drawing room, trying to build up enough courage to go round her flat pulling the rest of the curtains, fastening the other windows, Mrs. Fairlands heard sounds that instantly explained the situation. She heard, raggedly begun, out of tune, but reassuringly familiar, the strains of "Once in Royal David's City."

Carol singers! Of course. Why had she not thought of them instead of frightening herself to death with gruesome suspicions?

Mrs. Fairlands, always remembering her age, her gamble, went to the side window of the bay and, pulling back the edge of the curtain, looked out. A darkclad group stood there, six young people, four girls with scarves on their heads, two boys with woolly caps. They had a single electric torch directed onto a sheet of paper held by the central figure of the group.

Mrs. Fairlands watched them for a few seconds. Of course they had seen the light in her room, so they knew someone was in. How stupid of her to think of burglars. The light would have driven a burglar away if he was out looking for an empty house to break into. All her fears about the unanswered bell were a nonsense.

In her immense relief, and seeing the group straighten up as they finished the hymn, she tapped at the glass. They turned quickly, shining the torch in her face. Though she was a little startled by this, she smiled and nodded, trying to convey the fact that she enjoyed their performance.

"Want another, missis?" one boy shouted.

She nodded again, let the curtain slip into place, and made her way to her bureau, where she kept her handbag. Her purse in the handbag held very little silver, but she found the half crown she was looking for and took it in her hand. "The Holly and the Ivy" was in full swing outside. Mrs. Fairlands decided that these children must have been well taught in school. It was not usual for small parties to sing real carols. Two lines of "Come, All Ye Faithful," followed by loud knocking, was much more likely.

As she moved to the door with the half crown in one hand, Mrs. Fairlands put the other to her throat to pull together the folds of her cardigan before leaving her warm room for the cold passage and the outer hall door. She felt her brooch, and instantly misgiving struck her. It was a diamond brooch, a very valuable article, left to her by her mother. It would perhaps be a mistake to appear at the door offering half a crown and flaunting several hundred pounds. They might have seen it already, in the light of the torch they had shone on her.

Mrs. Fairlands slipped the half crown into her cardigan pocket, unfastened the brooch, and, moving quickly to the little Christmas tree on its table, reached up to the top and pinned the brooch to the very center of the silver tinsel star. Then, chuckling at her own cleverness, her quick wit, she went out to the front door just as the bell rang again in her flat. She opened it on a group of fresh young faces and sturdy young bodies standing on her steps.

"I'm sorry I was so slow," she said. "You must forgive me, but I am not very young."

"I'll say," remarked the younger boy, staring. He thought he had never seen anything as old as this old geyser.

"You shut up," said the girl next to him, and the tallest one said, "Don't be rude."

"You sing very nicely," said Mrs. Fairlands. "Very well indeed. Did you learn at school?"

"Mostly at the club," said the older boy, whose voice went up and down, on the verge of breaking, Mrs. Fairlands thought, remembering her brothers.

She held out the half crown. The tallest of the four

girls, the one who had the piece of paper with the words of the carols on it, took the coin and smiled.

"I hope I haven't kept you too long," Mrs. Fairlands said. "You can't stay long at each house, can you, or you would never get any money worth having."

"They mostly don't give anything," one of the other girls said.

"Tell us to get the 'ell out," said the irrepressible younger boy.

"We don't do it mostly for the money," said the tallest girl. "Not for ourselves, I mean."

"Give it to the club. Oxfam collection and that," said the tall boy.

"Don't you want it for yourselves?" Mrs. Fairlands was astonished. "Do you have enough pocket money without?"

They nodded gravely.

"I got a paper round," said the older boy.

"I do babysitting now and then," the tallest girl added.

"Well, thank you for coming," Mrs. Fairlands said. She was beginning to feel cold, standing there at the open door. "I must go back into my warm room. And you must keep moving, too, or you might catch colds."

"Thank you," they said in chorus. "Thanks a lot. Bye!"

She shut and locked the door as they turned, clattered down the steps, slammed the gate of the forecourt behind them. She went back to her drawing room. She watched from the window as they piled up the steps of the next house. And again she heard, more faintly because farther away, "Once in Royal David's City." There were tears in her old eyes as she left the window and stood for a few minutes staring down at the dull coals of her diminishing fire.

But very soon she rallied, took up the poker, mended her fire, went to her kitchen, and put on the kettle. Coming back to wait for it to boil, she looked again at her

Christmas tree. The diamond brooch certainly gave an added distinction to the star, she thought. Amused once more by her originality, she went into her bedroom and from her jewel box on the dressing table took her two other valuable pieces, a pearl necklace and a diamond bracelet. The latter she had not worn for years. She wound each with a tinsel string and hung them among the branches of the tree.

She had just finished preparing her combined tea and supper when the front doorbell rang again. Leaving the tray in the kitchen, she went to her own front door and opened it. Once again a carol floated to her, "Hark, the Herald Angels Sing" this time. There seemed to be only one voice singing. A lone child, she wondered, making the rounds by himself.

She hurried to the window of her drawing room, drew back the curtain, peeped out. No, not alone, but singing a solo. The pure, high boy's voice was louder here. The child, muffled up to the ears, had his head turned away from her towards three companions, whose small figures and pale faces were intent upon the door. They did not seem to notice her at the window as the other group had done, for they did not turn in her direction. They were smaller, evidently younger, very serious. Mrs. Fairlands, touched, willing again to defeat her loneliness in a few minutes' talk, took another half crown from her purse and went out to the main hall and the big door.

"Thank you, children," she said as she opened it. "That was very—"

Her intended praise died in her throat. She gasped, tried to back away. The children now wore black stockings over their faces. Their eyes glittered through slits; there were holes for their noses and mouths.

"That's a very silly joke," said Mrs. Fairlands in a high voice. "I shall not give you the money I brought for you. Go home. Go away."

She backed inside the door, catching at the knob to

close it. But the small figures advanced upon her. One of them held the door while two others pushed her away from it. She saw the fourth, the singer, hesitate, then turn and run out into the street.

"Stop this!" Mrs. Fairlands said again in a voice that had once been commanding but now broke as she repeated the order. Silently, remorselessly, the three figures forced her back; they shut and locked the main door, they pushed her, stumbling now, terrified, bewildered, through her own front door and into her drawing room.

It was an outrage, an appalling, unheard-of challenge. Mrs. Fairlands had always met a challenge with vigor. She did so now. She tore herself from the grasp of one pair of small hands to box the ears of another short figure. She swept round at the third, pulling the stocking halfway up his face, pushing him violently against the wall so his face met it with a satisfactory smack.

"Stop it!" she panted. "Stop it or I'll call the police!"

At that they all leaped at her, pushing, punching, dragging her to an upright chair. She struggled for a few seconds, but her breath was going. When they had her sitting down, she was incapable of movement. They tied her hands and ankles to the chair and stood back. They began to talk, all at once to start with, but at a gesture from one, the other two became silent.

When Mrs. Fairlands heard the voices, she became rigid with shock and horror. Such words, such phrases, such tones, such evil loose in the world, in her house, in her quiet room. Her face grew cold, she thought she would faint. And still the persistent demand went on.

"We want the money. Where d'you keep it? Come on. Give. Where d'you keep it?"

"At my bank," she gasped.

"That's no answer. Where?"

She directed them to the bureau, where they found and rifled her handbag, taking the three pound notes and five shillings' worth of small change that was all the currency she had in the flat.

Clearly they were astonished at the small amount. They threatened, standing round her, muttering threats and curses.

"I'm *not* rich," she kept repeating. "I live chiefly on the rents of the flats and a very small private income. It's all paid into my bank. I cash a check each week, a small check to cover my food and the wages of my daily help."

"Jewelry," one of them said. "You got jewelry. Rich old cows dolled up—we seen 'em. That's why we come. You got it. Give."

She rallied a little, told them where to find her poor trinkets. Across the room her diamond brooch winked discreetly in the firelight. They were too stupid, too savage, too—horrible to think of searching the room carefully. Let them take the beads, the dress jewelry, the amber pendant. She leaned her aching head against the hard back of the chair and closed her eyes.

After what seemed a long time they came back. Their tempers were not improved. They grumbled among themselves—almost quarreling—in loud harsh tones.

"Radio's worth nil. Prehistoric. No transistor. No record player. Might lift that old clock."

"Money stashed away. Mean old bitch."

"Best get going."

Mrs. Fairlands, eyes still closed, heard a faint sound outside the window. Her doorbell rang once. More carol singers? If they knew, they could save her. If they knew—

She began to scream. She meant to scream loudly, but the noise that came from her was a feeble croak. In her own head it was a scream. To her tormentors it was derisory, but still a challenge. They refused to be challenged.

They gagged her with a strip of sticking plaster, they pulled out the flex of her telephone. They bundled the few valuables they had collected into the large pockets of their overcoats and left the flat, pulling shut the two front doors as they went. Mrs. Fairlands was alone again, but gagged and bound and quite unable to free herself.

At first she felt a profound relief in the silence, the emptiness of the room. The horror had gone, and though she was uncomfortable, she was not yet in pain. They had left the light on—all the lights, she decided. She could see through the open door of the room the lighted passage and, beyond, a streak of light from her bedroom. Had they been in the kitchen? Taken her Christmas dinner, perhaps, the chicken her daily had cooked for her? She remembered her supper and realized fully, for the first time, that she could not open her mouth and that she could not free her hands.

Even now she refused to give way to panic. She decided to rest until her strength came back and she could, by exercising it, loosen her bonds. But her strength did not come back. It ebbed as the night advanced and the fire died and the room grew cold and colder. For the first time she regretted not accepting May's suggestion that she should spend Christmas with her, occupying the flat above in place of Dorothy. Between them they could have defeated those little monsters. Or she could herself have gone to Leatherhead. She was insured for burglary.

She regretted those things that might have saved her, but she did not regret the gamble of refusing them. She recognized now that the gamble was lost. It had to be lost in the end, but she would have chosen a more dignified finish than this would be.

She cried a little in her weakness and the pain she now suffered in her wrists and ankles and back. But the tears ran down her nose and blocked it, which stopped her breathing and made her choke. She stopped crying, resigned herself, prayed a little, considered one or two sins she had never forgotten but on whose account she had never felt remorse until now. Later on she lapsed into semiconsciousness, a half-dream world of past scenes and present cares, of her mother, resplendent in low-cut green chiffon and diamonds, the diamond brooch and bracelet now decorating the tree across the room. Of Bobbie, in a fever, plagued by itching spots, of Dorothy as a little girl, blotched with measles.

Towards morning, unable any longer to breathe properly, exhausted by pain, hunger, and cold, Mrs. Fairlands died.

The milkman came along the road early on Christmas morning, anxious to finish his round and get back to his family. At Mrs. Fairlands' door he stopped. There were no milk bottles standing outside and no notice. He had seen her in person the day before when she had explained that her daughter and family were not coming this year so she would only need her usual pint that day.

"But I'll put out the bottles and the ticket for tomorrow as usual," she had said.

"You wouldn't like to order now, madam?" he had asked, thinking it would save her trouble.

"No, thank you," she had answered. "I prefer to decide in the evening, when I see what milk I have left."

But there were no bottles and no ticket and she was a very, very old lady and had had this disappointment over her family not coming.

The milkman looked at the door and then at the windows. It was still dark, and the light shone clearly behind the closed curtains. He had seen it when he went in through the gate but had thought nothing of it, being intent on his job. Besides, there were lights in a good many houses and the squeals of delighted children finding Christmas stockings bulging on the posts of their beds. But here, he reminded himself, there were no children.

He tapped on the window and listened. There was no movement in the house. Perhaps she'd forgotten, being practically senile. He left a pint bottle on the doorstep.

But passing a constable on a scooter at the end of the road, he stopped to signal to him and told him about Mrs. Fairlands. "Know 'oo I mean?" he asked.

The constable nodded and thanked the milkman. No harm in making sure. He was pretty well browned off—nothing doing—empty streets—not a hooligan in sight—layabouts mostly drunk in the cells after last night's parties—villains all at the holiday resorts, casing jobs.

He left the scooter at the curb and tried to rouse Mrs. Fairlands. He did not succeed, so his anxiety grew. All the lights were on in the flat, front and back as far as he could make out. All her lights. The other flats were in total darkness. People away. She must have had a stroke or actually croaked, he thought. He rode on to the nearest telephone box.

The local police station sent a sergeant and another constable to join the man on the beat. Together they managed to open the kitchen window at the back, and when they saw the tray with a meal prepared but untouched, one of them climbed in. He found Mrs. Fairlands as the thieves had left her. There was no doubt at all what had happened.

"Ambulance," said the sergeant briefly. "Get the super first, though. We'll be wanting the whole works."

"The phone's gone," the constable said. "Pulled out."

"Bastard! Leave her like this when she couldn't phone anyway and wouldn't be up to leaving the house till he'd had plenty time to make six getaways. Bloody bastard!"

"Wonder how much he got?"

"Damn all, I should think. They don't keep their savings in the mattress up this way."

The constable on the scooter rode off to report, and before long, routine investigations were well under way. The doctor discovered no outward injuries and decided that death was probably due to shock, cold, and exhaustion, taking into account the victim's obviously advanced age. Detective-Inspector Brooks of the divisional CID found plenty of papers in the bureau to give him all the information he needed about Mrs. Fairlands' financial position, her recent activities, and her nearest relations. Leaving the sergeant in charge at the flat while the experts in the various branches were at work, he went back to the local station to get in touch with Mrs. Fairlands' daughter, Dorothy Evans.

In Devonshire the news was received with horror, indignation, and remorse. In trying to do the best for her mother by not exposing her to possible infection, Mrs. Evans felt she had brought about her death.

"You can't think of it like that," her husband Hugh protested, trying to stem the bitter tears. "If she'd come down, she might have had an accident on the way or got pneumonia or something. Quite apart from shingles."

"But she was all alone! That's what's so frightful!"

"And it wasn't your fault. She could have had what's-her-name—Miss Bolton, the old girl who lives at Leatherhead."

"I thought May Bolton was going to have *her*. But you couldn't make Mother do a thing she hadn't thought of herself."

"Again, that wasn't your fault, was it?"

It occurred to him that his wife had inherited to some extent this characteristic of his mother-in-law, but this was no time to remind her of it.

"You'll go up at once, I suppose?" he said when she was a little calmer.

"How can I?" The tears began to fall again. "Christmas Day and Bobbie's temperature still up and his spots itching like mad. Could *you* cope with all that?"

"I'd try," he said. "You know I'd do anything."

"Of course you would, darling." She was genuinely grateful for the happiness of her married life and at this moment of self-reproach prepared to give him most of the credit for it. "Honestly, I don't think I could face it.

There'd be identification, wouldn't there? And hearing detail—'' She shuddered, covering her face.

"Okay. I'll go up,'' Hugh told her. He really preferred this arrangement. "I'll take the car in to Exeter and get the first through train there is. It's very early. Apparently her milkman made the discovery.''

So Hugh Evans reached the flat in the early afternoon to find a constable on duty at the door and the house locked up. He was directed to the police station, where Inspector Brooks was waiting for him.

"My wife was too upset to come alone,'' he explained, "and we couldn't leave the family on their own. They've all got chicken pox; the youngest's quite bad with it today.''

He went on to explain all the reasons why Mrs. Fairlands had been alone in the flat.

"Quite,'' said Brooks, who had a difficult mother-in-law himself and was inclined to be sympathetic. "Quite. Nothing to stop her going to an hotel here in London over the holiday, was there?''

"Nothing at all. She could easily afford it. She isn't— wasn't—what you call rich, but she'd reached the age when she really *couldn't* spend much.''

This led to a full description of Mrs. Fairlands' circumstances, which finished with Hugh pulling out a list, hastily written by Dorothy before he left home, of all the valuables she could remember that were still in Mrs. Fairlands' possession.

"Jewelry,'' said the inspector thoughtfully. "Now where would she keep that?''

"Doesn't it say? In her bedroom, I believe.''

"Oh, yes. A jewel box, containing—yes. Well, Mr. Evans, there was no jewel box in the flat when we searched it.''

"Obviously the thief took it, then. About the only thing worth taking. She wouldn't have much cash there. She took it from the bank in weekly amounts. I know that.''

There was very little more help he could give, so Inspector Brooks took him to the mortuary where Mrs.
Fairlands now lay. And after the identification, which
Hugh found pitiable but not otherwise distressing, they
went together to the flat.

"In case you can help us to note any more objects of
value you find are missing," Brooks explained.

The rooms were in the same state in which they had
been found. Hugh found this more shocking, more disturbing, than the colorless, peaceful face of the very old
woman who had never been close to him, who had never
shown a warm affection for any of them, though with her
unusual vitality she must in her youth have been capable
of passion.

He went from room to room and back again. He
stopped beside the bureau. "I was thinking, on the way
up," he said diffidently. "Her solicitor—that sort of
thing. Insurances. I ought—can I have a look through this
lot?"

"Of course, sir," Inspector Brooks answered politely.
"I've had a look myself. You see, we aren't quite clear
about motive."

"Not—But wasn't it a burglar? A brutal, thieving
thug?"

"There is no sign whatever of breaking and entering.
It appears that Mrs. Fairlands let the murderer in herself."

"But that's impossible."

"Is it? An old lady, feeling lonely perhaps. The doorbell rings. She thinks a friend has called to visit her. She
goes and opens it. It's always happening."

"Yes. Yes, of course. It could have happened that way.
Or a tramp asking for money—Christmas—"

"Tramps don't usually leave it as late as Christmas
Eve. Generally smash a window and get put inside a day
or two earlier."

"What worries you, then?"

"Just in case she had someone after her. Poor relation. Anyone who had it in for her, if she knew something damaging about him. Faked the burglary."

"But he seems to have taken her jewel box, and according to my wife, it was worth taking."

"Quite. We shall want a full description of the pieces, sir."

"She'll make it out for you. Or it may have been insured separately."

"I'm afraid not. Go ahead, though, Mr. Evans. I'll send my sergeant in, and he'll bring you back to the station with any essential papers you need for Mrs. Fairlands' solicitor.

Hugh worked at the papers for half an hour and then decided he had all the information he wanted. No steps of any kind need, or indeed could, be taken until the day after tomorrow, he knew. The solicitor could not begin to wind up Mrs. Fairlands' affairs for some time. Even the date of the inquest had not been fixed and would probably have to be adjourned.

Before leaving the flat, Hugh looked round the rooms once more, taking the sergeant with him. They paused before the mantelpiece, untouched by the thieves, a poignant reminder of the life so abruptly ended. Hugh looked at the cards and then glanced at the Christmas tree.

"Poor old thing!" he said. "We never thought she'd go like this. We ought all to have been here today. She always decorated a tree for us—" He broke off, genuinely moved for the first time.

"So I understand," the sergeant said gruffly, sharing the wave of sentiment.

"My wife—I wonder—D'you think it'd be in order to get rid of it?"

"The tree, sir?"

"Yes. Put it out at the back somewhere. Less upsetting—Mrs. Evans will be coming up the day after tomorrow. By that time the dustmen may have called.''

''I understand. I don't see any harm—''

''Right.''

Hurrying, in case the sergeant should change his mind, Hugh took up the bowl, and turning his face away to spare it from being pricked by the pine needles, he carried it out to the back of the house where he stood it beside the row of three dustbins. At any rate, he thought, going back to join the sergeant, Dorothy would be spared the feelings that overcame him so unexpectedly.

He was not altogether right in this. Mrs. Evans traveled to London on the day after Boxing Day. The inquest opened on this day, with a jury. Evidence was given of the finding of the body. Medical evidence gave the cause of death as cold and exhaustion and bronchial edema from partial suffocation by a plaster gag. The verdict was murder by a person or persons unknown.

After the inquest, Mrs. Fairlands' solicitor, who had supported Mrs. Evans during the ordeal in court, went with her to the flat. They arrived just as the municipal dust cart was beginning to move away. One of the older dustmen came up to them.

''You for the old lady they did Christmas Eve?'' he asked, with some hesitation.

''I'm her daughter,'' Dorothy said, her eyes filling again, as they still did all too readily.

''What d'you want?'' asked the solicitor, who was anxious to get back to his office.

''No offense,'' said the man, ignoring him and keeping his eyes on Dorothy's face. ''It's like this 'ere, see. They put a Christmas tree outside, by the bins, see. Decorated. We didn't like to take it, seeing it's not exactly rubbish and her gone and that. Nobody about we could ask—''

Dorothy understood. The Christmas tree. Hugh's doing, obviously. Sweet of him.

"Of course you must have it, if it's any use to you now, so late. Have you got children?"

"Three, ma'am. Two younguns. I arsked the other chaps. They don't want it. They said to leave it."

"No, you take it," Dorothy told him. "I don't want to see it. I don't want to be reminded—"

"Thanks a lot, dear," the dustman said, gravely sympathetic, walking back round the house.

The solicitor took the door key from Dorothy and let her in, so she did not see the tree as the dustman emerged with it held carefully before him.

In his home that evening the tree was greeted with a mixture of joy and derision.

"As if I 'adn't enough to clear up yesterday and the day before," his wife complained, half angry, half laughing. "Where'd you get it, anyway?"

When he had finished telling her, the two children, who had listened, crept away to play with the new glittering toy. And before long Mavis, the youngest, found the brooch pinned to the star. She unfastened it carefully and held it in her hand, turning it this way and that to catch the light.

But not for long. Her brother Ernie, two years older, soon snatched it. Mavis went for him, and he ran, making for the front door to escape into the street where Mavis was forbidden to play. Though she seldom obeyed the rule, on this occasion she used it to make loud protest, setting up a howl that brought her mother to the door of the kitchen.

But Ernie had not escaped with his prize. His elder brother Ron was on the point of entering, and when Ernie flung wide the door, Ron pushed in, shoving his little brother back.

" 'E's nicked my star," Mavis wailed. "Make 'im give me back, Ron. It's mine. Off the tree."

Ron took Ernie by the back of his collar and swung him round.

"Give!" he said firmly. Ernie clenched his right fist, betraying himself. Ron took his arm, bent his hand over forwards, and, as the brooch fell to the floor, stooped to pick it up. Ernie was now in tears.

"Where'd 'e get it?" Ron asked over the child's doubled-up, weeping form.

"The tree," Mavis repeated. *"I* found it. On the star— on the tree."

"Wot the 'ell d'she mean?" Ron asked, exasperated.

"Shut up, the lot of you!" their mother cried fiercely from the kitchen where she had retreated. "Ron, come on in to your tea. Late as usual. Why you never—"

"Okay, Mum," the boy said, unrepentant. "I never—"

He sat down, looking at the sparkling object in his hand.

"What'd Mavis mean about a tree?"

"Christmas tree. Dad brought it in. I've a good mind to put it on the fire. Nothing but argument since 'e fetched it."

"It's pretty," Ron said, meaning the brooch in his hand. "Dress jewelry, they calls it." He slipped it into his pocket.

"That's mine," Mavis insisted. "I found it pinned on that star on the tree. You give it back, Ron."

"Leave 'im alone," their mother said, smacking away the reaching hands. "Go and play with your blasted tree. Dad didn't ought t'ave brought it. Ought t'ave 'ad more sense—"

Ron sat quietly, eating his kipper and drinking his tea. When he had finished, he stacked his crockery in the sink, went upstairs, changed his shirt, put a pair of shiny dancing shoes in the pockets of his mackintosh, and went off to the club where his current girlfriend, Sally, fifteen like himself, attending the same comprehensive school, was waiting for him.

"You're late," she said over her shoulder, not leaving the group of her girlfriends.

"I've 'eard that before tonight. Mum was creating. Not my fault if Mr. Pope wants to see me about exam papers."

"You're never taking G.C.E.?"

"Why not?"

"Coo!'Oo started that lark?"

"Mr. Pope. I just told you. D'you want to dance or don't you?"

She did and she knew Ron was not one to wait indefinitely. So she joined him, and together they went to the main hall where dancing was in progress, with a band formed by club members.

" 'Alf a mo!" Ron said as they reached the door. "I got something you'll like."

He produced the brooch.

Sally was delighted. This was no cheap store piece. It was slap-up dress jewelry, like the things you saw in the West End, in Bond Street, in the Burlington Arcade, even. She told him she'd wear it just below her left shoulder near the neck edge of her dress. When they moved on to the dance floor she was holding her head higher and swinging her hips more than ever before. She and Ron danced well together. That night many couples stood still to watch them.

About an hour later the dancing came to a sudden end with a sound of breaking glass and shouting that grew in volume and ferocity.

"Raid!" yelled the boys on the dance floor, deserting their partners and crowding to the door. "Those bloody Wingers again."

The sounds of battle led them, running swiftly, to the table-tennis and billiards room, where a shambles confronted them. Overturned tables, ripped cloth, broken glass were everywhere. Tall youths and younger lads were fighting indiscriminately. Above the din the club warden and the three voluntary workers, two of them women, raised their voices in appeal and admonishment, equally ignored. The young barrister who attended once a week to give legal advice free, as a form of social service, to those who asked for it plunged into the battle, only to be flung out again nursing a twisted arm. It was the club caretaker, old and experienced in gang warfare, who summoned the police. They arrived silently, snatched ringleaders with expert knowledge or recognition, hemmed in their captives while the battle melted, and waited while their colleagues, posted at the doors of the club, turned back all would-be escapers.

Before long complete order was restored. In the dance hall the line of prisoners stood below the platform where the band had played. They included club members as well as strangers. The rest, cowed, bunched together near the door, also included a few strangers. Murmurings against these soon added them to the row of captives.

"Now," said the sergeant, who had arrived in answer to the call, "Mr. Smith will tell me who belongs here and who doesn't."

The goats were quickly separated from the rather black sheep.

"Next, who was playing table tennis when the raid commenced?"

Six hands shot up from the line. Some disheveled girls near the door also held up their hands.

"The rest were in here dancing," the warden said. "The boys left the girls when they heard the row, I think."

"That's right," Ron said boldly. "We 'eard glass going, and we guessed it was them buggers. They been 'ere before."

"They don't learn," said the sergeant with a baleful glance at the goats, who shuffled their feet and looked sulky.

"You'll be charged at the station," the sergeant went

on, "and I'll want statements from some of your lads," he told the warden. "Also from you and your assistants. These other kids can all go home. Quietly, mind," he said, raising his voice. "Show us there's some of you can behave like reasonable adults and not childish savages."

Sally ran forward to Ron as he left the row under the platform. He took her hand as they walked towards the door. But the sergeant had seen something that surprised him. He made a signal over their heads. At the door they were stopped.

"I think you're wanted. Stand aside for a minute," the constable told them.

The sergeant was the one who had been at the flat in the first part of the Fairlands case. He had been there when a second detailed examination of the flat was made in case the missing jewelry had been hidden away and had therefore escaped the thief. He had formed a very clear picture in his mind of what he was looking for from Mrs. Evans' description. As Sally passed him on her way to the door with Ron, part of the picture presented itself to his astonished eyes.

He turned to the warden.

"That pair. Can I have a word with them somewhere private?"

"Who? Ron Sharp and Sally Biggs? Two of our very nicest—"

The two were within earshot. They exchanged a look of amusement instantly damped by the sergeant, who ordered them briefly to follow him. In the warden's office, with the door shut, he said to Sally, "Where did you get that brooch you're wearing?"

The girl flushed. Ron said angrily, "I give it 'er. So what?"

"So where did you come by it?"

Ron hesitated. He didn't want to let himself down in Sally's eyes. He wanted her to think he'd bought it specially for her. He said, aggressively, "That's my business."

"I don't think so." Turning to Sally, the sergeant said, "Would you mind letting me have a look at it, miss?"

The girl was becoming frightened. Surely Ron hadn't done anything silly? He was looking upset. Perhaps—

"All right," she said, undoing the brooch and handing it over. "Poor eyesight, I suppose."

It was feeble defiance, and the sergeant ignored it. He said, "I'll have to ask you two to come down to the station. I'm not an expert, but we shall have to know a great deal more about this article, and Inspector Brooks will be particularly interested to know where it came from."

Ron remaining obstinately silent in spite of Sally's entreaty, the two found themselves presently sitting opposite Inspector Brooks, with the brooch lying on a piece of white paper before them.

"This brooch," said the inspector sternly, "is one piece of jewelry listed as missing from the flat of a Mrs. Fairlands, who was robbed and murdered on Christmas Eve or early Christmas Day."

"Never!" whispered Sally, aghast.

Ron said nothing. He was not a stupid boy, and he realized at once that he must now speak, whatever Sally thought of him. Also that he had a good case if he didn't say too much. So, after careful thought, he told Brooks exactly how and when he had come by the brooch and advised him to check this with his father and mother. The old lady's son had stuck the tree out by the dustbins, his mother had said, and her daughter had told his father he could have it to take home.

Inspector Brooks found the tale too fantastic to be untrue. Taking the brooch and the two subdued youngsters with him, he went to Ron's home, where more surprises awaited him. After listening to Mr. Sharp's account of the Christmas tree, which exactly tallied with Ron's, he went into the next room where the younger children were playing and Mrs. Sharp was placidly watching television.

"Which of you two found the brooch?" Brooks asked. The little girl was persuaded to agree that she had done so.

"But I got these," the boy said. He dived into his pocket and dragged out the pearl necklace and the diamond bracelet.

" 'Struth!" said the inspector, overcome. "She must've been balmy."

"No, she wasn't," Sally broke in. "She was nice. She give us two and a tanner."

"She *what?*"

Sally explained the carol singing expedition. They had been up four roads in that part, she said, and only two nicker the lot.

"Mostly it was nil," she said. "Then there was some give a bob and this old gentleman and the woman with 'im ten bob each. We packed it in after that."

"This means you actually went to Mrs. Fairlands' house?" Brooks said sternly to Ron.

"With the others—yes."

"Did you go inside?"

"No."

"No." Sally supported him. "She come out."

"Was she wearing the brooch?"

"No," said Ron.

"Not when she come out, she wasn't," Sally corrected him.

Ron kicked her ankle gently. The inspector noticed this.

"When did you see it?" he asked Sally.

"When she looked through the window at us. We shone the torch on 'er. It didn't 'alf shine."

"But you didn't recognize it when Ron gave it to you?"

"Why should I? I never saw it close. It was pinned on 'er dress at the neck. I didn't think of it till you said."

Brooks nodded. This seemed fair enough. He turned to face Ron.

"So you went back alone later to get it? Right?"

"I never! It's a damned lie!" the boy cried fiercely.

Mr. Sharp took a step forward. His wife bundled the younger children out of the room. Sally began to cry.

" 'Oo are you accusing?" Mr. Sharp said heavily. "You 'eard 'ow I come by the tree. My mates was there. The things was on it. I got witnesses. If Ron did that job, would 'e leave the only things worth 'aving? It says in the paper nothing of value, don't it?"

Brooks realized the force of this argument, however badly put. He'd been carried away a little. Unusual for him; he was surprised at himself. But the murder had been a particularly revolting one, and until these jewels turned up, he'd had no idea where to look. Carol singers. It might be a line and then again it mightn't.

He took careful statements from Ron, Sally, Ron's father, and the two younger children. He took the other pieces of jewelry and the Christmas tree. Carol singers. Mrs. Fairlands had opened the door to Ron's lot, having taken off her brooch if the story was true. Having hidden it very cleverly. He and his men had missed it completely. A Christmas tree decorated with flashy bits and pieces as usual. Standing back against a wall. They'd ignored it. Seen nothing but tinsel and glitter for weeks past. Of course they hadn't noticed it. The real thief or thieves hadn't noticed it, either.

Back at the station he locked away the jewels, labeled, in the safe and rang up Hugh Evans. He did not tell him where the pieces had been found.

Afterwards he had to deal with some of the hooligans who had now been charged with breaking, entering, willful damage, and making an affray. He wished he could pin Mrs. Fairlands' murder on their ringleader, a most degenerate and evil youth. Unfortunately, the whole gang had been in trouble in the West End that night; most of them had spent what remained of it in Bow Street police station. So they were out. But routine investigations now had a definite aim. To collect a list of all those who had sung carols at the house in Mrs. Fairlands' road on Christmas Eve, to question the singers about the times they had appeared there and about the houses they had visited.

It was not easy. Carol singers came from many social groups and often traveled far from their own homes. The youth clubs in the district were helpful; so were the various student bodies and hostels in the neighborhood. Brooks's manor was wide and very variously populated. In four days he had made no headway at all.

A radio message went out, appealing to carol singers to report at the police station if they were near Mrs. Fairlands' house at any time on Christmas Eve. The press took up the quest, dwelling on the pathetic aspects of the old woman's tragic death at a time of traditional peace on earth and good will towards men. All right-minded citizens must want to help the law over this revolting crime.

But the citizens maintained their attitude of apathy or caution.

Except for one, a freelance journalist, Tom Meadows, who had an easy manner with young people because he liked them. He became interested because the case seemed to involve young people. It was just up his street. So he went first to the Sharp family, gained their complete confidence, and had a long talk with Ron.

The boy was willing to help. After he had got over his indignation with the law for daring to suspect him, he had had sense enough to see how this had been inevitable. His anger was directed more truly at the unknown thugs responsible. He remembered Mrs. Fairlands with respect and pity. He was ready to do anything Tom Meadows suggested.

The journalist was convinced that the criminal or crim-

inals must be local, with local knowledge. It was unlikely they would wander from house to house, taking a
chance on finding one that might be profitable. It was far
more likely that they knew already that Mrs. Fairlands
lived alone, would be quite alone over Christmas and
therefore defenseless. But their information had been in-
complete. They had not known how little money she kept
at the flat. No one had known this except her family. Or
had they?

Meadows, patient and amiable, worked his way from
the Sharps to the postman, the milkman, and through the
latter to the daily.

"Well, of course I mentioned 'er being alone for the
'oliday. I told that detective so. In the way of conversation, I told 'im. Why shouldn't I?"

"Why indeed? But who did you tell, exactly?"

"I disremember. Anyone, I suppose. If we was com-
paring. I'm on me own now meself, but I go up to me
brother's at the 'olidays."

"Where would that be?"

"Notting 'Ill way. 'E's on the railway. Paddington."

Bit by bit Meadows extracted a list of her friends and
relations, those with whom she had talked most often
during the week before Christmas. Among her various
nephews and nieces was a girl who went to the same
comprehensive school as Ron and his girlfriend Sally.

Ron listened to the assignment Meadows gave him.

"Sally won't like it," he said candidly.

"Bring her into it, then. Pretend it's all your own
idea."

Ron grinned.

"Shirl won't like that," he said.

Tom Meadows laughed.

"Fix it any way you like," he said. "But I think this
girl Shirley was with a group and did go to sing carols
for Mrs. Fairlands. I know she isn't on the official list,
so she hasn't reported it. I want to know why."

"I'm not shopping anymore," Ron said warily.

"I'm not asking you to. I don't imagine Shirley or her friends did Mrs. Fairlands. But it's just possible she knows or saw something and is afraid to speak up for fear of reprisals."

"Cor!" said Ron. It was like a page of his favorite magazine working out in real life. He confided in Sally, and they went to work.

The upshot was interesting. Shirley did have something to say, and she said it to Tom Meadows in her own home with her disapproving mother sitting beside her.

"I never did like the idea of Shirl going out after dark, begging at house doors. That's all it really is, isn't it? My children have very good pocket money. They've nothing to complain of."

"I'm sure they haven't," Meadows said mildly. "But there's a lot more to carol singing than asking for money. Isn't there, Shirley?"

"I'll say," the girl answered. "Mum don't understand."

"You can't stop her," the mother complained. "Self-willed. Stubborn. I don't know, I'm sure. Out after dark. My dad'd've taken his belt to me for less."

"There were four of us," Shirley protested. "It wasn't late. Not above seven or eight."

The time was right, Meadows noted, if she was speaking of her visit to Mrs. Fairlands' road. She was. Encouraged to describe everything, she agreed that her group was working towards the house especially to entertain the old lady who was going to be alone for Christmas. She'd got that from her aunt, who worked for Mrs. Fairlands. They began at the far end of the road on the same side as the old lady. When they were about six houses away, they saw another group go up to it or to one near it. Then they were singing themselves. The next time she looked round, she saw one child running away up the road. She did not know where he had come from. She did not see the others.

"You did not see them go on?"

"No. They weren't in the road then, but they might have gone right on while we were singing. There's a turning off, isn't there?"

"Yes. Go on."

"Well, we went up to Mrs. Fairlands' and rang the bell. I thought I'd tell her she knew my aunt and we'd come special."

"Yes. What happened?"

"Nothing. At least—"

"Go on. Don't be frightened."

Shirley's face had gone very pale.

"There were men's voices inside. Arguing like. Nasty. We scarpered."

Tom Meadows nodded gravely.

"That would be upsetting. *Men's* voices? Or big boys?"

"Could be either, couldn't it? Well, perhaps more like sixth form boys, at that."

"You thought it was boys, didn't you? Boys from your school."

Shirley was silent.

"You thought they'd know and have it in for you if you told. Didn't you? I won't let you down, Shirley. Didn't you?"

She whispered, "Yes," and added, "Some of our boys got knives. I seen them."

Meadows went to Inspector Brooks. He explained how Ron had helped him to get in touch with Shirley and the result of that interview. The inspector, who had worked as a routine matter on all Mrs. Fairlands' contacts with the outer world, was too interested to feel annoyed at the other's success.

"Men's voices?" Brooks said incredulously.

"Most probably older lads," Meadows answered.

"She agreed that was what frightened her group. They might have looked out and recognized them as they ran away."

"There'd been no attempt at intimidations?"

"They're not all *that* stupid."

"No."

Brooks considered.

"This mustn't break in the papers yet, you understand?"

"Perfectly. But I shall stay around."

Inspector Brooks nodded, and Tom went away. Brooks took his sergeant and drove to Mrs. Fairlands' house. They still had the key of the flat, and they still had the house under observation.

The new information was disturbing, Brooks felt. Men's voices, raised in anger. Against poor Mrs. Fairlands, of course. But there were no adult fingerprints in the flat except those of the old lady herself and of her daily. Gloves had been worn, then. A professional job. But no signs whatever of breaking and entering. Therefore, Mrs. Fairlands had let them in. Why? She had peeped out at Ron's lot, to check who they were, obviously. She had not done so for Shirley's. Because she was in the power of the "men" whose voices had driven this other group away in terror.

But there had been two distinct small footprints in the dust of the outer hall and a palmprint on the outer door had been small, childsize.

Perhaps the child that Shirley had seen running down the road had been a decoy. The whole group she had noticed at Mrs. Fairlands' door might have been employed for that purpose and the men or older boys were lurking at the corner of the house, to pounce when the door opened. Possible, but not very likely. Far too risky, even on a dark evening. Shirley could not have seen distinctly. The street lamps were at longish intervals in that road. But there were always a few passersby. Even on

Christmas Eve no professional group of villains would take such a risk.

Standing in the cold drawing room, now covered with a grey film of dust, Inspector Brooks decided to make another careful search for clues. He had missed the jewels. Though he felt justified in making it, his mistake was a distinct blot on his copybook. It was up to him now to retrieve his reputation. He sent the sergeant to take another look at the bedroom, with particular attention to the dressing table. He himself began to go over the drawing room with the greatest possible care.

Shirley's evidence suggested there had been more than one thief. The girl had said "voices." That meant at least two, which probably accounted for the fact, apart from her age, that neither Mrs. Fairlands nor her clothes gave any indication of a struggle. She had been overpowered immediately, it seemed. She had not been strong enough or agile enough to tear, scratch, pull off any fragment from her attackers' clothes or persons. There had been no trace of any useful material under her fingernails or elsewhere.

Brooks began methodically with the chair to which Mrs. Fairlands had been bound and worked his way outwards from that center. After the furniture, the carpet and curtains. After that the walls.

Near the door, opposite the fireplace, he found on the wall—two feet, three inches up from the floor—a small, round, brownish, greasy smear. He had not seen it before. In artificial light, he checked, it was nearly invisible. On this morning, with the first sunshine of the New Year coming into the room, the little patch was entirely obvious, slightly shiny where the light from the window caught it.

Inspector Brooks took a wooden spatula from his case of aids and carefully scraped off the substance into a small plastic box, sniffing at it as he did so.

"May I, too?" asked Tom Meadows behind him.

The inspector wheeled round with an angry exclamation.

"How did you get in?" he asked.

"Told the copper in your car I wanted to speak to you."

"What about?"

"Well, about how you were getting on, really," Tom said disarmingly. "I see you are. Please let me have one sniff."

Inspector Brooks was annoyed, both by the intrusion and the fact that he had not heard it, being so concentrated on his work. So he closed his box, shut it into his black bag, and called to the sergeant in the next room.

Meadows got down on his knees, leaned towards the wall, and sniffed. It was faint, since most of it had been scraped off, but he knew the smell. His freelancing had not been confined to journalism.

He was getting to his feet as the sergeant joined Inspector Brooks. The sergeant raised his eyebrows at the interloper.

"You can't keep the press's noses out of anything," said Brooks morosely.

The other two grinned. It was very apt.

"I'm just off," Tom said. "Good luck with your specimen, inspector. I know where to go now. So will you."

"Come back!" called Brooks. The young man was a menace. He would have to be controlled.

But Meadows was away, striding down the road until he was out of sight of the police car, then running to the nearest tube station where he knew he would find the latest newspaper editions. He bought one, opened it at the entertainments column, and read down the list.

He was a certain six hours ahead of Brooks, he felt sure, possibly more. Probably he had until tomorrow morning. He skipped his lunch and set to work.

Inspector Brooks got the report from the lab that evening, and the answer to his problem came to him as com-

pletely as it had done to Tom Meadows in Mrs. Fairlands'
drawing room. His first action was to ring up Olympia.
This proving fruitless, he sighed. Too late now to contact
the big stores; they would all be closed and the employees of every kind gone home.

But in the morning some very extensive telephone calls
to managers told him where he must go. He organized
his forces to cover all the exits of a big store not very far
from Mrs. Fairlands' house. With his sergeant he entered
modestly by way of the men's department.

They took a lift from there to the third floor, emerging
among the toys. It was the tenth day of Christmas, with
the school holidays in full swing and eager children, flush
with Christmas money, choosing long-coveted treasures.
A Father Christmas, white-bearded, in the usual red,
hooded gown, rather too short for him, was moving about
trying to promote a visit to the first of that day's perfor-
mances of "Snowdrop and the Seven Dwarfs." As his
insistence seeped into the minds of the abstracted young,
they turned their heads to look at the attractive cardboard
entrance of the little "theater" at the far end of the department. A gentle flow towards it began and gathered
momentum. Inspector Brooks and the sergeant joined the
stream.

Inside the theater there were small chairs in rows for
the children. The grownups stood at the back. A gram-
ophone played the Disney film music.

The early scenes were brief, mere tableaux with a line
thrown in here and there for Snowdrop. The queen spoke
the famous doggerel to her mirror.

The curtain fell and rose again on Snowdrop, surrounded by the Seven Dwarfs. Two of them had beards,
real beards. Dopey rose to his feet and began to sing.

"Okay," whispered Brooks to the sergeant. "The child
who sang and ran away."

The sergeant nodded. Brooks whispered again. "I'm

going round the back. Get the audience here out quietly if the balloon goes up before they finish.''

He tiptoed quietly away. He intended to catch the dwarfs in their dressing room immediately after the show, arrest the lot, and sort them out at the police station.

But the guilty ones had seen him move. Or rather Dopey, more guilt-laden and fearful than the rest, had noticed the two men who seemed to have no children with them, had seen their heads close together, had seen one move silently away. As Brooks disappeared, the midget's nerve broke. His song ended in a scream; he fled from the stage.

In the uproar that followed, the dwarf's scream was echoed by the frightened children. The lights went up in the theater, the shop assistants and the sergeant went into action to subdue their panic and get them out.

Inspector Brooks found himself in a maze of lathe and plaster backstage arrangements. He found three bewildered small figures, with anxious, wizened faces, trying to restrain Dopey, who was still in the grip of his hysteria. A few sharp questions proved that the three had no idea what was happening.

The queen and Snowdrop appeared, highly indignant. Brooks, now holding Dopey firmly by the collar, demanded the other three dwarfs. The two girls, subdued and totally bewildered, pointed to their dressing room. It was empty, but a tumbled heap of costumes on the floor showed what they had done. The sergeant appeared, breathless.

"Take this chap," Brooks said, thrusting the now fainting Dopey at him. "Take him down. I'm shopping him. Get onto the management to warn all departments for the others."

He was gone, darting into the crowded toy department, where children and parents stood amazed or hurried towards the lifts, where a dense crowd stood huddled, anxious to leave the frightening trouble spot.

Brooks bawled an order.

The crowd at the lift melted away from it, leaving three small figures in overcoats and felt hats, trying in vain to push once more under cover.

They bolted, bunched together, but they did not get far. Round the corner of a piled table of soft toys Father Christmas was waiting. He leaped forward, tripped up one, snatched another, hit the third as he passed and grabbed him, too, as he fell.

The tripped one struggled up and on as Brooks appeared.

"I'll hold these two," panted Tom Meadows through his white beard, which had fallen sideways.

The chase was brief. Brooks gained on the dwarf. The latter knew it was hopeless. He snatched up a mallet lying beside a display of camping equipment and, rushing to the side of the store, leaped on a counter, from there clambered up a tier of shelves, beat a hole in the window behind them, and dived through. Horrified people and police on the pavement below saw the small body turning over and over like a leaf as it fell.

"All yours," said Tom Meadows, handing his captives, too limp now to struggle, to Inspector Brooks and tearing off his Father Christmas costume. "See you later."

He was gone, to shut himself in a telephone booth on the ground floor of the store and hand his favorite editor the scoop. It had paid off, taking over from the old boy, an ex-actor like himself, who was quite willing for a fiver to write a note pleading illness and sending a substitute. "Your reporter, Tom Meadows, dressed as Father Christmas, today captured and handed over to the police two of the three murderers of Mrs. Fairlands—"

Inspector Brooks, with three frantic midgets demanding legal aid, scrabbling at the doors of their cells, took a lengthy statement from the fourth, the one with the treble voice whose nerve had broken on the fatal night, as it had again that day. Greasepaint had betrayed the little fiends, Brooks told him, privately regretting that Meadows had been a jump ahead of him there. Greasepaint left on in the rush to get at their prey. One of the brutes must have fallen against the wall, pushed by the old woman herself perhaps. He hoped so. He hoped it was her own action that had brought these squalid killers to justice.

MURDER UNDER THE MISTLETOE

by Margery Allingham

Murder under the mistletoe—and the man who must have done it couldn't have done it. That's my Christmas and I don't feel merry thank you very much all the same.'' Superintendent Stanislaus Oates favored his old friend Mr. Albert Campion with a pained smile and sat down in the chair indicated.

It was the afternoon of Christmas Day and Mr. Campion, only a trifle more owlish than usual behind his horn rims, had been fetched down from the children's party which he was attending at his brother-in-law's house in Knightsbridge to meet the Superintendent, who had moved heaven and earth to find him.

"What do you want?" Mr. Campion inquired facetiously. "A little armchair miracle?"

"I don't care if you do it swinging from a trapeze. I just want a reasonable explanation." Oates was rattled. His dyspeptic face with the perpetually sad expression was slightly flushed and not with festivity. He plunged into his story.

"About eleven last night a crook called Sampson was found shot dead in the back of a car in a garage under a small drinking club in Alcatraz Mews—the club is named The Humdinger. A large bunch of mistletoe which had been lying on the front seat ready to be driven home had been placed on top of the body partially hiding it—which was why it hadn't been found before. The gun, fitted with a silencer, but wiped of prints, was found under the front seat. The dead man was recognized at once by the owner of the car who is also the owner of the club. He was the owner's current boyfriend. She is quite a well-known West End character called 'Girlski.' What did you say?''

"I said, 'Oo-er','' murmured Mr. Campion. "One of the Eumenides, no doubt?''

"No.'' Oates spoke innocently. "She's not a Greek. Don't worry about her. Just keep your mind on the facts. She knows, as we do, that the only person who wanted to kill Sampson is a nasty little snake called Kroll. He has been out of circulation for the best of reasons. Sampson turned Queen's evidence against him in a matter concerning a conspiracy to rob Her Majesty's mails and when he was released last Tuesday Kroll came out breathing retribution.''

"Not the Christmas spirit,'' said Mr. Campion inanely.

"That is exactly what *we* thought,'' Oates agreed. "So about five o'clock yesterday afternoon two of our chaps, hearing that Kroll was at The Humdinger, where he might have been expected to make trouble, dropped along there and brought him in for questioning and he's been in custody ever since.

"Well, now. We have at least a dozen reasonably sober witnesses to prove that Kroll did not meet Sampson at the Club. Sampson had been there earlier in the afternoon but he left about a quarter to four saying he'd got to do some Christmas shopping but promising to return. Fifteen minutes or so later Kroll came in and stayed there in full view of Girlski and the customers until our men turned up and collected him. *Now* what do you say?''

"Too easy!'' Mr. Campion was suspicious. "Kroll killed Sampson just before he came in himself. The two met in the dusk outside the club. Kroll forced Sampson into the garage and possibly into the car and shot him. With the way the traffic has been lately, he'd hardly have attracted attention had he used a mortar, let alone a gun with a silencer. He wiped the weapon, chucked it in the car, threw the mistletoe over the corpse, and went up to Girlski to renew old acquaintance and establish an alibi. Your chaps, arriving when they did, must have appeared welcome.''

Oates nodded. ''We thought that. *That is what happened.* That is why this morning's development has set me glibbering. We now have two unimpeachable witnesses who swear that the dead man was in Chipperwood West at six last evening delivering some Christmas purchases he had made on behalf of a neighbor. That is *a whole hour* after Kroll was pulled in.

''The assumption is that Sampson returned to Alcatraz Mews sometime later in the evening and was killed by someone else—which we know is not true. Unfortunately, the Chipperwood West witnesses are not the kind of people we are going to shake. One of them is a friend of yours. She asked our Inspector if he knew you because you were 'so good at crime and all that nonsense'.''

''Good Heavens!'' Mr. Campion spoke piously as the explanation of the Superintendent's unlikely visitation was made plain to him. ''I don't think I know Chipperwood West.''

''It's a suburb which is becoming fashionable. Have you ever heard of Lady Larradine?''

''Old Lady 'ell?'' Mr. Campion let the joke of his salad days escape without its being noticed by either of them. ''I don't believe it. She must be dead by this time!''

''There's a type of woman who never dies before you do,'' said Oates with apparent sincerity. ''She's quite a dragon, I understand from our Inspector. However, she isn't the actual witness. There are two of them. Brigadier Brose is one. Ever heard of *him?*''

''I don't think I have.''

''My information is that you'd remember him if you'd

met him. Well, we'll find out. I'm taking you with me, Campion. I hope you don't mind?''

"My sister will hate it. I'm due to be Santa Claus in about an hour.''

"I can't help that." Oates was adamant. "If a bunch of silly crooks want to get spiteful at the festive season, someone must do the homework. Come and play Santa Claus with me. It's your last chance. I'm retiring this summer.''

Oates continued in the same vein as he and Mr. Campion sat in the back of a police car threading their way through the deserted Christmas streets where the lamps were growing bright in the dusk.

"I've had bad luck lately," the Superintendent said seriously. "Too much. It won't help my memoirs if I go out in a blaze of no-enthusiasm.''

"You're thinking of the Phaeton Robbery," Mr. Campion suggested. "What are you calling your memoirs? *Man-Eaters of the Yard?*''

Oates's mild old eyes brightened, but not greatly.

"Something of the kind," he admitted. "But no one could be blamed for not solving that blessed Phaeton business. Everyone concerned was bonkers. A silly old musical star, for thirty years the widow of an eccentric Duke, steps out into her London garden one autumn morning leaving the street door wide open and all her most valuable jewelry collected from strong-rooms all over the country lying in a brown paper parcel on her bureau in the first room off the hall. Her excuse was that she was just going to take it to the Bond Street auctioneers and was carrying it herself for safety! The thief was equally mental to lift it.''

"It wasn't saleable?''

"Saleable? It couldn't even be broken up. The stuff is just about as well-known as the Crown Jewels. Great big enamels which the old Duke had collected at great expense. No fence would stay in the same room with them, yet, of course, they are worth the Earth as every newspaper has told us at length ever since they were pinched!''

''He didn't get anything else either, did he?''

''He was a madman.'' Oates dismissed him with contempt. ''All he gained was the old lady's housekeeping money for a couple of months which was in her handbag—about a hundred and fifty quid—and the other two items which were on the same shelf, a soapstone monkey and a plated paperknife. He simply wandered in, took the first things he happened to see and wandered out again. Any sneak thief, tramp, or casual snapper-upper could have done it and who gets blamed? *Me!*''

He looked so woebegone that Mr. Campion hastily changed the subject. ''Where are we going?'' he inquired. ''To call on her ladyship? Do I understand that at the age of one hundred and forty-six or whatever it is she is cohabiting with a Brig? Which war?''

''I can't tell you.'' Oates was literal as usual. ''It could be the South African. They're all in a nice residential hotel—the sort of place that is very popular with the older members of the landed gentry just now.''

''When you say landed, you mean as in Fish?''

''Roughly, yes. Elderly people living on capital. About forty of them. This place used to be called *The Haven* and has now been taken over by two ex-society widows and renamed *The CCraven*—with two Cs. It's a select hotel—cum—Old Ducks' Home for Mother's Friends. You know the sort of place?''

''I can envisage it. Don't say your murdered chum from The Humdinger lived there too?''

''No, he lived in a more modest place whose garden backs on the CCraven's grounds. The Brigadier and one of the other residents, a Mr. Charlie Taunton, who has become a bosom friend of his, were in the habit of talking to Sampson over the wall. Taunton is a lazy man who seldom goes out and has little money but he very much wanted to get some gifts for his fellow guests—something in the nature of little jokes from the chain stores, I understand; but he dreaded the exertion of shopping for them and Sampson appears to have offered to get him some little items wholesale and to deliver them by six o'clock on Christmas Eve—in time for him to package them up and hand them to Lady Larradine who was dressing the tree at seven."

"And did you say Sampson actually did this?" Mr. Campion sounded bewildered.

"Both old gentlemen—the Brigadier and Taunton—swear to it. They insist they went down to the wall at six and Sampson handed the parcel over as arranged. My Inspector is an experienced man and he doesn't think we'll be able to shake either of them."

"That leaves Kroll with a complete alibi. How did these Chipperwood witnesses hear of Sampson's death?"

"Routine. The local police called at Sampson's home address this morning to report the death, only to discover the place closed. The landlady and her family are away for the holiday and Sampson himself was due to spend it with Girlski. The police stamped about a bit, making sure of all this, and in the course of their investigations they were seen and hailed by the two old boys in the adjoining garden. The two were shocked to hear that their kind acquaintance was dead and volunteered the information that he had been with them at six."

Mr. Campion looked blank. "Perhaps they don't keep the same hours as anybody else," he suggested. "Old people can be highly eccentric."

Oates shook his head. "We thought of that. My Inspector, who came down the moment the local police reported, insists that they are perfectly normal and quite positive. Moreover, they had the purchases. He saw the packages already on the tree. Lady Larradine pointed them out to him when she asked after you. She'll be delighted to see you, Campion."

"I can hardly wait!"

"You don't have to," said Oates grimly as they pulled up before a huge Edwardian villa. "It's all yours."

"My dear Boy! You haven't aged any more than I have!"

Lady Larradine's tremendous voice—one of her chief terrors, Mr. Campion recollected—echoed over the crowded first-floor room where she received them. There she stood in an outmoded but glittering evening gown looking, as always, exactly like a spray-flecked seal.

"I *knew* you'd come," she bellowed. "As soon as you got my oblique little S.O.S. How do you like our little hideout? Isn't it *fun!* Moira Spryg-Fysher and Janice Poole-Poole wanted something to do, so we all put our pennies in it and here we are!"

"Almost too marvelous," murmured Mr. Campion in all sincerity. "We really want a word with Brigadier Brose and Mr. Taunton."

"Of course you do and so you shall! We're all waiting for the Christmas tree. Everybody will be there for that in about ten minutes in the drawing room. My dear, when *we* came they were calling it the Residents' Lounge!"

Superintendent Oates remained grave. He was startled to discover that the dragon was not only fierce but also wily. The news that her apparently casual mention of Mr. Campion to the Inspector had been a ruse to get hold of him shocked the innocent Superintendent. He retaliated by insisting that he must see the witnesses at once.

Lady Larradine silenced him with a friendly roar. "My dear man, you can't! They've gone for a walk. I always turn men out of the house after Christmas luncheon. They'll soon be back. The Brigadier won't miss his Tree! Ah. Here's Fiona. This is Janice Poole-Poole's daughter, Albert. Isn't she a pretty girl?"

Mr. Campion saw Miss Poole-Poole with relief, knowing of old that Oates was susceptible to the type. The newcomer was young and lovely and even her beehive hair and the fact that she appeared to have painted herself with two black eyes failed to spoil the exquisite smile she bestowed on the helpless officer.

"Fabulous to have you really here," she said and sounded as if she meant it. While he was still recovering, Lady Larradine led Oates to the window.

"You can't see it because it's pitch-dark," she said, "but out there, down in the garden, there's a wall and it was over it that the Brigadier and Mr. Taunton spoke to Mr. Sampson at six o'clock last night. No one liked the man Sampson—I think Mr. Taunton was almost afraid of him. Certainly he seems to have died very untidily!"

"But he *did* buy Mr. Taunton's Christmas gifts for him?"

The dragon lifted a webby eyelid. "You have already been told that. At six last night Mr. Taunton and the Brigadier went to meet him to get the box. I got them into their mufflers so I know! I had the packing paper ready, too, for Mr. Taunton to take up to his room . . . Rather a small one on the third floor."

She lowered her voice to reduce it to the volume of distant traffic. "Not many pennies, but a dear little man!"

"Did you *see* these presents, Ma'am?"

"Not before they were wrapped! That would have spoiled the surprise!"

"I shall have to see them." There was a mulish note in the Superintendent's voice which the lady was too experienced to ignore.

"I've thought how to do that without upsetting anybody," she said briskly. "The Brigadier and I will cut the presents from the Tree and Fiona will be handing them round. All Mr. Taunton's little gifts are in the very distinctive black and gold paper I bought from Millie's Boutique and so, Fiona, you must give every package in black and gold not to the person to whom it is addressed but to the Superintendent. Can you do that, dear?"

Miss Poole-Poole seemed to feel the task difficult but not impossible and the trusting smile she gave Oates cut short his objection like the sun melting frost.

"Splendid!" The dragon's roar was hearty. "Give me your arm, Superintendent. You shall take me down."

As the procession reached the hall, it ran into the Brigadier himself. He was a large, pink man, affable enough, but of a martial type and he bristled at the Superintendent. "Extraordinary time to do your business—middle of Christmas Day!" he said after acknowledging the introductions.

Oates inquired if he had enjoyed his walk.

"Talk?" said the Brigadier. "I've not been talking. I've been asleep in the card room. Where's old Taunton?"

"He went for a walk, Athole dear," bellowed the dragon gaily.

"So he did. You sent him! Poor feller."

As the old soldier led the way to the open door of the drawing room, it occurred to both the Superintendent and Mr. Campion that the secret of Lady Larradine's undoubted attraction for the Brigadier lay in the fact that he could hear *her* if no one else. The discovery cast a new light altogether on the story of the encounter with Sampson in the garden.

Meanwhile, they had entered the drawing room and the party had begun. As Mr. Campion glanced at the company, ranged in a full circle round a magnificent tree loaded with gifts and sparkling like a waterfall, he saw face after familiar face. They were elder acquaintances of the dizzy 1930s whom he had mourned as gone forever, when he thought of them at all. Yet here they all were, not only alive but released by great age from many of the restraints of convention.

He noticed that every type of headgear from night-cap to tiara was being sported with fine individualistic enthusiasm. But Lady Larradine gave him little time to look about. She proceeded with her task immediately.

Each guest had been provided with a small invalid table beside his armchair, and Oates, reluctant but wax in Fiona's hands, was no exception. The Superintendent found himself seated between a mountain in flannel and a wraith in mauve mink, waiting his turn with the same beady-eyed avidity.

Christmas Tree procedure at the CCraven proved to be well organized. The dragon did little work herself. Armed with a swagger stick, she merely prodded parcel after parcel hanging amid the boughs while the task of detaching them was performed by the Brigadier who handed them to Fiona. Either to add to the excitement or perhaps to muffle any unfortunate comment on gifts received by the uninhabited company, jolly Christmas music was played throughout, and under cover of the noise Mr. Campion was able to tackle his hostess.

"Where is Taunton?" he whispered.

"Such a nice little man. Most presentable, but just a little teeny-weeny bit dishonest."

Lady Larradine ignored the question in his eyes and continued to put him in the picture at great speed, while supervising the Tree at the same time. "Fifty-seven convictions, I believe, but only small ones. I only got it all out of him last week. Shattering! He'd been so *useful*, amusing the Brigadier. When he came, he looked like a lost soul with no luggage, but after no time at all he settled in perfectly."

She paused and stabbed at a ball of colored cellophane with her stick before returning to her startled guest.

"Albert, I am terribly afraid that it was poor Mr. Taunton who took that dreadful jewelry of Maisie Phaeton's. It appears to have been entirely her fault. He was merely wandering past her house, feeling in need of care and attention. The door was wide open and Mr. Taunton suddenly found himself inside, picking up a few odds and ends. When he discovered from all that fuss in the news-papers what he had got hold of—how well-known it was, I mean—he was quite horrified and had to hide. And where better place than here with us where he never had to go out?''

''Where indeed!'' Mr. Campion dared not glance across the room at the Superintendent unwrapping his black and gold parcels. ''Where is he now? Poor Mr. Taunton, I mean.''

''Of course I hadn't the faintest idea what was worry-ing the man until he confessed,'' the dragon went on stonily. ''Then I realized that something would have to be done at once to protect everybody. The wretch had hidden all that frightful stuff in our toolshed for three months, not daring to keep it in the house; and to make matters worse, the impossible person at the end of the garden, Mr. Sampson, had recognized him and *would* keep speaking. Apparently people in the—er—underworld all know each other just like those of us in—er—other closed circles do.''

Mr. Campion, whose hair was standing on end, had a moment of inspiration. ''This absurd rigmarole about Taunton getting Sampson to buy him some Christmas gifts wholesale was *your* idea!'' he said accusingly.

The dragon stared. ''It seemed the best way of getting Maisie's jewelry back to her without any *one* person be-ing involved,'' she said frankly. ''I knew we should all recognize the things the moment we saw them and I was certain that after a lot of argument we should decide to pack them up and send them round to her. But, if there *were* any repercussions, we should *all* be in it—quite a formidable array, dear Boy—and the blame could be traced to Mr. Sampson if absolutely necessary. You see, the Brigadier is convinced that Sampson *was* there last night. Mr. Taunton very cleverly left him on the lawn and went behind the toolshed and came back with the box.''

"How completely immoral!" Mr. Campion couldn't restrain himself.

The dragon had the grace to look embarrassed.

"I don't think the Sampson angle would ever have arisen," she said. "But if it had, Sampson was quite a terrible person. Almost a blackmailer. Utterly dishonest and inconsiderate. Think how he has spoiled everything and endangered us all by getting himself killed on the *one* afternoon when we said he was here, so that the police were brought in. Just the *one* thing I was trying to avoid. When the Inspector appeared this morning I was so upset I thought of you!"

In his not unnatural alarm Mr. Campion so far forgot himself as to touch her sleeve. "Where is Taunton now?"

The dragon threshed her train. "Really, Boy! What a fidget you are! If you must know, I gave him his Christmas present—every penny I had in cash for he was broke again, he told me—and sent him for a nice long walk after lunch. Having seen the Inspector here this morning he was glad to go."

She paused and a granite gleam came into her hooded eyes. "If that Superintendent friend of yours has the stupidity to try to find him once Maisie has her monstrosities back, none of us will be able to identify him, I'm afraid. And there's another thing. If the Brigadier should be *forced* to give evidence, I am sure he will stick to his guns about Mr. Sampson being down in the garden here at six o'clock last night. That would mean that the man Kroll would have to go unpunished for his revenge murder, wouldn't it? Sampson was a terrible person—but *no one* should have killed him."

Mr. Campion was silenced. He glanced fearfully across the room.

The Superintendent was seated at his table wearing the strained yet slap-happy expression of a man with concussion. On his left was a pile of black and gold wrappings, on his right a rajah's ransom in somewhat specialized form.

From where he stood, Mr. Campion could see two examples amid the rest—a breastplate in gold, pearl, and enamel in the shape of a unicorn and an item which looked like a plover's egg in tourmaline encased in a ducal coronet. There was also a soapstone monkey and a solid-silver paperknife.

Much later that evening Mr. Campion and the Superintendent drove quietly back to headquarters. Oates had a large cardboard box on his knee. He clasped it tenderly.

He had been silent for a long time when a thought occurred to him. "Why did they take him into the house in the first place?" he said. "An elderly crook looking lost! And no luggage!"

Mr. Campion's pale eyes flickered behind his spectacles.

"Don't forget the Duchess' housekeeping money," he murmured. "I should think he offered one of the widows who really run that place the first three months' payment in cash, wouldn't you? That must be an impressive phenomenon in that sort of business, I fancy."

Oates caught his breath and fell silent once more. Presently he burst out again.

"Those people! That woman!" he exploded. "When they were younger they led me a pretty dance—losing things or getting themselves swindled. But now they're old they take the blessed biscuit! Do you see how she's tied my hands, Campion?"

Mr. Campion tried not to grin.

"Snapdragons are just permissible at Christmas," he said. "Handled with extreme caution they burn very few fingers, it seems to me."

Mr. Campion tapped the cardboard box. "And some of them provide a few plums for retiring coppers, don't they, Superintendent?"

THE ADVENTURE
OF THE BLUE CARBUNCLE
by Sir Arthur Conan Doyle

I had called upon my friend Sherlock Holmes upon the second morning after Christmas, with the intention of wishing him the compliments of the season. He was lounging upon the sofa in a purple dressing-gown, a pipe-rack within his reach upon the right, and a pile of crumpled morning papers, evidently newly studied, near at hand. Beside the couch was a wooden chair, and on the angle of the back hung a very seedy and disreputable hard-felt hat, much the worse for wear, and cracked in several places. A lens and a forceps lying upon the seat of the chair suggested that the hat had been suspended in this manner for the purpose of examination.

"You are engaged," said I; "perhaps I interrupt you."

"Not at all. I am glad to have a friend with whom I can discuss my results. The matter is a perfectly trivial one"—he jerked his thumb in the direction of the old hat—"but there are points in connection with it which are not entirely devoid of interest and even of instruction."

I seated myself in his armchair and warmed my hands before his crackling fire, for a sharp frost had set in, and the windows were thick with the ice crystals. "I suppose," I remarked, "that, homely as it looks, this thing has some deadly story linked on to it—that it is the clue which will guide you in the solution of some mystery and the punishment of some crime.''

"No, no. No crime," said Sherlock Holmes, laughing. "Only one of those whimsical little incidents which will happen when you have four million human beings all jostling each other within the space of a few square miles. Amid the action and reaction of so dense a swarm of humanity, every possible combination of events may be expected to take place, and many a little problem will be presented which may be striking and bizarre without being criminal. We have already had experience of such.''

"So much so," I remarked, "that of the last six cases which I have added to my notes, three have been entirely free of any legal crime.''

"Precisely. You allude to my attempt to recover the Irene Adler papers, to the singular case of Miss Mary Sutherland, and to the adventure of the man with the twisted lip. Well, I have no doubt that this small matter will fall into the same innocent category. You know Peterson, the commissionaire?''

"Yes.''

"It is to him that this trophy belongs.''

"It is his hat.''

"No, no; he found it. Its owner is unknown. I beg that you will look upon it not as a battered billycock but as an intellectual problem. And, first, as to how it came here. It arrived upon Christmas morning, in company with a good fat goose, which is, I have no doubt, roasting at this moment in front of Peterson's fire. The facts are these: about four o'clock on Christmas morning, Peterson, who, as you know, is a very honest fellow, was returning from some small jollification and was making his way homeward down Tottenham Court Road. In front of him he saw, in the gaslight, a tallish man, walking with a slight stagger, and carrying a white goose slung over his shoulder. As he reached the corner of Goodge

Street, a row broke out between this stranger and a little knot of roughs. One of the latter knocked off the man's hat, on which he raised his stick to defend himself, and swinging it over his head, smashed the shop window behind him. Peterson had rushed forward to protect the stranger from his assailants; but the man, shocked at having broken the window, and seeing an official-looking person in uniform rushing towards him, dropped his goose, took to his heels, and vanished amid the labyrinth of small streets which lie at the back of Tottenham Court Road. The roughs had also fled at the appearance of Peterson, so that he was left in possession of the field of battle, and also of the spoils of victory in the shape of this battered hat and a most unimpeachable Christmas goose.''

''Which surely he restored to their owner?''

''My dear fellow, there lies the problem. It is true that 'For Mrs. Henry Baker' was printed upon a small card which was tied to the bird's left leg, and it is also true that the initials 'H.B.' are legible upon the lining of this hat; but as there are some thousands of Bakers, and some hundreds of Henry Bakers in this city of ours, it is not easy to restore lost property to any of them.''

''What, then, did Peterson do?''

''He brought round both hat and goose to me on Christmas morning, knowing that even the smallest problems are of interest to me. The goose we retained until this morning, when there were signs that, in spite of the slight frost, it would be well that it should be eaten without unnecessary delay. Its finder has carried it off, therefore, to fulfil the ultimate destiny of a goose, while I continue to retain the hat of the unknown gentleman who lost his Christmas dinner.''

''Did he not advertise?''

''No.''

''Then, what clue could you have as to his identity?''

''Only as much as we can deduce.''

"From his hat?"

"Precisely."

"But you are joking. What can you gather from this old battered felt?"

"Here is my lens. You know my methods. What can you gather yourself as to the individuality of the man who has worn this article?"

I took the tattered object in my hands and turned it over rather ruefully. It was a very ordinary black hat of the usual round shape, hard and much the worse for wear. The lining had been of red silk, but was a good deal discoloured. There was no maker's name; but, as Holmes had remarked, the initials "H.B." were scrawled upon one side. It was pierced in the brim for a hat-securer, but the elastic was missing. For the rest, it was cracked, exceedingly dusty, and spotted in several places, although there seemed to have been some attempt to hide the discoloured patches by smearing them with ink.

"I can see nothing," said I, handing it back to my friend.

"On the contrary, Watson, you can see everything. You fail, however, to reason from what you see. You are too timid in drawing your inferences."

"Then, pray tell me what it is that you can infer from this hat?"

He picked it up and gazed at it in the peculiar introspective fashion which was characteristic of him. "It is perhaps less suggestive than it might have been," he remarked, "and yet there are a few inferences which are very distinct, and a few others which represent at least a strong balance of probability. That the man was highly intellectual is of course obvious upon the face of it, and also that he was fairly well-to-do within the last three years, although he has now fallen upon evil days. He had foresight, but has less now than formerly, pointing to a moral retrogression, which, when taken with the decline of his fortunes, seems to indicate some evil influence, probably drink, at work upon him. This may account also for the obvious act that his wife has ceased to love him.''

''My dear Holmes!''

''He has, however, retained some degree of self-respect,'' he continued, disregarding my remonstrance. ''He is a man who leads a sendentary life, goes out little, is out of training entirely, is middle-aged, has grizzled hair which he has had cut within the last few days, and which he anoints with lime-cream. These are the more patent facts which are to be deduced from his hat. Also, by the way, that it is extremely improbable that she has gas laid on in his house.''

''You are certainly joking, Holmes.''

''Not in the least. Is it possible that even now, when I give you these results, you are unable to see how they are attained?''

''I have no doubt that I am very stupid, but I must confess that I am unable to follow you. For example, how did you deduce that this man was intellectual?''

For answer Holmes clapped the hat upon his head. It came right over the forehead and settled upon the bridge of his nose. ''It is a question of cubic capacity,'' said he; ''a man with so large a brain must have something in it.''

''The decline of his fortunes, then?''

''This hat is three years old. These flat brims curled at the edge came in then. It is a hat of the very best quality. Look at the band of ribbed silk and the excellent lining. If this man could afford to buy so expensive a hat three years ago, and has had no hat since, then he has assuredly gone down in the world.''

''Well, that is clear enough, certainly. But how about the foresight and the moral retrogression?''

Sherlock Holmes laughed. ''Here is the foresight,'' said he, putting his finger upon the little disc and loop of the hat-securer. ''They are never sold upon hats. If this man ordered one, it is a sign of a certain amount of foresight, since he went out of his way to take this precaution against the wind. But since we see that he has broken the elastic and has not troubled to replace it, it is obvious that he has less foresight now than formerly, which is a distinct proof of a weakening nature. On the other hand, he has endeavored to conceal some of these stains upon the felt by daubing them with ink, which is a sign that he has not entirely lost his self-respect.''

"Your reasoning is certainly plausible.''

"The further points, that he is middle-aged, that his hair is grizzled, that it has been recently cut, and that he uses lime-cream, are all to be gathered from a close examination of the lower part of the lining. The lens discloses a large number of hair-ends, clean cut by the scissors of the barber. They all appear to be adhesive, and there is a distinct odour of lime-cream. This dust, you will observe, is not the gritty, gray dust of the street but the fluffy brown dust of the house, showing that it has been hung up indoors most of the time; while the marks of moisture upon the inside are proof positive that the wearer perspired very freely, and could therefore, hardly be in the best of training.''

"But his wife—you said that she had ceased to love him.''

"This hat has not been brushed for weeks. When I see you, my dear Watson, with a week's accumulation of dust upon your hat, and when your wife allows you to go out in such a state, I shall fear that you also have been unfortunate enough to lose your wife's affection.''

"But he might be a bachelor.''

"Nay, he was bringing home the goose as a peace-offering to his wife. Remember the card upon the bird's leg.''

"You have an answer to everything. But how on earth do you deduce that the gas is not laid on in his house?''

"One tallow stain, or even two, might come by chance; but when I see no less than five, I think that there can be little doubt that the individual must be brought into frequent contact with burning tallow—walks upstairs at night probably with his hat in one hand and a guttering candle in the other. Anyhow, he never got tallow-stains from a gas-jet. Are you satisfied?''

''Well, it is very ingenious,'' said I, laughing; ''but since, as you said just now, there has been no crime committed, and no harm done save the loss of a goose, all this seems to be rather a waste of energy.''

Sherlock Holmes had opened his mouth to reply, when the door flew open, and Peterson, the commissionaire, rushed into the apartment with flushed cheeks and the face of a man who is dazed with astonishment.

''The goose, Mr. Holmes! The goose, sir!'' he gasped.

''Eh? What of it, then? Has it returned to life and flapped off through the kitchen window?'' Holmes twisted himself round upon the sofa to get a fairer view of the man's excited face.

''See here, sir! See what my wife found in its crop!'' He held out his hand and displayed upon the center of the palm a brilliantly scintillating blue stone, rather smaller than a bean in size, but of such purity and radiance that it twinkled like an electric point in the dark hollow of his hand.

Sherlock Holmes sat up with a whistle. ''By Jove, Peterson!'' said he, ''this is treasure trove indeed. I suppose you know what you have got?''

''A diamond, sir? A precious stone. It cuts into glass as though it were putty.''

''It's more than a precious stone. It is *the* precious stone.''

''Not the Countess of Morcar's blue carbuncle!'' I ejaculated.

''Precisely so. I ought to know its size and shape, seeing that I have read the advertisement about it in *The Times* every day lately. It is absolutely unique, and its value can only be conjectured, but the reward offered of one thousand pounds is certainly not within a twentieth part of the market price.''

''A thousand pounds! Great Lord of mercy!'' The commissionaire plumped down into a chair and stared from one to the other of us.

''That is the reward, and I have reason to know that there are sentimental considerations in the background which would induce the Countess to part with half her fortune if she could but recover the gem.''

''It was lost, if I remember aright, at the Hotel Cosmopolitan,'' I remarked.

''Precisely so, on December 22nd, just five days ago. John Horner, a plumber, was accused of having abstracted it from the lady's jewel-case. The evidence against him was so strong that the case has been referred to the Assizes. I have some account of the matter here, I believe.'' He rummaged amid his newspapers, glancing over the dates, until at last he smoothed one out, doubled it over, and read the following paragraph:

''Hotel Cosmopolitan Jewel Robbery. John Horner, 26, plumber, was brought up upon the charge of having upon the 22d inst., abstracted from the jewel-case of the Countess of Morcar the valuable gem known as the blue carbuncle. James Ryder, upper-attendant at the hotel, gave his evidence to the effect that he had shown Horner up to the dressing-room of the Countess of Morcar upon the day of the robbery in order that he might solder the second bar of the grate, which was loose. He had remained with Horner some little time, but had finally been called away. On returning, he found that Horner had disappeared, that the bureau had been forced open, and that the small morocco casket in which, as it afterwards transpired, the Countess was accustomed to keep her jewel, was lying empty upon the dressing-table. Ryder instantly gave the alarm, and Horner was arrested the same evening; but the stone could not be found either upon his person or in his rooms. Catherine Cusack, maid to the Countess, de-

posed to having heard Ryder's cry of dismay on dis-
covering the robbery, and to having rushed into the
room, where she found matters as described by the
last witness. Inspector Bradstreet, B division, gave evidence as to the arrest of Horner, who struggled frantically, and protested his innocence in the strongest
terms. Evidence of a previous conviction for robbery
having been given against the prisoner, the magistrate
refused to deal summarily with the offence, but referred it to the Assizes. Horner, who had shown signs
of intense emotion during the proceedings, fainted away
at the conclusion and was carried out of the court.

"Hum! So much for the police-court," said Holmes
thoughtfully, tossing aside the paper. "The question for
us now to solve is the sequence of events leading from a
rifled jewel-case at one end to the crop of a goose in
Tottenham Court Road at the other. You see, Watson,
our little deductions have suddenly assumed a much more
important and less innocent aspect. Here is the stone;
the stone came from the goose, and the goose came from
Mr. Henry Baker, the gentleman with the bad hat and all
the other characteristics with which I have bored you. So
now we must set ourselves very seriously to finding this
gentleman and ascertaining what part he has played in
this little mystery. To do this, we must try the simplest
means first, and these lie undoubtedly in an advertisement in all the evening papers. If this fails, I shall have
recourse to other methods."

"What will you say?"

"Give me a pencil and that slip of paper. Now, then:

"Found at the corner of Goodge Street, a goose and a
black felt hat. Mr. Henry Baker can have the same by
applying at 6:30 this evening at 221B Baker Street.

That is clear and concise."

"Very. But will he see it?"

"Well, he is sure to keep an eye on the papers, since,

to a poor man, the loss was a heavy one. He was clearly
so scared by his mischance in breaking the window and
by the approach of Peterson that he thought of nothing
but flight, but since then he must have bitterly regretted
the impulse which caused him to drop his bird. Then,
again, the introduction of his name will cause him to see
it, for everyone who knows him will direct his attention
to it. Here you are, Peterson, run down to the advertising
agency and have this put in the evening papers.''

"In which sir?''

"Oh, in the *Globe, Star, Pall Mall, St. James's, Evening
News Standard, Echo,* and any others that occur to
you.''

"Very well, sir. And this stone?''

"Ah, yes, I shall keep the stone. Thank you. And, I
say, Peterson, just buy a goose on your way back and
leave it here with me, for we must have one to give to
this gentleman in place of the one which your family is
now devouring.''

When the commissionaire had gone, Holmes took up
the stone and held it against the light. "It's a bonny
thing,'' said he. "Just see how it glints and sparkles. Of
course it is a nucleus and focus of crime. Every good
stone is. They are the devil's pet baits. In the larger and
older jewels every facet may stand for a bloody deed.
This stone is not yet twenty years old. It was found in
the banks of the Amoy River in southern China and is
remarkable in having every characteristic of the carbuncle,
save that it is blue in shade instead of ruby red. In
spite of its youth, it has already a sinister history. There
have been two murders, a vitriol-throwing, a suicide, and
several robberies brought about for the sake of this forty-
grain weight of crystallized charcoal. Who would think
that so pretty a toy would be a purveyor to the gallows
and the prison? I'll lock it up in my strong box now and
drop a line to the Countess to say that we have it.''

"Do you think that this man Horner is innocent?''

"I cannot tell."

"Well, then, do you imagine that this other one, Henry Baker, had anything to do with the matter?"

"It is, I think, much more likely that Henry Baker is an absolutely innocent man, who had no idea that the bird which he was carrying was of considerably more value than if it were made of solid gold. That, however, I shall determine by a very simple test if we have an answer to our advertisement."

"And you can do nothing until then?"

"Nothing."

"In that case I shall continue my professional round. But I shall come back in the evening at the hour you have mentioned, for I should like to see the solution of so tangled a business."

"Very glad to see you. I dine at seven. There is a woodcock, I believe. By the way, in view of recent occurrences, perhaps I ought to ask Mrs. Hudson to examine its crop."

I had been delayed at a case, and it was a little after half-past six when I found myself in Baker Street once more. As I approached the house I saw a tall man in a Scotch bonnet with a coat which was buttoned up to his chin waiting outside in the bright semicircle which was thrown from the fanlight. Just as I arrived the door was opened, and we were shown up together to Holmes's room.

"Mr. Henry Baker, I believe," said he, rising from his armchair and greeting his visitor with the easy air of geniality which he could so readily assume. "Pray take this chair by the fire, Mr. Baker. It is a cold night, and I observe that your circulation is more adapted for summer than for winter. Ah, Watson, you have just come at the right time. Is that your hat, Mr. Baker?"

"Yes, sir, that is undoubtedly my hat."

He was a large man with rounded shoulders, a massive head, and a broad, intelligent face, sloping down to a

pointed beard of grizzled brown. A touch of red in nose
and cheeks, with a slight tremor of his extended hand,
recalled Holmes's surmise as to his habits. His rusty
black frock-coat was buttoned right up in front, with the
collar turned up, and his lank wrists protruded from his
sleeves without a sign of cuff or shirt. He spoke in a slow
staccato fashion, choosing his words with care, and gave
the impression generally of a man of learning and letters
who had had ill-usage at the hands of fortune.

"We have retained these things for some days," said
Holmes, "because we expected to see an advertisement
from you giving your address. I am at a loss to know
now why you did not advertise."

Our visitor gave a rather shamefaced laugh. "Shillings
have not been plentiful with me as they once were," he
remarked. "I had no doubt that the gang of roughs who
assaulted me had carried off both my hat and the bird. I
did not care to spend more money in a hopeless attempt
at recovering them."

"Very naturally. By the way, about the bird, we were
compelled to eat it."

"To eat it!" Our visitor half rose from his chair in his
excitement.

"Yes, it would have been of no use to anyone had we
not done so. But I presume that this other goose upon
the sideboard, which is about the same weight and perfectly fresh, will answer your purpose equally well?"

"Oh, certainly, certainly," answered Mr. Baker with
a sigh of relief.

"Of course, we still have the feathers, legs, crop, and
so on of your own bird, so if you wish—"

The man burst into a hearty laugh. "They might be
useful to me as relics of my adventure," said he, "but
beyond that I can hardly see what use the *disjecta mem-
bra* of my late acquaintance are going to be to me. No,
sir, I think that, with your permission, I will confine my

attentions to the excellent bird which I perceive upon the sideboard.''

Sherlock Holmes glanced sharply across at me with a slight shrug of his shoulders.

"There is your hat, then, and there your bird," said he. "By the way, would it bore you to tell me where you got the other one from? I am somewhat of a fowl fancier, and I have seldom seen a better grown goose."

"Certainly, sir," said Baker, who had risen and tucked his newly gained property under his arm. "There are a few of us who frequent the Alpha Inn, near the Museum—we are to be found in the Museum itself during the day, you understand. This year our good host, Windigate by name, instituted a goose club, by which, on consideration for some few pence every week, we were each to receive a bird at Christmas. My pence were duly paid, and the rest is familiar to you. I am much indebted to you, sir, for a Scotch bonnet is fitted neither to my years nor my gravity." With a comical pomposity of manner he bowed solemnly to both of us and strode off upon his way.

"So much for Mr. Henry Baker," said Holmes when he had closed the door behind him. "It is quite certain that he knows nothing whatever about the matter. Are you hungry, Watson?"

"Not particularly."

"Then I suggest that we turn our dinner into a supper and follow up this clue while it is still hot."

"By all means."

It was a bitter night, so we drew on our ulsters and wrapped cravats about our throats. Outside, the stars were shining coldly in a cloudless sky, and the breath of the passers-by blew out into smoke like so many pistol shots. Our footfalls rang out crisply and loudly as we swung through the doctors' quarter, Wimpole Street, Harley Street and so through Wigmore Street into Oxford Street. In a quarter of an hour we were in Bloomsbury at the

Alpha Inn, which is a small public-house at the corner of one of the streets which runs down into Holborn. Holmes pushed open the door of the private bar and ordered two glasses of beer from the ruddy-faced, white-aproned landlord.

"Your beer should be excellent if it is as good as your geese," said he.

"My geese!" The man seemed surprised.

"Yes. I was speaking only half an hour ago to Mr. Henry Baker, who was a member of your goose club."

"Ah! yes, I see. But you see, sir, them's not *our* geese."

"Indeed! Whose, then?"

"Well, I got the two dozen from a salesman in Covent Garden."

"Indeed? I know some of them. Which was it?"

"Breckinridge is his name."

"Ah! I don't know him. Well, here's your good health, landlord, and prosperity to your house. Good-night.

"Now for Mr. Breckinridge," he continued, buttoning up his coat as we came out into the frosty air. "Remember, Watson, that though we have so homely a thing as a goose at one end of this chain, we have at the other a man who will certainly get seven years' penal servitude unless we can establish his innocence. It is possible that our inquiry may but confirm his guilt; but, in any case, we have a line of investigation which has been missed by the police, and which a singular chance has placed in our hands. Let us follow it out to the bitter end. Faces to the south, then, and quick march!"

We passed across Holborn, down Endell Street, and so through a zigzag of slums to Covent Garden Market. One of the largest stalls bore the name of Breckinridge upon it, and the proprietor, a horsy-looking man, with a sharp face and trim side-whiskers, was helping a boy to put up the shutters.

"Good-evening. It's a cold night," said Holmes.

The salesman nodded and shot a questioning glance at my companion.

"Sold out of geese, I see," continued Holmes, pointing at the bare slabs of marble.

"Let you have five hundred to-morrow morning."

"That's no good."

"Well, there are some on the stall with the gas-flare."

"Ah, but I was recommended to you."   •

"Who by?"

"The landlord of the Alpha."

"Oh, yes; I sent him a couple of dozen."

"Fine birds they were, too. Now where did you get them from?"

To my surprise the question provoked a burst of anger from the salesman.

"Now, then, mister," said he, with his head cocked and his arms akimbo, "what are you driving at? Let's have it straight, now."

"It is straight enough. I should like to know who sold you the geese which you supplied to the Alpha."

"Well, then, I shan't tell you. So now!"

"Oh, it is a matter of no importance; but I don't know why you should be so warm over such a trifle."

"Warm! You'd be as warm, maybe, if you were as pestered as I am. When I pay good money for a good article there should be an end of the business; but it's 'Where are the geese?' and 'Who did you sell the geese to?' and 'What will you take for the geese?' One would think they were the only geese in the world, to hear the fuss that is made over them."

"Well, I have no connection with any other people who have been making inquiries," said Holmes carelessly. "If you won't tell us the bet is off, that is all. But I'm always ready to back my opinion on a matter of fowls, and I have a fiver on it that the bird I ate is country bred."

"Well, then, you've lost your fiver, for it's town bred," snapped the salesman.

"It's nothing of the kind."

"I say it is."

"I don't believe it."

"D'you think you know more about fowls than I, who have handled them ever since I was a nipper? I tell you, all those birds that went to the Alpha were town bred."

"You'll never persuade me to believe that."

"Will you bet, then?"

"It's merely taking your money, for I know that I am right. But I'll have a sovereign on with you, just to teach you not to be obstinate."

The salesman chuckled grimly. "Bring me the books, Bill," said he.

The small boy brought round a small thin volume and a great greasy-backed one, laying them out together beneath the hanging lamp.

"Now then, Mr. Cocksure," said the salesman, "I thought that I was out of geese, but before I finish you'll find that there is still one left in my shop. You see this little book?"

"Well?"

"That's the list of the folk from whom I buy. D'you see? Well, then, here on this page are the country folk, and the numbers after their names are where their accounts are in the big ledger. Now, then! You see this other page in red ink? Well, that is a list of my town suppliers. Now, look at that third name. Just read it out to me."

" 'Mrs. Oakshott, 117, Brixton Road—249,' " read Holmes.

"Quite so. Now turn that up in the ledger."

Holmes turned to the page indicated. "Here you are, 'Mrs. Oakshott, 117 Brixton Road, egg and poultry supplier.' "

"Now, then, what's the last entry?"

" 'December 22d. Twenty-four geese at 7s. 6d.' "

"Quite so. There you are. And underneath?"

" 'Sold to Mr. Windigate of the Alpha, at 12s.' "

"What have you to say now?"

Sherlock Holmes looked deeply chagrined. He drew a sovereign from his pocket and threw it down upon the slab, turning away with the air of a man whose disgust is too deep for words. A few yards off he stopped under a lamp-post and laughed in the hearty, noiseless fashion which was peculiar to him.

"When you see a man with whiskers of that cut and the 'Pink 'un' protruding out of his pocket, you can always draw him by a bet," said he. "I daresay that if I had put £100 down in front of him, that man would not have given me such complete information as was drawn from him by the idea that he was doing me on a wager. Well, Watson, we are, I fancy, nearing the end of our quest, and the only point which remains to be determined is whether we should go on to this Mrs. Oakshott to-night, or whether we should reserve it for to-morrow. It is clear from what that surly fellow said that there are others besides ourselves who are anxious about the matter, and I should—"

His remarks were suddenly cut short by a loud hubbub which broke out from the stall which we had just left. Turning round we saw a little rat-faced fellow standing in the centre of the circle of yellow light which was thrown by the swinging lamp, while Breckinridge, the salesman, framed in the door of his stall, was shaking his fists fiercely at the cringing figure.

"I've had enough of you and your geese," he shouted. "I wish you were all at the devil together. If you come pestering me any more with your silly talk I'll set the dog at you. You bring Mrs. Oakshott here and I'll answer her, but what have you do to with it? Did I buy the geese off you?"

"No; but one of them was mine all the same," whined the little man.

"Well, then, ask Mrs. Oakshott for it."

"She told me to ask you."

"Well, you can ask the King of Proosia, for all I care. I've had enough of it. Get out of this!" He rushed fiercely forward, and the inquirer flitted away into the darkness.

"Ha! this may save us a visit to Brixton Road," whispered Holmes. "Come with me, and we will see what is to be made of this fellow." Striding through the scattered knots of people who lounged round the flaring stalls, my companion speedily overtook the little man and touched him upon the shoulder. He sprang round, and I could see in the gas-light that every vestige of colour had been driven from his face.

"Who are you, then? What do you want?" he asked in a quavering voice.

"You will excuse me," said Holmes blandly, "but I could not help overhearing the questions which you put to the salesman just now. I think that I could be of assistance to you."

"You? Who are you? How could you know anything of the matter?"

"My name is Sherlock Holmes. It is my business to know what other people don't know."

"But you can know nothing of this?"

"Excuse me, I know everything of it. You are endeavoring to trace some geese which were sold by Mrs. Oakshott, of Brixton Road, to a salesman named Breckinridge, by him in turn to Mr. Windigate, of the Alpha, and by him to his club, of which Mr. Henry Baker is a member."

"Oh, sir, you are the very man whom I have longed to meet," cried the little fellow with outstretched hands and quivering fingers. "I can hardly explain to you how interested I am in this matter."

Sherlock Holmes hailed a four-wheeler which was

passing. "In that case we had better discuss it in a cosy room rather than in this wind-swept market-place," said he. "But pray tell me, before we go further, who it is that I have the pleasure of assisting."

The man hesitated for an instant. "My name is John Robinson," he answered with a sidelong glance.

"No, no; the real name," said Holmes sweetly. "It is always awkward doing business with an alias."

A flush sprang to the white cheeks of the stranger. "Well, then," said he, "my real name is James Ryder."

"Precisely so. Head attendant at the Hotel Cosmopolitan. Pray step into the cab, and I shall soon be able to tell you everything which you would wish to know."

The little man stood glancing from one to the other of us with half-frightened, half-hopeful eyes, as one who is not sure whether he is on the verge of a windfall or of a catastrophe. Then he stepped into the cab, and in half an hour we were back in the sitting-room at Baker Street. Nothing had been said during our drive, but the high, thin breathing of our new companion, and the claspings and unclaspings of his hands, spoke of the nervous tension within him.

"Here we are!" said Holmes cheerily as we filed into the room. "The fire looks very seasonable in this weather. You look cold, Mr. Ryder. Pray take the basket-chair. I will just put on my slippers before we settle this little matter of yours. Now, then! You want to know what became of those geese?"

"Yes, sir."

"Or rather, I fancy, of that goose. It was one bird, I imagine, in which you were interested—white, with a black bar across the tail."

Ryder quivered with emotion. "Oh, sir," he cried, "can you tell me where it went to?"

"It came here."

"Here?"

"Yes, and a most remarkable bird it proved. I don't

wonder that you should take an interest in it. It laid an
egg after it was dead—the bonniest, brightest little blue
egg that ever was seen. I have it here in my museum.''

Our visitor staggered to his feet and clutched the
mantel-piece with his right hand. Holmes unlocked his
strongbox and held up the blue carbuncle, which shone
out like a star, with a cold, brilliant, many-pointed radiance. Ryder stood glaring with a drawn face, uncertain
whether to claim or to disown it.

"The game's up, Ryder," said Holmes quietly. "Hold
up, man, or you'll be into the fire! Give him an arm back
into his chair, Watson. He's not got blood enough to go
in for felony with impunity. Give him a dash of brandy.
So! Now he looks a little more human. What a shrimp it
is, to be sure!"

For a moment he had staggered and nearly fallen, but
the brandy brought a tinge of colour into his cheeks, and
he sat staring with frightened eyes at his accuser.

"I have almost every link in my hands, and all the
proofs which I could possibly need, so there is little
which you need tell me. Still, that little may as well be
cleared up to make the case complete. You had heard,
Ryder, of this blue stone of the Countess of Morcar's?"

"It was Catherine Cusack who told me of it," said he
in a crackling voice.

"I see—her ladyship's waiting-maid. Well, the temp-
tation of sudden wealth so easily acquired was too much
for you, as it has been for better men before you; but you
were not very scrupulous in the means you used. It seems
to me, Ryder, that there is the making of a very pretty
villain in you. You knew that this man Horner, the
plumber, had been concerned in some such matter before, and that suspicion would rest the more readily upon
him. What did you do, then? You made some small job
in my lady's room—you and your confederate Cusack—
and you managed that he should be the man sent for.
Then, when he had left, you rifled the jewel-case, raised

the alarm, and had this unfortunate man arrested. You then—''

Ryder threw himself down suddenly upon the rug and clutched at my companion's knee. ''For God's sake, have mercy!'' he shrieked. ''Think of my father! of my mother! It would break their hearts. I never went wrong before! I never will again. I swear it. I'll swear it on a Bible. Oh, don't bring it into court! For Christ's sake, don't!''

''Get back into your chair!'' said Holmes sternly. ''It is very well to cringe and crawl now, but you thought little enough of this poor Horner in the dock for a crime of which he knew nothing.''

''I will fly, Mr. Holmes. I will leave the country, sir. Then the charge against him will break down.''

''Hum! We will talk about that. And now let us hear a true account of the next act. How came the stone into the goose, and how came the goose into the open market? Tell us the truth, for there lies your only hope of safety.''

Ryder passed his tongue over his parched lips. ''I will tell you it just as it happened, sir,'' said he. ''When Horner had been arrested, it seemed to me that it would be best for me to get away with the stone at once, for I did not know at what moment the police might not take it into their heads to search me and my room. There was no place about the hotel where it would be safe. I went out, as if on some commission, and I made for my sister's house. She had married a man named Oakshott, and lived in Brixton Road, where she fattened fowls for the market. All the way there every man I met seemed to me to be a policeman or a detective; and, for all that it was a cold night, the sweat was pouring down my face before I came to the Brixton Road. My sister asked me what was the matter, and why I was so pale; but I told her that I had been upset by the jewel robbery at the hotel. Then I went into the back yard and smoked a pipe, and wondered what it would be best to do.

"I had a friend once called Maudsley, who went to the bad, and has just been serving his time in Pentonville. One day he had met me, and fell into talk about the ways of thieves, and how they could get rid of what they stole. I knew that he would be true to me, for I knew one or two things about him; so I made up my mind to go right on to Kilburn, where he lived, and take him into my confidence. He would show me how to turn the stone into money. But how to get to him in safety? I thought of the agonies I had gone through in coming from the hotel. I might at any moment be seized and searched, and there would be the stone in my waistcoat pocket. I was leaning against the wall at the time and looking at the geese which were waddling about round my feet, and suddenly an idea came into my head which showed me how I could beat the best detective that ever lived.

"My sister had told me some weeks before that I might have the pick of her geese for a Christmas present, and I knew that she was always as good as her word. I would take my goose now, and in it I would carry my stone to Kilburn. There was a little shed in the yard, and behind this I drove one of the birds—a fine big one, white, with a barred tail. I caught it, and, prying its bill open, I thrust the stone down its throat as far as my finger could reach. The bird gave a gulp, and I felt the stone pass along its gullet and down into its crop. But the creature flapped and struggled, and out came my sister to know what was the matter. As I turned to speak to her the brute brook loose and fluttered off among the others.

" 'Whatever were you doing with that bird, Jem?' says she.

" 'Well,' said I, 'you said you'd give me one for Christmas, and I was feeling which was the fattest.'

" 'Oh,' says she, 'we've set yours aside for you—Jem's bird, we call it. It's the big white one over yonder. There's twenty-six of them, which makes one for you, and one for us, and two dozen for the market.'

" 'Thank you, Maggie,' says I; 'but if it is all the same to you, I'd rather have that one I was handling just now.'

" 'The other is a good three pound heavier,' said she, 'and we fattened it expressly for you.'

" 'Never mind. I'll have the other, and I'll take it now,' said I.

" 'Oh, just as you like,' said she, a little huffed. 'Which is it you want, then?'

" 'That white one with the barred tail, right in the middle of the flock.'

" 'Oh, very well. Kill it and take it with you.'

"Well, I did what she said, Mr. Holmes, and I carried the bird all the way to Kilburn. I told my pal what I had done, for he was a man that it was easy to tell a thing like that to. He laughed until he choked, and we got a knife and opened the goose. My heart turned to water, for there was no sign of the stone, and I knew that some terrible mistake had occurred. I left the bird, rushed back to my sister's, and hurried into the back yard. There was not a bird to be seen there.

" 'Where are they all, Maggie?' I cried.

" 'Gone to the dealer's, Jem.'

" 'Which dealer's?'

" 'Breckinridge, of Covent Garden.'

" 'But was there another with a barred tail?' I asked, 'the same as the one I chose?'

" 'Yes, Jem; there were two barred-tailed ones, and I could never tell them apart.'

"Well, then, of course I saw it all, and I ran off as hard as my feet would carry me to this man Breckinridge; but he had sold the lot at once, and not one word would he tell me as to where they had gone. You heard him yourselves to-night. Well, he has always answered me like that. My sister thinks that I am going mad. Sometimes I think that I am myself. And now—and now I am myself a branded thief, without ever having touched the

wealth for which I sold my character. God help me! God
help me!'' He burst into convulsive sobbing, with his
face buried in his hands.

There was a long silence, broken only by his heavy
breathing, and by the measured tapping of Sherlock
Holmes's finger-tips upon the edge of the table. Then my
friend rose and threw open the door.

''Get out!'' said he.

''What, sir! Oh, Heaven bless you!''

''No more words. Get out!''

And no more words were needed. There was a rush,
a clatter upon the stairs, the bang of a door, and the crisp
rattle of running footfalls from the street.

''After all, Watson,'' said Holmes, reaching up his
hand for his clay pipe, ''I am not retained by the police
to supply their deficiencies. If Horner were in danger it
would be another thing; but this fellow will not appear
against him, and the case must collapse. I suppose that I
am commuting a felony, but it is just possible that I am
saving a soul. This fellow will not go wrong again; he is
too terribly frightened. Send him to jail now, and you
make him a jail-bird for life. Besides, it is the season of
forgiveness. Chance has put in our way a most singular
and whimsical problem, and its solution is its own reward. If you will have the goodness to touch the bell,
Doctor, we will begin another investigation, in which,
also, a bird will be the chief feature.''

MASTERS OF MYSTERY

Buy them at your local

bookstore or use coupon

on next page for ordering.

There's an epidemic with 27 million victims. And no visible symptoms.

It's an epidemic of people who can't read.

Believe it or not, 27 million Americans are functionally illiterate, about one adult in five.

The solution to this problem is you... when you join the fight against illiteracy. So call the Coalition for Literacy at toll-free **1-800-228-8813** and volunteer.

Volunteer Against Illiteracy. The only degree you need is a degree of caring.